Other books by E. Jade Lomax.

The Alliance Trilogy
Sneak
Liar
Traitor

The Leagues and Legends series
Beanstalk: the adventures of a Jack of All Tales

For Marina

ISBN 978-1-304-74802-7

4

SNEAK

Book One of the Alliance Trilogy

by E. Jade Lomax

Table of Contents

Eight years before.

High in the mountains, two boys scampered with dirt between their toes and together they dreamed adventures.

In the royal palace, far lowland, the captain of the Royal Guard gave a young princess a wooden sword, for lack of anything better to distract her with.

She would have blisters that night, and calluses later.

Past the royal white walls, the streets of the capital city circled, crossed, and clashed.

Far too far from the palace walks to hear and far too close for comfort, the chaos of the lower city broke to silence as a young girl's father was hung for treason.

Chapter One
The Old Oak Tree

The lead carriage of the caravan rocked with every bump and pothole in the mountain pass. The head hostler had given a long grumbling sigh when they had turned onto the rocky trail and, a half day later, he hadn't quite stopped. "*Northerners,*" the hostler told his horses mournfully and gritted his teeth before the next jarring impact.

With each jostle, the young woman tucked atop the carriage bit back glee. She nestled smugly further between a dark wood trunk and a leather bag, holding tightly to the ropes that lashed the baggage to the roof.

A black-and-silver squad of the Royal Guard rode in front of the caravan. Another kept watch behind the servants' wagons in the back. A redheaded guardsman a few years older than the young woman on the roof munched an apple, watching the stone hills roll slowly by.

When she heard the hostler stop grumbling and start muttering in anticipation of their arrival, the young woman swung herself down from the roof, catching herself by the tips of her toes on the carriage window sill.

(Upon hearing the scrap of boots on wood, the head hostler gave another resigned grumble. Luckily, however, controlling the behavior of bored young royals was not within his job description).

The girl eased the wooden shutters open and then lingered, a hand on the roof's edge, ten booted toes pressed firmly against the window sill, until the redheaded guard caught sight of her. He hurled the half-eaten apple and a curse in her direction.

The girl swallowed her laugh to keep from waking the two sisters she'd left sleeping inside, and then slipped into the carriage. She had had hours in the stale air of the box on wheels to push at floorboards with her feet, listening for which ones creaked, so the girl from the roof stepped carefully as she moved to a cushioned corner beside her youngest sister and settled down for a nap herself.

She left the window open. A chill blue sky crowned the rocky mountainside.

In one of the flatbed wagons following closely behind the royal caravan, servants sat twelve abreast, shaded by tented white canvas, facing inward, knees knocking together. Will Rocole turned away from the view out the open back of the wagon, where the stone skeleton of hills had been looking dreadfully more and more familiar as they travelled on.

Some maids giggled, leaning out the front, pestering the hostler who drove the wagon's sturdy plowhorses. A young boy sat on the floor, dangling his feet off the back edge, watching the line of pack mules trundling behind.

Beside Will, a tall young maid stared into space, slender fingers tapping her knee, a black-haired off-duty guardsman's arm slung around her shoulders. The guardsman was telling the man next to him, "My cousin picked it up for me, off a merchant ship in the Panet province."

"A pirate ship, no doubt," his listener said, leaning back with a grin.

"The gold of fruits, he said." The guardsman passed the other man his bag, inviting him to admire the orange globe resting inside, and puffed up his chest like an overfed hen. "Only nobles get to eat like this." Will rolled his eyes.

On the other side of the wagon, a few men and a pinched-faced matron slept, leaning back against the sagging canvas, their legs stretched and feet crossed in the narrow aisle.

Will shifted in his seat and stretched. Almost there, he thought. The wagon bumped and jostled.

He tapped the tall, bored maid's knee, softly, and she looked up at him like a startled rabbit. Will pushed his brown hair out of his eyes, and then, as though he'd plucked it from his skull, brought his hand around, two fingers holding a greened copper coin in front of her nose. Her eyes lit up.

He passed the coin (or, rather, had a coin in each hand and hid the other in his sleeve or slipped between his fingers—but it was all the same to her) from hand to hand, found it behind her small ears, in the boots of the stable hand snoring thunderously across from them. She laughed and clapped her hands. He grinned crookedly, half his face a smile.

"Oy there," said her black-haired guardsman, finally catching on. Will rolled the coin across the backs of his fingers, glancing once to the frowning guardsman and then back to his coin. "Leave her alone, kid."

"She can look if she wants to." Will tossed the coin up, caught it and slipped it down his sleeve. He slipped a second coin into his left hand and spun that across the back of his fingers, too, but more slowly.

"I'll not have you flirting with my girl, you mountain hick."

"*Your* girl?" Will glanced at the arm slung around her shoulders and smiled. "Ah, yes. I see you're doing your best to make *that* clear." He threw his coin in the air, caught it in a cupped hand, and opened it—palm up and empty. "If she's so surely your girl, mate," said Will, leaning forward and snatching the coin back into sight as though out of the guard's ear, "then you shouldn't worry about me and my tricks."

The guard scowled and snatched at his ear as Will whisked his hand away. The wagon swayed and creaked underneath them. "You should show more respect, hick. I'm with the Royal Guard," he added, glancing at Will's palace uniform—cleaned and paid for by his employers—and his own shabby shoes beneath it. "You probably don't even know what that means."

"I'm not a hick."

"Oh?" The guardsman leaned back with a laugh, glancing over to his friend and tightening his arm around the tall maid's shoulders. She sent an apologetic look at Will. "You sure *sound* like a mountain hick. Even if you are a little brown for the north."

Across the way, an older woman clutched her bag and gave the guardsman a deeply unimpressed look.

Will's eye marked the silhouette of hills visible out the back of the wagon and then he said, "And you sound like a drunken bore, but I'm giving *you* the benefit of the doubt."

The guardsman started to his feet, one hand shoved against the slanted canvas, and lunged for Will. The maid squeaked and ducked, but the guard never made it past her—the wagon groaned to a halt, throwing him off balance. He thudded back into his seat, glaring at Will.

The older woman across the way grinned into her bag.

The hostler who'd reined in the horses reported obliviously back, "We're here, folks—Willow Tree Castle."

Will hopped up, grabbing the worn leather bag stashed under his seat. He moved to exit quickly, visibly ignoring the guard, but trying to keep him in the corner of his eye. Passing by the tall maid, he tossed her the little greenish coin with a wink. The guard's angry sweep of his feet caught him, knocking his legs out from under him and sending Will crashing to his hands and knees on the top of the boots and bags that marked the aisle.

His chin stung where it had smacked the ground. Will shoved himself up off of the guardsman's cloth bag and back onto his feet, brushing off his pants.

The guard looked smug. "Well, *hick*?" His fists balled and his eyes darted, ready for Will's next move. Will could feel the bruises already.

Instead, Will smiled, friendly-like, and shifted his own bag's strap further up on his shoulder. He told the maid, "You'll not have much to spend that on." A few more steps and a hop down brought him out into the pale sunlight. He shaded his eyes, looking around dourly. "Not here," he finished.

Behind him, he heard the guard bluster something about scaring him off. He grinned. Above him, Willow Tree Castle squatted in a yellow-green meadow like a grey and lopsided toad. Four stout towers were joined by thick walls, hovering defensively. The scent of crushed pine was thick in the air from the wheels of the wagon train and the hooves of horses grinding green and brown needles into the rocky soil.

Twenty paces from Will Rocole, groomsmen pulled the horses of the royal carriage to a stop. The girl from the roof unlatched the carriage door before the wheeled wooden box had stopped swaying. "*Sasha*," she heard her older sister sigh. The two other carriages had their doors opened, properly, by the bowing groomsmen, and in a moment elegant skirts and polished shoes stirred the dry grass. The five other nobles, all around Lia's twenty-one years, glanced at each other and their winter residence doubtfully.

Sasha surveyed the slopes that rose steeply around the castle, choked in scraggly pines and jagged rocks peeking between tall dry grass. "One could really get lost in that, don't you think, Eli?" she commented to the shadow at her side.

The redheaded guard, holding his horse's reins in one hand, said dryly, "Lost in the mountains, freezing the death? Yes, sounds like large wicker baskets filled with glory and excitement."

"I'll leave you at home, then," she said. Sasha turned to him and grinned. "You must have been asleep in your saddle today. And that apple core was miles off its target."

"You thought that apple was for you?" Elijah said. "Would a Royal guard try to hit his princess?" His horse flicked its tail, looking longingly at the other animals, which were being led toward a steep-roofed stable connected to the castle by a long enclosed walkway, and also presumably toward dinner.

"I know a squad that tries to, every morning," she said. Sasha looked Elijah up and down, the horse sweat and dirt on his silver and black uniform, the half-smile on his face. "Not all of them manage."

Elijah's grin spread. "I thought you could use the apple," he said. "You're scrawny, highness. You should work on that."

Sasha caught sight of some maids and footmen unloading the baggage mules. "Blessed bones," she said. "They'll unpack my trousers and then I'll never see them again." She took off at a run and Elijah went to stable his grateful horse.

A voice cleared itself behind her. "Your *highness*." Sasha sighed, dropping to a more ladylike walk, and mournfully eyed the baggage mules across the meadow.

"Your *dress*," said the voice—a baroness, a little older, one of Lia's flunkies. "It's ripped." The baroness's dark hair was done up in a tight bun, her skin brown like many of the citizens from the more southern provinces of Neria.

18

Sasha's hand dropped to a tear and a scuff mark on the yellow fabric, probably gained climbing back into the carriage. "Well," she began.

Lia looked up from where she was talking to a young duchess. The duchess stepped back to banter with the two male nobles while Lia made her way over to her sister.

"It's just a rip," said Sasha.

"Yes, but I can't imagine what you were doing to get it," said Lia. "Oh, Sasha. What are we going to do with you?"

"You don't need to do anything," Sasha said with false cheer. "It's just a rip. I'll ask one of the maids to look at it."

"You were on the roof, or in a—a— *tussle*," said Lia, fishing for vocabulary she rarely needed in her silk-lined life. Long dark hair fell around Lia's face and down her back, as carefully straight as the best smithed sword. "You can't keep doing this, Sasha. The way you act matters. *Sasha*," said Lia, and waited until Sasha lifted her eyes from her boots to her sister's face. "I don't understand you. Don't you understand that you represent something larger than yourself?"

"If I go crazy from being stuck in a box on wheels, how good am I going to be able to *represent* then? Besides, who's here to see? I won't tell Mother if you won't."

"It's not about what you seem, Sasha. It's about what we are. Just—" Lia sighed prettily, fingers brushing lightly against the bridge of her nose like she wanted to squeeze a headache away. "I worry about you. You aren't nine anymore. This isn't a quaint little quirk of yours, not anymore." She waved a graceful hand, referring as much to the rip in Sasha's dress and her scuffed boots as the black and silver backs of the guardsmen disappearing past the stable doors. "You are seventeen. You are a princess. You *matter*."

"And when it comes to it, don't I always do as I should?" said Sasha. "I know what I'm needed for, I *know*. I dance with whom I'm told, I don't slurp my soup, I curtsy to the proper depths, I wave from the carriage window on parades. I mean, maybe I've forgotten a ball or two? And there was that incident with the Kainen ambassador's son. But I'm not going to run off and join a circus, Lia, or set the palace aflame. I just need to *breathe* sometimes."

"Corsets do take practice," the baroness told her gravely.

"That's not quite what she meant," Lia said. "And Sasha, you broke his arm."

"I put him in an arm lock, and then knocked him down," said Sasha. "I didn't break anything. And he deserved it, he tried to put his hand—"

"Well!" said the baroness. "I think we should explore the rest of this, ehm, *quaint* abode." She scuttled away as fast as her skirts would let her.

Lia looked after her and sighed gently. "I care about what happens to you," she said.

20

"You have so much potential." Lia touched her chin lightly and said, "You're important, Sasha."

Sasha shrugged, fingering the rip in her skirt.

Lia dropped her hand and said, "Shall we go inside, then?"

Sasha peered up at the lumpy stone walls and twisted her nose with a grimace, to Lia's audible sigh of admonishment. "Might as well," she said. She looked over at Lia and straightened her face quickly into something more seemly.

Lia smiled at her, softly, a polite and well-trained expression. "You'll be alright," she said, more like a prayer than a promise.

Sasha walked slower, dragging her boots through trampled yellow grass, while Lia moved ahead in a swish of skirts to rejoin her peers. They accepted her back into their ranks with a seamless parting of silks and brocade.

Sasha heard quiet footsteps behind her. Elijah had finished stabling his horse.

"I don't *feel* like I matter," she told Elijah.

"You do," he said, without hesitation. She looked at him. Eli shrugged, hiding a smile. "If we had even numbers for sparring in the mornings, then no one would ever have time to rest."

"Just on the practice field," Sasha said, a laugh gathering in her. "Just on one square of earth. I can live with that."

The flatbed wagons where the servants had ridden, packed in with extra food stuffs and baggage, were rapidly being emptied and the goods carted up to the castle.

Will Rocole jumped up onto the back of one—one which did not hold a tall, bored maid or her disgruntled black-haired guardsman—and eyed the castle above him with obvious misgivings.

Will then switched his gaze to the royal swarm—royally blooded (debatably), affiliated, or employed—that lapped at the knees of the castle. His target was not difficult to find: a sturdy, barrel-chested man with a warrior's bearing, dressed in the Guard's black and silver. The captain's badge was secured to his upper left arm.

Will leapt down lightly and hurried towards him, snatching up a parcel so he wouldn't be the only servant not toting luggage or hauling livestock. "Captain Harston," Will said, quietly, when he was close enough to be heard. "A word with you?" He hefted the weight of his parcel to one side and offered a hand to shake.

Harston looked puzzled, wild grey eyebrows—the only wild thing about the rather square man—raised. "Do I know you?" He took the young man's hand and his eyebrows rose higher as he felt something slipped into his palm.

"Will," he said. "Will Rocole. I don't believe we've met."

"No," Harston agreed, glancing carefully down at the wax seal slipped in his hand.

"Minister Westel thought someone should keep an eye on the situation," Will said. "A few too many variables are unknown." He smiled. "And he knows you're never against a little extra protection for your charges."

"Westel didn't inform me he was lending me an agent." The captain looked Will over, slowly.

Will said, "With all the ruckus in the capital, I'm afraid the minister hadn't the resources to warn you about me." He smiled ruefully. "I'm just another man at your service, sir. Don't worry about me."

Harston ignored the seal in his hand, watching Will. After a moment, he nodded.

"Let me know if you need me for anything," Will said. "Otherwise, I'll just keep my eyes open and report to you if I find anything."

"I will have my second in command, Frederick Brown, contact you," Harston said. He paused, a quirk in the edge of his mouth that might have been a smile, if Will believed old knights had senses of humor. "Don't let him ruffle you. He's a bit stiff, but he gets things done."

"I don't ruffle easy," said Will with an comfortable grin.

"A pleasure meeting you, Will Rocole," the captain said, shaking his hand and slipping the seal back to him with surprising grace.

Will bowed. As he walked away he dug into his bag, grinning. The story was holding up, so far.

Will dropped the peel of the black-haired guardsman's orange on the dry grass at his feet and chewed a segment thoughtfully. Tasty, he supposed, but hardly *gold*.

The next morning, the Royal Guard had marked out a square of rocky earth beside the castle's barn. A broad-shouldered, tawny-haired guardsman was lugging a barrel of wooden swords out to its edge when Sasha stepped out into the cold and laughed.

"Tell me," said Sasha, "*tell* me you made the practice field, Gideon." She wore a cotton shirt and trousers, the same white practice gear that was worn by the guardsmen on the field. She'd had to bribe the maids generously to unpack her practice clothes into her wardrobe and not into the composting heaps.

The tawny-haired guard thumped the barrel of swords down beside the edge of the field. "Well," said Gideon. "Second Squad is the first to practice, mornings, so who else was going to do it?"

Elijah popped out of the barn door behind her, sleepily garbed in black and silver— they'd come down through the covered path from the castle to the barn. Sasha turned to him, gleeful. "*Look* at that."

The sun hadn't managed to overcome the mountainous horizon, but the sky was streaked purple and dusty blue with the promise of it. Eli said, reflectively, "You know, Gideon, if the practice yard had been a few inches—feet, even—off in some direction, I don't think anyone would've tripped and broken anything because of it."

Sasha hopped down to the field to stand toe-to-toe with the square's edge. "It looks exactly the same. You've even got the barn standing in for the Guardhouse!"

Gideon cleared his throat. "Are you done admiring my work?"

"Yes, let's start," she said. "Before Nathaniel has time to really get to sleep."

A lanky redhead who shared Elijah's cheekbones, but had a few inches on his younger brother in height, called out, "I'm awake!" from where he leaned against the barn wall, eyes closed and arms crossed. A few other guardsmen, enough to make a total of ten, and all in plain cotton trousers and shirts, stood about or wandered in.

(One, a black-haired young man, looked melancholy—he had been looking forward to enjoying an orange for breakfast).

Elijah, pulling off his outer black jacket as he headed back into the barn, knocked Nathaniel in the arm as he walked by. "You're not awake," he told his brother.

"Why Second Squad?" said Nathaniel to the pre-dawn chill. "*Why* out of all the miserable squads of the Royal Guard did I have to get stuck with *Second*?"

"Oh, the sun's out and everything," said Sasha. "Just wait until midwinter when we start practice in pitch."

"The sun," said Nathaniel gravely, "is *not* out." Sasha elbowed him, and he grinned and lunged to ruffle the top of her head.

"You'd think," said a crackling voice, "after eight years he'd have the sense to get used to it—or quit."

"Stearnes," Gideon said to the blond guardsman who'd spoken. "You're implying Nathaniel has sense."

"Ah," said Stearnes. "That explains it."

Elijah slipped back out of the barn, dressed like the others in light practice gear. Gideon, Second's squad leader, addressed the ten-man squad plus one princess. "Exercises, boys, but first a few laps around the castle base."

"Sasha," said Nathaniel. "You're bouncing."

"Yes," she said.

"Stop it. You're making me dizzy."

"But we get to *spar*." She added, in grumpy explanation, "I just spent three days stuck in a carriage, Nate."

Elijah sidled up beside them, adjusting the plain white cloth. Sasha glanced at him and said, "You didn't need to get all uniformed up to

26

come get me. You don't need to come at all—I can walk myself, you know."

"So you've said," said a new voice—a square jawed man with wild, bushy eyebrows approached. "Often."

"Captain," said Elijah. Harston inclined his head.

"Harston!" Sasha said. "You're late."

Gideon came up beside them. "Captain," he said to the new arrival. And, to the others, "You're not moving. I want five laps about the castle base. If they beat you back it's an extra hour of practice—and Stearnes gets to choose what your shifts will be for the week, Nate."

Nathaniel was sprinting before his squad leader finished the threat. Sasha shook out each foot and then jogged after him. Elijah hesitated, as though he wanted to say something more, and then followed his brother and the princess.

Gideon and Harston were left standing. "She doesn't know," said Gideon, running fingers over the seams of his shirt. "Are you going to tell her?"

Harston hesitated. "The king told me not to."

"Ah," said Gideon, as though that sentence was the same as *I'm not going to.* Gideon sighed. "Well," he said. "She'll sleep better at night."

Some breathless challenges provoked a sixth and seventh lap, and then the Second Squad of the Royal Guard and the princess met the Guard captain and Second's squad leader in Gideon's perfect square for stretches, exercises, and one impromptu wrestling match.

Guard practices were three hours each, every morning. Second Squad had theirs first, so in late winter, most of theirs happened in darkness. Second's mostly commonborn men had less fathers to complain to in high places than those assigned to squads like First (the king's squad) or Fourth (the queen's)—except for their unofficial eleventh practice partner, but Sasha liked early mornings much more than she liked asking favors of her father.

Nathaniel tossed Sasha a sword—Gideon, nearby, winced at the lack of weapons etiquette, even with a wooden practice sword. "Go hit something with it," said Nate. "If that'll make you be still."

"You?" Sasha suggested.

He grinned. "If you think you can reach me."

She narrowed her eyes and pointed with the sword. "The corner with the scraggly oak, now." (The scraggly oak was back in the palace, casting a shadow on a different practice field. Gideon, hearing her, muttered, "What other size should I have made it?").

Harston stood at the edge of the practice field. He shifted a little, watching. "Watch your stance," he said to a guardsman. He rolled gravel under his feet and commented quietly, "Elijah, you're not sparring."

The redhead behind him gave a soft, amused exhale. "And you're observant as always, sir."

"I hear that's the fun part," said Harston, nodding toward the field. Elijah moved up beside him. Eli looked as though he wanted to shove his hands in his pockets but wanted to have them ready, too.

"She doesn't know," said Elijah. Harston looked at him. "She doesn't know, and she's going to do something stupid, because she thinks everything's the same as it's always been."

"Is that all?" said Harston blandly. He turned back to the field. "I believe your job is to *keep* her from doing stupid things, isn't it?"

Elijah held his breath for a moment and didn't say anything.

Harston sighed. "I apologize. That was uncalled for. The ministers—"

"And the king, and the queen, and palace chef, and everyone who got lucky enough to catch wind of the latest intrigue has been breathing down your neck. I understand, sir." Elijah added, reluctantly, "And I admit maybe I've been one of those few, too."

"Thank you," said Harston. He paused, then said, reflectively, "I thought about not telling you and Nathaniel about the attempt."

Elijah held his breath again, then said, "That would rather have gotten in the way of us, as you said, doing our job."

"I know," said Harston, kneading one eye with the palm of his hand. "And our job's hard enough as it is."

"She should know," said Elijah.

Harston laughed, softly, and said, "She *will* do something stupid and dangerous. But there are things I am not supposed to tell—even to you, Eli. You will just have to watch her, while I work on weathering our latest storm."

Elijah watched Harston watching the spars. Yellow streaked the morning sky and the crags in the captain's face. "It *will* be alright, sir," Eli said. "We'll manage."

"We have to," said Harston.

"We will." Somewhere, a fight was ending. Elijah stretched each arm briefly. As he hailed a guardsman with a sword and stepped into the marked-off square of ground, he hesitated. He added quietly to Harston, "If you hadn't told me about the attempt, sir—" Elijah shook his head, once. "I'm not sure I would've forgiven you that."

Harston laughed, deep in the pit of his stomach. Sasha, by the oak's corner, raised a weighted wooden practice sword and demanded a fight.

A Royal guard stood stiffly at the door of Willow Tree's sole courtyard, and he watched Will's approach suspiciously.

Will said cheerily, a disgruntled sigh in the back of his mind, "Whatcha guarding that for? It doesn't go anywhere." When Westel had given him his orders, Will had dropped the careful lowland accent he'd cultivated for the past year. The old mountain lilt felt thick with unwanted familiarity on his tongue.

The guard blinked at him, and then apparently wrote him off as harmless, because he shrugged. "Orders. Why do you want to go in?"

"Breath of fresh air," Will lied.

The courtyard might not lead anywhere, but it was a lovely if chilly place for private conversations—as long as you stayed away from the wooden-shuttered window in one of the walls—

"Ah," said Will. "You gave the royals that freezing-cold room, didn't you?" They must think a window made it a higher class of room. He nodded his head to the guard and walked away, whistling and amused. *They*'d never lived through a Willow Tree winter.

Will spotted a boy coming down the corridor. He hurried to intercept him, before the boy tried to enter the courtyard, too.

The boy's curly brown hair was squashed under a red cap. His skin was much darker than the rather pale mountain norm. The boy's mother had been an immigrant from the south. She had travelled to Willow Tree with a merchant's caravan and fallen in love with the idea of staying still.

The boy slowed as he spotted Will.

Will swept past him, grinning, and the boy turned when he passed and followed Will back down the hall. "The courtyard's closed," Will confided.

"I know," said the boy. "I *live* here, remember?" He scrambled to keep up pace with him—Will was taller, but the boy was faster.

"So do I, for now," said Will. He ducked into a narrow side corridor, then down another. A few more turns and they passed by the door of a small cobwebbed room and then another. Willow Tree was a small castle, but the number of folk who wanted to live between its crumbling, isolated walls was even smaller.

"Will," said the boy, following. "*Will*." He dug in his heels and stopped. Will turned a corner, disappearing, then popped his head back around a moment later, when he figured out he'd lost his tail. The boy crossed his arms over his chest and said, "You're *back*."

Will ambled back to him, slipping his hands into his pockets. He shrugged. "I'm back," he said, and the boy leapt forward and threw his arms around Will's neck. Will laughed and spun the kid around. "Good to see you, too, Gregory."

"I didn't miss you at *all*," said Gregory, muffled into the front of his best friend's shirt.

"Of course you didn't," said Will. He stepped back and grabbed the boy's shoulders to examine him—a smattering of dark freckles over his cheekbones, a smudge of torch soot, a familiar bewildered expression.

"Come on," said Will, continuing down the corridor. "We need some privacy."

"You're *back*." Gregory kept up pace with him. "I didn't quite believe it when I stuck my hand in my pocket this morning and found a note from you."

"I haven't been gone *that* long," said Will.

"It's been two years."

"Just one," said Will.

Gregory said, "It'll be two years in the spring."

"And it's fall," said Will. He grinned at the younger boy.

Will kicked imaginary pebbles down the narrow hallway. There was a slight slope in the floor, just up ahead, where a real pebble would have to be kicked with extra force to get it over the hump. Will made a face at this easy knowledge and grabbed a torch from an iron wall bracket. He took two quick turns, then stopped in front of a battered row of old tapestries. He paused before them with a flourished bow to Gregory. There was no one in sight.

Gregory ducked behind the third tapestry down, slipped his hand between two massive building stones and pulled the latch between them. With a slight shove, a door-sized portion of the wall swung inward creakily. Will slung an arm around Gregory's shoulder. "Ah, I've missed you, mate."

Gregory rolled his eyes. "You've missed *these*," he said.

"You have to admit," said Will, "they make mischief a bit easier." He ruffled

Gregory's curls and earned a scrunched-nose face from him. "But, then, having you around's a big part of that, too. I haven't stuck a frog in anyone's bed in *ages*."

After they stepped inside, they latched the wall-door shut behind them and Will lifted the torch. They stood in a slender, arched corridor. Will could reach out with both arms and touch the brick walls with flat palms. He didn't.

Will stuffed one hand in a pocket and strolled along the narrow brick passage hidden between the massive stones of the castle walls, torch lighting the way. Will ducked instinctively under a cobweb that wasn't there. He brushed the now-empty space with his fingers. "Huh." They'd made a game, for years, of letting that spiderweb be.

They stopped by a short flight of stairs inside the narrow passage. Will flung himself down to sit on them, dangling long legs.

Gregory hovered at the top of the stairs, his face working. Finally he settled on an emotion. "Will, you're *here*." A grin split his face. "I knew you'd come back." He rocked onto tip-toes excitedly. "Cook bought a guard pup off a peddler as came up here, summer last. It's great fun t' get past him to the pantry these days. Chased me all the way to south tower one night—hey, you moving back to our room soon? Jens got made carpenter and moved out—"

Will moved the torch from one hand to the other. "I'm staying in the visiting servant's quarters," he said. "What kind of pup?"

"Some sort of scruffy black one," said Gregory absently, working out the implications of "visiting." He fidgeted, then said, "This private enough? What, you got a girl to tell me about or something?" He settled on the stairs next to Will, drawing his knees up under his chin. "What're you up to, Will?"

"Me?" Will said innocently.

"None more likely. Why're you back?"

"Orders," said Will and couldn't contain a grin as he added, "From the ministry of intelligence."

"How—?" said Gregory. He spluttered for a moment, then decided on, "They let a mountain lad like you in?"

"Certainly did," said Will.

"What were they, desperate?"

Will grinned. "I'll have to tell you that story sometime. But, for now—"

"Wait, are you here for the *princesses*?" asked Gregory. "What have you been doing, that they're sending you off watching royals after less than two years? What did you *do*, Will?"

"I *am* watching princesses," said Will, "but, ah, I'm not really supposed to." He scratched the back of his head. "I'm s'posed to be just keeping an eye on the half a dozen of petty nobles they got with them; correspondence and such. There's a policy—" One of constant noble surveillance, which was probably a good idea, coming from a king who was the grandson of a usurping noble himself. "And old Westel likes to put journeymen he don't like on boring duty like this paper-sniffing."

"But you're not sticking to that, are you?" the boy said, with experience.

"There are assassins!" Will said, spreading his arms wide. "Rebels, or usurpers, or something." He shrugged and said eagerly, "There's things to do, secrets to ferret out, enemies to catch—and Westel wants me to sit it out and keep an eye on a bunch of lovesick noble puppies."

"Lies to tell, mischief to get into…"

Will grinned at Gregory and shrugged. "*You* wouldn't know anything about that," he said.

Gregory grinned back. "Nothing at all." He flicked a pebble and sent it bouncing down the short flight of stairs.

Will leaned back. He laced his fingers behind his skull and asked the ceiling, "What are you still doing here, Gregory?"

Gregory leaned forward, elbows on his knees. "Have you forgotten that much already?"

"What do you mean?" Will shrugged horizontally. "I just figured, why would you stay? I know you were hesitant to leave when I did, but once it had all sunk in, I thought you'd come to your senses. I kept expecting you to show up on my doorstep in the city."

Gregory shook his head, frowning. "I don't see why *you* left."

Will pushed himself up again, spreading his hands wide. "There's a *world* out there, Gregory. How can you not want to see it? The capital city—you can't imagine it, the size! And the palace. How can you hide in these mountains when there's so much to see out there?"

"I like it here," said Gregory. "I'm sorry you didn't."

"Once you see the capital, once you leave these mountains, you'll understand. You'll never want to come back, I promise. After seeing the world, this place will seem so small."

"It is small," said Gregory. "But I'm small."

Will laughed. "Well, for now I need a second pair of eyes up here," he said, "to look for folk that might have been bought. You game?"

Gregory nodded. "See if any of the old folk changes, acts suspicious, now that the royals are here."

Will shook his head. "Not changes," he said. "If they were bought, they were bought awhiles ago. I don't know if it'll be in the Willow Tree folk, or the royal servants—or even the Guard—but the royals' enemies have got folk up here already."

"They can't already have people up here," said Gregory. "We only heard about this royal visit a week ago. And a week's not what you mean by 'awhiles.'" The boy frowned at Will, who was keeping a smug smile carefully off his face. "And we're too small and too far away from anything for them to want anything to do with us, if it weren't for the royals' surprise visit. What are you thinking, Will?"

"Trust me," said Will. "They sent their people up here, or planned to have 'em sent with us. Or maybe they turned some of the Willow Tree servants already. Months ago maybe. A year."

Gregory shook his head.

"They *knew* we were coming," Will said, "and coming *here*. Westel didn't even blink when the king said the princesses were going to some castle no one but me had ever heard of. This is where royalty goes when it's threatened—and these people threatened them."

"Because my passages are here," said Gregory. "It's *got* to be. They're for the royals, they must be. Why else would they come here?" Then he blinked. "Threaten? What's happened then?"

"They tried to poison the royal family at her majesty's autumn ball. The ministry of Intelligence caught on before it reached their table. We didn't get the culprit."

"But Will, if the plan was to poison them dead a week ago, then they wouldn't have been working seeding the castle with traitors."

"No," Will said. "You see—that was never the plan. They never wanted the princesses dead. The poison, it was a botch job, sloppy and stupid. They were gambling we'd catch that, and we did. Now I want to know what they were gambling to win."

That day, two hours before, Sasha had slipped away from the temporarily-royal suite of rooms and its window, which was leaking cold. In the pale, deep blue of early morning, she'd pressed warm toes against greedy stone and pulled on cotton breeches and a shirt, then tiptoed past her rumpled bed, past the small sitting room and Gabrielle's closed door, and out to meet Elijah in the hall.

Now, there was sweat dried to salt across the bridge of her nose. Her clothing, well-worn and well-loved, stuck damply to her sides. Sasha turned the chill knob and stepped inside, shutting the door quietly behind her.

Sasha padded over stone tiles, pulled off her sweaty gear and scrubbed down with a cloth, wiping away red-brown grit. She looked for a moment at the damp wad on the floor, then picked it up and laid the shirt and trousers out over a chair.

She took a long breath.

Next, a pair of high stockings. A shift, a petticoat, layers of skirts; a light corset, breath sucked in and ribbons tied tight, and an overdress dropped down atop it all. Sasha yanked a brush through her hair with one hand and worked at pulling on her boots with the other.

She dug through a box on the desk, muttering. "A strip of leather? Come on, a bit of grungy string…" Finally she tugged out a long yellow ribbon. She eyed it, dubiously, in her palm for a moment, then tied her brown hair back.

A long mirror, only a little warped, hung along one wall. Sasha pushed back the thin tapestry covering it. Fabric whispered across stone. She tilted her head at the groomed young stranger in it, then nodded, businesslike, and left.

There was no one to impress in this tiny castle, *surely*. (And even when there was, Sasha liked to have a touch or two—weathered boots peeking from beneath her embroidered skirts, a bit of old string tucked in her thin tresses—that were *hers*).

In the sitting room of the suite, a young girl with black curls waited in a pale gown. She hadn't been there when Sasha had come in. "Where did you go?" asked Gabrielle.

"Practice," said Sasha, shrugging. "What are you reading?"

Her little sister turned a page. "I didn't realize you did that sword thing of yours so early," Gabrielle said.

"Sword," said Sasha, "*and* baton, and knife, and hand to hand." Gabrielle grinned up at her and shrugged. Sasha leaned over the back of the couch. "Geste's *Trade and economy in modern times: the lower continent*?" Sasha plopped her chin down on her hands. "Gabe, you do realize you're twelve, right?"

"I," said Gabrielle, turning another page, "am twelve and a half." She paused. "You said Geste's name wrong."

Sasha kissed her on the top of the head. "I'm hungry," she said. "Let's go."

Two guards stood outside the door of the suite of the two younger princesses. Gabrielle tucked her book under one arm.

"Nice ribbon," said Elijah. The other guard (not a member of Second Squad) looked, startled, at him.

"I will hurt you," Sasha said. The other guard looked, startled, at her.

"Don't," said Harston, rounding a corner. "I'm feeling a little short on men, having to split them between this castle and the palace." The other guard looked, the startled edge beginning to wear off into weary confusion, at him.

"Now," said Sasha, "it would break my heart, but if it really makes you uncomfortable, Harston, we can just turn around and head straight back for the capital."

"It *would* break the queen's," said Harston.

"A winter holiday she's not going on? Hardly." Sasha shrugged.

Gabrielle, ahead of them, dropped her book open in her hands and said briefly, "It gets Lia locked in a little castle with the two most eligible prospects of the country. Mother has her priorities."

Sasha made a face. "Lia better not get married—"

"She's twenty-one," murmured Gabrielle.

"—else Mother's going to try it in earnest on *me* next."

Gabrielle chuckled, a little girl hiccup in the back of her throat. "I hear the crown prince of the Sylian royal family is good looking," she said brightly.

"I love the weather in Sylia this time of year," said Elijah blandly. "Frigid."

"It's frigid *here*," said Sasha, looking around at the walls. "Is Mother hoping Lia will get so cold she has choose a suitor just so she won't freeze to death?"

Harston glanced at her, and hesitated, the expression looking odd on his square face. His steps slowed and Sasha shortened hers to fall back with him, Elijah at her shoulder. Gabrielle, reading, got ahead of them.

"Are you planning on lecturing me again?" said Sasha. "Harston, no one's going to shoot me off the top of a carriage—Elijah can't hit me with an apple—"

"There was wind," said Elijah. "I don't like these mountain things." He glanced at the captain as he spoke; the captain was watching his feet.

"Sasha, there's—" Harston stopped, then took a long, deep breath, mind made up. "There's more here than there seems. I think," said the captain. "I think there's something I should tell you." He took a breath—and an arrow flew into the stone wall behind them.

Harston knocked Sasha down and out of the way. Elijah knelt beside her before she could

42

catch her breath, his hand on his sword hilt as he hauled her to her feet. Two more arrows whistled towards them from the bows of the two masked figures down the hallway.

Sasha reached out and pulled Gabrielle behind her, looking around for something to duck behind. The arched hallway was ribbed with stone outcroppings; she pulled her sister behind one, pushing her into the corner where ridge met wall. The brief barrier was not enough to hide even both Sasha and Gabrielle from arrows, let alone their three guardsmen as well.

"Are you alright?" Elijah asked, seizing her shoulder. His eyes flicked away from her pale face, to the assassins, to his captain's haggard visage, to the distant light of the dining hall door where guards, summoned by Gabrielle's shriek, grabbed what weapons they could.

But there were several long corridors between their highnesses and the reinforcements.

Eli's eyes flicked back to Sasha. An arrow clattered on the floor behind them and they both jumped. "Stay behind me," he ordered, turning to face the assassins.

"I'm fine," she said, her eyes on the two assassins, her thoughts on the small knife tucked into her boot. "We need to get to the next rib, come on." Adrenaline raced through her veins, making her breath come quick and shallow. Incongruously, she thought she could smell burning paint and paper thick in the air.

Sasha shivered while she pushed Gabrielle along, one hand on a crumpled bow at the back of her dress. As they hurried to the next stone rib, toward the safety of the too-faraway dining hall, a whistling bolt sliced through Gabrielle's guard's upper arm. He stumbled a little and Gabrielle squeaked into the front of Sasha's dress.

"Get out of here," gritted Harston over his shoulder.

Sasha stashed Gabrielle behind the rib and then knelt and ripped a strip from her skirt. She darted past Elijah and tied it as tight as she could around the guard's bleeding arm. The guard gave her a pained thanks, his eyes on the archers. Eli yanked her back just as an arrow whistled by her head. "I told you to stay behind me," he said. "Do you know how much trouble I'd be in if one of those hit you?"

"They're just as likely to hit you!"

"I'm a little less valuable!"

Harston, who stood between them and the assassins, turned towards the enemy that still hovered behind their corner. He drew his sword, the steely sound shivering over the stone.

"Captain," said Elijah, taking a step after him, his sword half-drawn, his other hand behind him to hold Sasha back.

"Elijah, stay with the princesses," said Harston. "I will deal with these."

"But, captain," Eli began.

"Get them out of here. Keep them safe; that's an order."

"Harston," called Sasha. He didn't look back. Her heart thudded in her chest. She ached for a sword in her hand; her skirts clung to her legs like kindly hands.

"Come on, Sash," said Elijah, his face nearly as pale as his injured comrade as he watched his captain's back. Elijah dragged her away; Gabrielle was clasped tightly to her side. A thunder of footsteps reached them: the guards from the dining room.

Gabrielle's guard had his hand clamped to his injured arm. Blood stained through Sasha's makeshift bandage and tight relief drained over his features as the guards reached them.

Armed guards surrounded the two princesses, pulling them toward the dining hall and safety. Sasha released Gabrielle to their care, but pushed back through the crowd, trying to catch a glimpse of their attackers.

A handful of the guards charged toward the assassins, Elijah not among them. Eli shoved through the guards behind Sasha, grabbing her shoulder to keep her from leaving the guards' circle. She pushed at him, her heart pounding dreadfully. She had almost tugged out of his hold.

Harston charged. The guards who rushed behind him lent their shouts to the general noise. The two assassins let loose their arrows once more before turning to dart away. One bolt swished harmlessly between two of the guards, clattering to the floor behind them.

The second buried itself in Harston's chest.

Harston jerked to a stop and so did Sasha, breath stopping in her chest. The captain reached up a hand to brush his chest. The red stained the silver of his uniform; the black of it shone wetly.

Harston sagged to his knees, took a long, jarring breath as though making his mind up once again; and then collapsed to the ground where he lay, very still.

Sasha struggled through the restricting circle of bodies around her. Elijah's numb fingers had let her go. She was just able to push past the edge of the guards when Elijah caught up to her again, wrapping his hands around her shoulders. She could feel his fingers shaking.

"Sash, we've got to get you someplace more secure." Elijah's fingers tightened and then he slipped around her, standing between her and the black and silver body on the floor.

Guards raced after the retreating assassins, the clamor fading down the hall while Sasha fought to breathe.

"That's Harston," she said, numb. "Elijah, did you see that, they just *shot Harston*—" Her voice rose and broke. She darted forward and he caught her with an arm across the front of her shoulders.

"We have to go," he said. "They could be back. There could be more of them." When she tried to push past him, Elijah picked her up by the shoulders and walked her three feet back before he dropped her. "We have to go," Eli said, again, trying to force her back by walking forward.

Sasha shoved at his chest, dark with the lightweight armor of the Guard, which would turn a glancing shot, perhaps, but never a head-on blow. That was Elijah's chest under there, Elijah's, which maybe one day too would sprout an arrow shaft and stop beating.

"*That's Harston*," she said, and hit him in the chest again, hard enough to bruise if it hadn't been for the leather padding. "How can you—I won't leave him! I'm not going anywhere!"

Eli took another step forward, forcing her back. "At least to the mess hall, c'mon, it's got doors."

At any other moment, Sasha might have noticed the tension in Eli's voice, the way his eyes flicked to the corridors that joined the hallway, looking for dangers, but for now she couldn't even notice her own tears cutting through the dirt on her cheeks.

She still had dirt on her cheeks from Gideon's perfectly square practice field.

She'd missed a few spots, when she'd been scrubbing off her face in her room, ten minutes ago—that had only been ten minutes ago—how could that have only been ten minutes ago—

"Sash, we have to go."

She shoved at him, wept without noticing, and tried to get past the solid black and silver presence that was keeping her from the captain. She could see a man bending over Harston, feeling for a pulse. Her own heart beat loud enough she thought she could feel it shake her ribs. The man reached out two worn fingers and slid Harston's eyelids closed.

"Come on, Sash, just to the mess hall."

Sasha threw herself against Elijah's hold and screamed at him to let her go, that they couldn't leave with the captain lying on the floor, looking like he'd never get up again. "That's Harston!"

"Do you think I don't know?" roared Elijah, and she stopped, breath coming in shallow hiccups, and stared. His eyes were as red-rimmed as hers. "It's not safe," Eli said, his voice returned to normal levels, clipped and tense, hoarse and barely hiding it.

"We have to go," he said, and she let him pull her down the hallway, to someplace with entrances and exits to guard, away from the man lying dead on the stone floor behind them.

Chapter Two
A Chill in the Air

"You *idiots*," said a thin man named Doulings, shattering the quiet of the underground jumble of storage rooms. "I told you to *shadow* them, not to shoot arrows at them. What if you had killed one of the girls?" His frame was taut with anger. He glared at the two standing before him; their black masks were discarded on one of the storage barrels.

"Shout a little quieter, would you? Someone will hear us," a young woman with a long blond braid said, leaning on a crate and examining her fingernails. Andrea had snagged one, in the panic of the chase and the frantic yanking at a passage door with guards close on their heels. The jagged edge was poking annoyingly into the skin of her finger.

"Do you have any idea how far it is to the nearest living person?" Doulings demanded, turning on her. Her eyes flicked up to meet his but she didn't change her stance. "These storage rooms are bigger than the castle itself. I can yell at you idiots as *loud* and for as *long* as I want!" Doulings's forearms were run up and down with white scars, reminders of old fights, old losses and victories.

"We didn't plan it," Andrea said. "But the opportunity was there—"

Yohan, the second assassin, said over her, "He was about to tell the princesses something—perhaps the passages. We thought we should prevent that." He was a barrel chested man at least twenty years older than the younger woman.

Andrea shrugged, brushing her hands along her pants. She had a servant's skirt and blouse slung over a barrel, to change into later. "Anyway, getting that bloody loyalist ought to make it all worthwhile."

There was a long moment, then Doulings said to Andrea, "If you hadn't been planning on killing anyone, *why did you bring bows?*"

She sniffed.

"We're not here for personal revenge, chit. You're here for your precious Ceren; I'm here for the money. The big picture! That's more important than settling the score with one man."

Andrea stiffened. Yohan sat resignedly down to wait it out.

"How would *you* know?" Andrea said. "You know how to murder and cheat and steal.

You don't know about sacrifice; you don't know about duty. You know *nothing* of this."

"Is that your problem with me? That I don't believe in whatever idealistic junk you lot prescribe to?"

Andrea stood—she came up to about his collarbone. "My problem with you is that you don't belong here and we don't *need* you—"

"Andie!" Yohan interrupted.

Andrea sat abruptly down on the crate.

Doulings raised an eyebrow smugly. "Your elders seemed to think that you needed me."

Andrea leaned back and crossed her ankles, her legs straight out in front of her. "They're wrong," she said.

"Have you informed them of this?"

Andrea said, "Yes," as Yohan said, "They didn't ask her opinion."

Doulings smirked. "Well, in any case," he said, stepping forward so she'd have to look up to meet his eyes. "Your elders put me in charge, so, no matter what you think, chit, you've got to listen to me. What? Never had to be obedient before? Just know this," he said, his voice falling to a whisper as he leaned in close to her, "if you mess this up for me, I *will* rain misery down on your pretty little head."

Yohan stepped between them. "Leave her be, Doulings. You're in charge of the plan, yes, but stop with the threats." The older man was a few inches shorter than Doulings, but what he lacked in height he made up for in sturdy strength. The elders, after all, had chosen to send him here for the most monumental task the Ceren rebels had attempted in eight years.

Doulings backed off warily and Andrea gazed at him with a flat expression. The thin man cleared his throat. "We should have waited until winter to make a move," said Doulings. "They'd let their guard down, thinking we were stuck outside of this miserable snowed-in valley. But that advantage is gone now, thanks to your foolery. They're not idiots enough to think that we'll flock south when winter comes. Besides that, we need to hold off on getting the princesses until we are sure our noble is the chosen suitor. It doesn't help us if the two little ones die now, and the eldest marries someone who is not under our influence."

Yohan nodded solemnly while Andrea rolled her eyes. "I'm going to go back to the kitchen," the young woman said. "They'll miss me if I stay away too long."

Yohan stood as well. "And I'm sure the hostlers are noticing my absence." He held a fisted hand to his chest in a Ceren gesture of respect before he left the room. Andrea simply let her gaze rest on Doulings for a moment before turning and leaving after Yohan.

Outside, Yohan eyed his young compatriot, a frown etched between his brows. "I can't say I'm upset that Old Harston's not around to plague us, but you will *never* lie to me again, miss. Not about something this important."

Her cheeks going bright red, Andrea said, "I thought it—"

"I don't want your excuses," he said. "Just know I won't cover for you again."

She nodded mutely.

"And we *should* listen to him," said Yohan. "He knows far more about this sort of thing than we do."

Andrea crossed her arms over her chest, scowling. "We're not totally helpless, Yohan. We've done resistance work before, you know that. Just because he's a bit more experienced—"

Yohan gave her a sympathetic smile. "Andie, kidnapping tax collectors and raiding warehouses isn't the same as a royal assassination and a secret coup."

She shook her head. "We've taken down people before, Yohan. What do you call me getting Harston?"

"Have you killed anyone before that?" Yohan asked. Andrea glanced away. "Face it, we need Doulings. He's the one who found the noble for us."

"We could've found someone," Andrea said. "We don't need this faithless murderer."

Yohan shook his head. "We can't do it alone." He sighed, putting a hand on her shoulder. "He's helping us to free Ceren. You have to deal with him. Put your country above yourself. It's what your father would've done."

Andrea's chin lifted and they continued on.

The next morning saw Sasha up in the early darkness of before dawn. She lay quietly in her bed, staring upwards at the ceiling, which faded into black. The darkness seemed to muffle sound; the castle was silent around her.

With a sigh, Sasha pushed herself up into a seated position. Her blankets fell around her. "You still have to go to practice," she said quietly.

She slipped out of bed, the cold biting in her feet, hands, the tip of her nose. She got dressed quietly in the dark. She rubbed her arms to warm herself and wiggled her toes in her soft boots.

The funeral had been yesterday.

She slipped into the corridor outside where their two guards waited—one for her and one for Gabrielle—standing sleepily on either side of the door. She nodded to them both, a Fourth and a Fifth Squader. All of First Squad had been left at home, as that was where the king was, but a few the queen's Fourth Squad had come along because the queen's squad also watched the princess heir. Third, the prison watch, was entirely left behind as well.

At home, Second and Fifth guarded the walls and filled in the gaps—most of the gaps involving Sasha got filled by Second, because they knew how to handle her, or she knew how to handle them. All of Second had come to the mountains with the royal children and most of Fifth had, too. Harston had asked, grudgingly, for the ministry of war to have the army help to fill in the gaps back home.

There was supposed to be a Second Squader, now, coming to relieve one of these two from their shift, and to walk her out to Gideon's practice yard in the cold, where they would whack each other with sticks, or hone battle skills, depending on their attitude. Sasha leaned against the wall, looking down the hallway with a tired sort of curiosity.

One of the men shifted. She asked, "You wouldn't know who was replacing you for the next shift?"

Her guard stood straighter, addressing her. "I just began my shift, your highness."

She blinked at him. "Hmph," she said. Sasha straightened and made her way down the hallway. Torches flickered.

"Uh, princess?" said her guard, hurriedly taking a step toward her.

She sighed. "Walk with me? I'm trying to get to practice."

Sasha moved swiftly through the castle and down the sloped-roof passage to the barn. The barn was almost as cold as the outside. She shoved through the thick wooden door. Sasha wrapped her arms around herself, chill leaking through light practice gear, and looked at the empty yard.

Someone cleared his throat behind her—not her guard, coming out of the barn, it was too sure of itself for that. "Your highness?" said the man behind her. Sasha turned around.

"Vice-captain Brown," she said. Over his shoulder, she saw ten practice-clothing-colored dots racing each other for the crown of a dry yellow slope.

Frederick Brown paused, allowing her time to edit her phrase, then said, "*Captain* Brown."

"Yes," she said. "I suppose so."

His eyes brushed over Guard-issue practice gear. "Out for a morning stroll?" Brown asked. The guard at Sasha's shoulder was trying his best to look dutiful and invisible.

Sasha hooked her thumbs in the belt of her trousers. She gave him time to edit his phrase, too. "Morning *practice*," she said. She looked over his shoulder again. The dots had reached the top of the slope and were coming back down. "I guess I slept in a little today."

"I don't think," said Brown, but Sasha was ignoring him. He finished anyway. "I don't think princesses *have* anything to practice with guardsmen." She turned back to him, slowly. "Other than being guarded."

"I'm not very good at that one," said Sasha. "I like arms practice much better, thank you."

Nathaniel was almost the first back, loping long-legged. He slowed to a walk before he reached them. The men chasing him swept past shouting victory calls. Elijah slipped in with the bulk of the group.

Sasha took a breath, ignoring new additions and absences. "You started without me,

Gideon," she said. "Were you afraid I'd beat you to the top of the mountain?"

"With those length legs, highness?" said Elijah. "Hardly likely." He looked at Gideon.

And Gideon hesitated and looked to Brown.

Sasha felt all the ugly pieces falling into place.

"Exercises?" she said. "C'mon, boys, my lazy bums, we just going to stand around?" Sasha stepped over the line that edged the practice field, carefully drawn, and spun to face them all, who were standing outside it. Her hands on her hips, she said, "Well, if you're not gonna—"

"Your highness," said Brown. "You're disrupting a Guard practice."

"You're disrupting it," Sasha said. "Normally we're well into sets by this point. Look at the sky. Gideon, make 'em move, will you? Was I not the only sleepy one this morning?"

"I'm afraid this can't continue, your highness," said Captain Brown.

Practice clothes were made for practicing, not standing still. The dawn chill cut through the cloth. Sasha crossed her arms across her chest and said, "Excuse me?"

Brown sighed, as though he were hoping she'd be smarter, but hadn't expected it. "I don't know why he let this continue for so long, Second Squad and their little mascot. Your highness, this is a Guard practice. You are not of the Guard."

Sasha raised her chin and looked at him stonily. Second Squad shifted where they stood. A few opened their mouths and shut them, swallowing.

"You are royalty," said Brown. "You're a girl." He stepped forward and offered a hand to escort her off the field. "I'm sure we can find an activity to better suit your situation."

"I belong here," she said. "I've been a part of this for eight years. I belong on this field, with this squad, *captain*."

"I'm afraid, your highness," said Brown, "you are mistaken. Please accompany me off the field. You've been a distraction to these men long enough."

She ignored the hand, still held up before her, and looked past him, at the ten men bunched up behind him, standing in parade rest. Elijah met her eyes with a question. Gideon watched his shoes.

"*You*'re mistaken," said Nathaniel. Elijah looked at his brother. "Sasha's one of us, you see," said Nate. "You can't kick her out."

"I'm not kicking her out of anything," said Brown. "I'm taking her back to where she should be. Your highness," he said. She hoped the arm he was holding out was starting to ache.

"Gideon," said Nathaniel. "Tell him."

Gideon kept watching his feet. He didn't say anything. Nathaniel said, "*Gideon*."

Sasha looked at Gideon's profile and exhaled slowly. She walked past Brown's outstretched hand and off the field. The men parted way for her, half of them looking like they wanted to say something, to her or to Brown.

She patted Nathaniel's arm as she passed. Elijah was still quietly asking if she needed his defense and she shook her head at him. Brown narrowed his eyes at the exchange.

Gideon lifted his head and met her eyes with an effort. She paused beside him, any expression of hers carefully hid behind a single raised, unconcerned eyebrow. "He's the captain," said Gideon softly, in explanation.

Sasha swallowed. "I was looking forward to beating you to the top of that hill today," she said and left.

Sasha took a deep, slow breath. She could make it to the privacy of her room, surely, before she burst out in tears or curses or broke a finger slamming her fist into the wall. She took another breath and thought about what Brown's face might look like with a broken nose. It helped.

Her guard was quivering a little bit, somewhere behind her. The sun was barely peeking over the horizon and he'd already spent far too much time in the company of individuals who were both very angry and very superior to him in rank. Gabrielle's guard, standing beside the two younger princess's rooms tried not to look too curious as the pair approached.

Sasha slipped inside the room and slammed the door behind her with a ringing thud. Her guard nodded to his slightly shell-shocked fellow and took up his post with a very quiet sigh of relief.

Inside the room, Sasha kicked at the throw rugs on the ground and tangled her feet in them. "Hook-nosed, big-eared son of a dockside—"

A door creaked open and Gabrielle peeked her head out, wreathed in a fuzzy black halo. "What is it?" she asked sleepily.

"Nothing!" said Sasha, stomping on a rug tassle. "Go back to bed!"

Sasha crossed the room in two great strides and flung open the shutters, letting a cool rush of morning air seep in. Above the courtyard, the square of sky she could see was streaked with color. She held the sill of the window in her hands until her knuckles turned white.

Well, that was it then. No Guard, no Harston, no— She slammed a kick into the wall, and then hopped up and down on the other leg, holding her foot in both hands and cursing at it. She staggered around one-legged for a moment, then collapsed onto a stiff couch.

Sasha wiggled the toe cautiously. It stung but didn't seem to be actually broken. She grumbled something, then hopped with a wince to her feet and stomped out of the room. "Your highness?" said her guard, following.

"I'm not just going to *sit* there," said Sasha.

"Of course not," he said with confusion.

She passed waking servants and a curly-headed boy changing out yesterday's torches for new ones. She was trying to think where Brown's office might be—not in Harston's already, *surely*—when she turned the corner. The soles of her boots shushed to stillness on the stone.

Sasha wrapped her arms around herself, staring at the place where the captain of the Royal Guard had died. It was cold in her light practice wear. If Brown had let her spar, she wouldn't be this cold.

Her guard drew to a stop behind her, quietly.

Sasha walked over to the wall, put her back to it, and slid down to sit at its base, the palms of hands flat on her knees. Rock pressed into her shoulder blades. The stones of Willow Tree were grey like the rock peeking out of the mountainside, stones the size of carriage wheels and smaller. In the palace, the walls were sanded smooth and whitewashed, but these walls were more like giant, upright replicas of the cobblestone streets of the capital city.

At home, in every free moment, or just when she couldn't stand one more dress fitting or fawning official or lesson on the proper way to hold a fan, she would be off in a breath to the city that surrounded the palace, wide and bright and dirty. Harston had tried to stop her until—

no, he'd always tried to stop her. After a few failed attempts he'd just started training her, too, for the times when he couldn't keep her behind white-washed walls.

The floor was cold. She wrapped her loose leggings tight around her calves. The ground had been almost frozen when they'd lowered Harston into it.

She stayed there until the change of guard.

"You're blue," said Elijah.

"And you're red," said Sasha. She looked up at him with half a smile. She'd heard him send the other guard away ten minutes ago and settle into place beside her. "Does that mean we're at war?"

Eli reached down to take her by the wrists and pulled her to her feet. "Always."

He walked down the hall and she followed, with one glance over her shoulder at an empty patch of stone.

Elijah turned down a hallway, then into a small corridor. "I did a little exploring," he said. "No one uses this room."

"What are we doing?" said Sasha.

Elijah creaked the door open, then looked over his shoulder at her. "I," he said. "Well, I thought you'd want to spar."

The force of her hug sent him stumbling backwards into the room.

"I hate Brown," she said into his shirt.

"He certainly makes it easy," said Elijah.

Sasha sprung back again, seizing Elijah's shoulders. "Do you know what happened? To the archers, the ones in black?"

Elijah hesitated and the door banged open.

Another redhead bounded into the room behind them. Nathaniel skidded to a stop and grinned at his little brother and the princess. "I got Rogers to cover my shift," he said. "Now, what are we going to do?"

"How? Did you bribe him?" said Sasha.

"Did you threaten him?" said Elijah.

"He lost at cards to me, awhiles back," said Nate.

"So, both," said Eli.

"So, this Brown fellow," began Nate.

"We dislike him greatly," said Sasha. "But I want to know about Harston."

"Sasha," said Nate.

"I was so angry about Brown and the fact that he's an idiot," said Sasha. "But— someone *murdered* Harston. I'm angry about *that*." Something was caught in her throat, sharp and hot. Nathaniel shrugged off his coat and handed it to her. "Did we catch them?" she asked, wrapping herself in the Royal Guard's silver and black.

Elijah sighed. "They disappeared," he said.

Nathaniel flicked his fingers. "Vanished, melted, wisped away, I don't know," he said. He flicked his fingers again, like he was rolling a pair of dice, to hide the tremble in them.

"I was at the other end of the palace," he said to his fingertips. "If I'd have been there, I'd have got them."

Elijah gave her a little more information. "They chased them into a dead end, but when they got to the end, they'd lost them."

Sasha crossed her arms. "What really happened?" she said.

"That's all we know," said Elijah. "That's all they've told us."

Sasha hopped up onto a sturdy old table, a puff of dust enveloping her light practice wear. "That's not all you know," she said. "You hear things, you make guesses. I want to know what's going on."

"So do we," said Eli.

"And we *have* been thinking," said Nathaniel. He elbowed Elijah. "C'mon, little brother."

The two redheads looked at each other. Elijah stuck his hands in his pockets, then took them out again.

"Option one," said Elijah. "The pursuit lost them somewhere before the dead end. Option two: It wasn't a dead end."

"Two doesn't make any sense," said Sasha. She pulled her knees up and propped her chin up on them. "They said it was a dead end."

"They said they didn't lose them, too," said Elijah. "So someone's wrong somewhere."

"Never trust what you haven't seen with your own two eyes," said Nathaniel.

"Gideon was in the pursuit," said Sasha. "Let's trust his eyes." She hopped off the table. "Do you know when he's off shift?"

Elijah said, "I already talked to him."

She hopped back up onto the table, making a new mark in the dust. "What'd he say?"

"They were following right behind the archers—they could hear them around the corner. Gideon knew it was a dead end up ahead; he'd reviewed the castle maps earlier. But when they came round into the corridor, it was empty."

Nathaniel said, "So they lost them along the way, and didn't report it."

Sasha snorted. "Like there's anything Gideon wouldn't report."

"If Brown tells him to jump," said Nate with a shrug.

Sasha smacked him in the shoulder. "Ow," said Nathaniel, rubbing the spot.

"Brown *is* the captain," said Sasha. "It's not Gideon's fault."

"Why isn't it?" said Nathaniel.

"Shush," said Sasha. "So, Gideon says they didn't lose them. Maybe he was at the back of the pack."

Elijah shook his head. "First one into the hall."

"Mmph," said Sasha.

Nathaniel said, "I was talking to some of the ladies in the kitchens."

"Flirting," said Sasha. Elijah snorted.

"Yes," said Nathaniel. "And they mentioned something interesting—a castle myth."

"Excellent dramatic delivery," said Elijah. "Just tell us, would you?"

Nathaniel grinned at him. "Passages," he said. "A network of secret passages built into the castle." He shrugged. "If the assassins had access to those, then it would be easy for them to disappear."

Elijah nodded, running his fingers over his chin. Sasha shook her head. "But, *passages*?" she said. "That's like a play. Why would this castle have secret passages?"

"Actually," said Elijah, "it makes sense."

"What?" said Sasha.

"They must be for you," said Elijah. Then he hesitated. "Uh."

"This is a royal castle," said Nathaniel easily. "It's one of the safehouses for your family. That's why we're here."

"And that's *classified*," said Elijah.

"So?"

"How do you two know then?" said Sasha.

"We're part of Harston's planning commission," said Elijah reluctantly. "Safehouses, protection plans, guard contingents."

Nate laughed. "We *are* his planning commission. It's why old man Harston hired the pair of us in the first place." He grinned. "We're good at figuring out the holes in security plans."

"So we know what Willow Tree is," said Elijah. "It's on the list."

"You know where the passages are?"

"No," said Eli slowly. "Harston didn't say a word about any of that. But—it makes sense. This place is high up on the list of safehouses, but if you just look at it straight on, there isn't any reason for there to be. It's got to be hiding something."

Sasha pulled the jacket tighter around herself. "What exactly is going on?" she said. "Why are we spending winter in a safehouse?" She scowled at the younger redhead. "Stop *hesitating,* Eli! I want to know."

"Elijah?" Nate said sweetly. "The lady asked a question."

"They tried poison, back at the palace," said Elijah reluctantly, with a glare for his brother. "And they got a bit too close. The king decided to send you here while the ministry of Intelligence works out who was behind it."

"So we'll have to find them," murmured Sasha.

"The killers?" said Nate.

Her eyes flicked up to him. "The passages," she said. "Those're holes in security, certainly."

"Mm."

She slid off the table, balancing on the balls of her feet. "I think I'll go see if Gabrielle's hungry," she said.

"No spar?" said Eli.

She hesitated. "My head's too full right now, I think."

"That's when I'd think you'd like to give bruises the most," said Nathaniel, opening the door for her.

Sasha stepped through it, slipping off the jacket and handing it back to him. "And, it's not quite the same."

Nathaniel, the jacket tossed over one hand, headed toward the kitchens. Sasha brushed off her trousers unsuccessfully and turned in the direction of her room. Eli followed her through the hallways with cat's feet quiet.

Outside the door, Elijah and Sasha paused. "Why're we doing this?" said Elijah.

Sasha looked over at him. "You're joking," she said. "You know why."

"I want to hear it from you." Eli crossed his arms and leaned back against the stone.

"Not knowing where those passages are is dangerous."

"Yes," said Eli. He waited.

She scowled at the floor. "Someone murdered Harston," said Sasha. "I want to find out *who*."

"And what're you going to do then?" said Elijah.

"I—" She lifted her head, chin firm and stubborn.

"These are *killers*, Sash," said Elijah. "You're going to get yourself killed."

"I can take care of myself!" she said. "I've been in trouble before, and I've gotten my own self out of it."

"Not like this," said Eli. "Not people trained to kill, not people who are especially out to kill *you*. Sash—"

"And have *you*?" said Sasha. Elijah opened his mouth and shut it. "You're a guardsman, is that what you were going to say? You're trained for this, right? Well so am I!"

She slammed the door and left him standing in the hall.

Standing before the vice-captain's study with a covered platter in one hand and a half-decanter of good wine and a goblet tucked under the other arm, Will raised a fist and knocked on the door.

It hadn't been hard to get Cook to give Will the job of delivering the new captain's dinner to his study. Captain Brown opened the door and peered down at the young man dressed in serviceable castle livery. "Come in," he said.

"Does your lordship wish for me to set it all up for you?" Will asked cheerily.

Brown blinked. "Alright." Will stepped inside and Brown shut the door behind him. "Are you the one who…?" Brown trailed off, gazing doubtfully at Will.

Will put the tray down on Brown's desk and pulled a piece of paper from his pocket. He passed it to Brown who unfolded it and held it up to the oil lamp's light, examining the seal pressed upon it.

"It's authentic," Will said, uncovering the tray, and laying the cover to the side. "Yeah, I'm the one who sent you the note."

Brown harrumphed. "It seemed a very odd request, *have your supper in your study tonight*, especially coupled with the ministry of Intelligence's seal."

Will chuckled. "Well, thank you for trusting it." He cleared a space on the desk and set down the plate of the new captain's supper.

"So why all the bother?" Brown asked, stepping over to stand at the front of the desk and to peer down at Will, who looked back at him with amused brown eyes. "Couldn't you just have asked me to be here, alone, at a certain time, and that you'd come to call?"

"A manservant having a secret conference with the captain of the Royal Guard would be suspicious—and someone would notice; they always do. I had to have a reason to be here." Will gestured to the tray in front of him. "Delivering your supper gives me a few moments of discussion with you without raising suspicion. We do have limited time, however, so we'd better get straight to the point."

Brown nodded.

Will placed the glass beside the plate, and the fork and knife on the other side. "I'm one of minister Westel's men." Brown looked doubtful at the word *men*. Will continued, "I assume you know what this entails. I'm here to

70

help with the protection of the princesses. If I gather any necessary information, I will pass it on to you. If you gain any, please pass it to me." He waited for Brown's slow nod of acceptance then went on. "Now, for our present dilemma. How did those assassins breach our defenses, do you think?"

Brown scowled. "Traitors, if I had to choose an option." He shook his head. "Harston was too soft on the men. Soft, and that leads to lack of respect, especially among the commonborn, and lack of respect creates sedition, and treason."

Will looked down and busied himself with unstoppering the decanter of wine. He poured the glass half-full of red liquid. "I will research that possibility, sir," he said.

Brown huffed. "You don't *know*? Isn't information your business?"

"Isn't keeping assassins out of the castle yours?" Will asked, as he put the stopper back into the wine decanter. With a hidden wince, he buried feelings of ruffled feathers. "I don't know how they got in," he went on. Brown had gone red in the face. "But I'm examining the possibilities. It is rather certain that they left the castle, but, perhaps not." He shook his head.

"Of course they left! We chased them into a dead end. The only place they could've gone was *out*."

"You can never be certain, unless you have all the information," Will said. Will picked up the metal cover and the tray and left the decanter on the desk. "If you fear traitors: put men in pairs on all the doors. It's unlikely that two randomly chosen fellows would both defect to the enemy—but randomly chosen. Don't let anyone influence the duty rosters."

"Are you *telling* me what to do?" Brown demanded.

"Yes," Will responded absently, heading to the door. He glanced back at Brown's tight, outraged face. He sighed. "I meant: I *recommend* you put men in pairs on all the doors." Will opened the door and bowed, his hands full with tray and cover. "Good night, my lord. I hope you enjoy the meal."

Ruffled. Damn.

Andrea glanced down the hallway, checking for anyone out walking, this late at night. She pulled a ring of lock picks from her pocket, a gift from her father for her seventh birthday. Inserting the first one in the door, she went to work, one ear listening for approaching guards, a thrill in her veins.

She knew it was selfish of her, but she was glad for the illness that had let her go in Nik's place on this mission. Her adoptive brother would've done as well (better) than she, but this would be a fight she would remember for a lifetime—as short as a rebel's lifetime tended to be.

And Nik was Nik—he'd find himself plenty of adventures without this one, and drag her and the rest of their brothers bruisingly along.

The passages remained unguarded despite the rebels' mysterious disappearance so close to one of the entrances. That said, to Andrea, that no one else had known of the passages except the old loyalist murderer. She was here, picking the lock on Harston's old rooms, to make sure their secret stayed kept.

The door swung open and she stepped inside, smiling. No one had disturbed his things yet. It had been a couple of days since his death but apparently his soldiers were too busy grieving him to sort through his possessions. She couldn't imagine why.

Andrea shut the door behind her and began glancing through Harston's papers. Careful to disturb as little as possible, she went through his desk, flicking papers and creaking open drawers. No map. Harston had had to have one somewhere. As long as she could find it, it would be easy to make certain that no one would be able to discover the passages anew.

Her only fear was that the locals might know of it already—what if they told the guards? She had mentioned this idea to Doulings, but he had passed it off as unlikely—his mocking laugh still grated on her ears.

Whatever Doulings said, she was still going to check out the possibility. He hadn't wanted her stealing Harston's map, either.

Andrea checked the obvious hiding places: under the mattress, in a drawer with a false bottom, buried in his bags. She searched the floor for a loose stone—the castle masons had, after all, been obsessed with secrets. Andrea stiffened, her eyes darting to the door as she heard footsteps in the hall, but continued her search. A smile crept across her face as the stone she stepped on wobbled beneath her.

A few seconds later, a green-eyed shadow slipped out of the room, a paper clutched in its fist.

"He's gone," said Sasha.

She, Elijah, and Nathaniel had found themselves in the little-used storeroom again. It was late; Gabrielle was fast asleep back in her and Sasha's shared suite. But Sasha hadn't been able to do anything but stare up at the ceiling while her toes froze in the draft seeping in the shuttered window, and the boys had just gotten off a night shift.

"I've barely had time to miss him yet," Sasha said. She was sitting cross-legged on the storeroom floor,

Elijah leaned against the wall, a few feet from her. Nathaniel, with all the excess energy of a long-legged yearling foal, paced, hopping up to perch on barrels and tables, and then hopping down.

Sasha said, "I've had stretches longer than two days before where I didn't see him at all, before, of course, but it's—it's not the same at all. We'll never see him again."

Sasha looked up. Nate was flicking his fingers, studying them like he'd never thought about throwing dice before.

"And that really, really hasn't sunk in yet." Sasha groped for words. "But it will, won't it? And there's a part of me—I can feel it—just waiting to break over that." Sasha ground the heels of her hands into her forehead. "And what am I doing? I'm supposed to be mourning Harston, and I'm thinking about how it makes *me* feel. I feel so selfish and I hate that—and here I go talking about me again." She dropped her forehead onto her raised knees.

"He saved my life," said Elijah into the silence. "Nate's and mine."

"I didn't know that," Sasha said, softly. She lifted her head.

Elijah nodded. Nathaniel hopped up onto a different part of the table, swinging his legs like a boy on a dock on a summer's day.

Sasha said, "Was that before I met you? You were so little then, though. What, eleven? And three weeks into a Guard apprenticeship."

"Before we were apprentices," said Elijah. "He gave us a chance when he didn't have to. It changed my life, becoming a guard."

"And what about, you, Nate?" said Sasha. "The uniform change your life, too?"

Nate grinned at her, shrugged. "It's been fun."

"Well," said Elijah. "I'm not sure anyone's got the power to make Nathaniel anything different than himself. He's a bit stagnant, my brother."

"Oy!" said Nate. "I'm flexible. I'm as flexible as the best nightside dancer in Neria City—I've got proof, too, just ask her about—"

"I don't want to hear!" Sasha and Eli protested together. Nathaniel grinned with well-earned pride.

"We are what we do," said Elijah. "We are what we do to other people. I'm here because of Theodore Harston." Elijah reached over with a hesitation only a handful of people would have had the experience to recognize (two of them were in the room) and took one of Sasha's hands, running a thumb over the ridged calluses on her palm. "And so are you."

Sasha blinked rapidly. A long breath just made her chest shake; there was a matching quiver in Elijah's chin. She wrapped her stolen hand around Elijah's and squeezed.

"Missing him is mourning him," Elijah said. "Being heartbroken means he had your heart to break. That's the opposite of selfish, Sasha."

She scooted closer to him, skirt catching on the grit of the unused floor, and buried her face in his shoulder. After a moment, Sasha felt Nathaniel settle down on her other side, an arm around her shoulders, one foot still tapping an erratic rhythm, never still.

Elijah's hand was warm in hers; she held on tight. She didn't let go for a long time.

Chapter Three
Yes, Sir

Snow fell, coating the meadow in a frigid blanket. The trees' green bows turned white, dripping with icicles, and cold drafts whispered through Willow Tree's halls. Sasha understood why a covered stone walkway had been built leading to the stables. The steep roof of the stable kept it from falling in.

A squad snow-shoed out and confirmed the pass had been blocked. Until the thaws came, Willow Tree would be home.

Sasha woke before the sun rose, rolled out of bed, and pulled on her practice clothes. She tied back her hair and grabbed the weighted practice sword she'd had Nathaniel smuggle out for her. In the adjoining room between her bedroom and Gabrielle's, she bunched the throw rugs up against the walls and began basic stretches and strength exercises on the bare stone floor. The weight of the sword and the feel of worn wood in her hand were familiar, comforting, and strange in this soft room.

After a particularly long pattern dance, she opened the wooden shutters. The sun was rising. It was out of sight below the walls of the small courtyard at the heart of the castle, but there was color in the one square of sky that she could see. With the rush of chill air on her back, she raised the sword again and continued, the weight of it seeming heavier than it had been at the beginning of the exercise.

Gabrielle had tip-toed out sometime after Sasha's muscles had warmed up and sometime before sweat started dripping off the tip of her nose. The littlest princess drew her knees up on the couch and watched her sister with open curiosity.

When Sasha had had her fill of defeating ghost enemies, she cleaned up herself and the room, tossing the crumpled rugs back into a semblance of tidiness. Gabrielle chuckled, rising from her perch. "I'll do that," she said. Gabrielle squatted down to shift a rug. "So, did you let the Guard sleep in today?"

Sasha had opened her room door and was taking off a damp shirt. "Something like that."

Gabrielle twitched a rug into place and scrambled over to straighten another. "Changes in administration?"

"Something like that."

In ten minutes, Sasha was ready to go and Gabrielle was barefoot in her nightgown. "I'll meet you there," she offered.

"I'm not hungry," said Sasha, settling on the couch. "I'll wait for you."

"*I'm* starving," said Gabrielle. "So are you." Sasha closed her eyes and leaned back. "I *do* have a well-trained guard, you know." Gabrielle went back to her room, calling out, "You think you're going to take the whole enemy army out by yourself if they come to call?" When her sister didn't answer, Gabrielle looked over her shoulder at the patterns of throw rugs on the floor and nudged one thoughtfully.

On the couch, Sasha tapped her feet and thought. Gabrielle returned a little while later, finding her sister half-asleep, and they stepped outside together.

As they did, a scratchy woolen shawl dropped around Sasha's shoulders. She turned to see Elijah slipping back to standing properly square-shouldered and stiff against the wall, cocking an eyebrow at her. "Morning, highness," he said. She nodded.

"Gabrielle's hungry," said Sasha. "Let's go." She stalked down the corridor, watched Gabrielle eat while she shredded bread in her own hands and gulped down the autumn's apple cider.

After, she walked to the room Lia had commandeered for the three princesses and five nobles who had come north. A half-squad of guards stood outside with nods to Elijah and a few with a nod to Sasha. Inside, the nobles who were up to see the morning hours eyed the castle's walls with courtly titters behind their fans.

Lia raised her head and looked at Sasha, who hadn't stepped inside.

"I'll see you later, Gabe," said Sasha. Gabrielle went inside and her guard joined the others by the door. Elijah followed Sasha down the corridor.

Willow Tree was not a very large castle. The four watchtowers marked the corners of the square. Sasha took the hall that walked the perimeter inside the walls. They walked two and a half circuits before she said, "Stop tiptoeing along back there. I'm not angry with *you*."

Sasha could almost hear one eyebrow raise. "Oh?"

She snorted. "Of course not, you silly." She scuffed her feet along the floor, glancing at the walls on each side of her, and then lengthened her stride. She turned down the wide central hall of the castle. The two main halls crossed at the center. Her and Gabrielle's courtyard, the only one in Willow Tree, was not in the center of the castle's square, but a little to one side. It did not intersect with the wider halls.

"I'm not tiptoeing," Eli said. "That would be unbalanced."

Sasha flicked her fingers at him over her shoulder while she walked that hall until the end, and then turned and walked it again.

"You're trying to disappear, which you always do, but never to *me*."

Elijah moved a few feet up, so he was walking beside her shoulder, instead of trailing properly behind her. "You had that look in your eyes," he said, "like you were searching for someone's liver to rip out."

Sasha smiled faintly. "Yes, but not yours."

She ran her fingers along the wall as they walked down the hall. She watched the turns of the corridor and peeked inside open doors while Elijah watched for possible threats and watched her.

"Your highness."

Sasha hesitated, and then stopped, turning around to face the speaker. Captain Brown bowed slightly and approached her. "Are you lost?" Brown asked. He ignored Elijah, who'd moved to stand properly in her wake.

"It's not a very big castle," said Sasha. "Are you?"

"I believe your sisters and friends have gathered in a drawing room on the east side," said Brown. "If I might escort you there?"

"It's not a drawing room," said Sasha.

Brown looked long-suffering, but said, "Did they find a room more to their liking?"

"It's the weaving room. The weaver and his apprentice had to haul the looms and spinning wheel out of it once Lia had her mind set. They've set up the loom in the castle library now, so my sister may hold court with her cronies. This place doesn't *have* drawing rooms." She glanced at Elijah, then said to Brown, "Sir?"

"Your highness."

"Do you know how they got in?" said Sasha. "The assassins?"

"Your highness, I assure you the Guard has everything under control."

"I'm sure you do," said Sasha. "That wasn't my question."

Brown hesitated. "We are pursuing the possibilities."

Sasha said, "There may be hidden passages in this castle, for the use of my family. If the assassins knew of them too, that would be problematic. Are you pursuing *that* possibility?"

Brown looked like maybe he wanted to laugh. "I think it would be best if you rejoined your sisters," he said. "I can escort you there, if you wish."

"I don't," she said. "I want to walk some more. Don't worry, Eli will take good care of me." She nodded to him curtly and Elijah gave a brief bow, and they both moved on.

"I'm not sure that was smart," said Elijah.

"Bringing up the passages or walking away?" she said and shrugged.

Eli sighed, loudly, at her shrug and she elbowed him. "Walking away," he said. "He's the captain; he needed to know about the passages. I just wish we had someone who wasn't a Second Squader or a lady who could tell him about it and make him listen." He frowned. "But I'd have thought he'd know about them already. I'm sure Harston did, if they exist."

"I don't think Harston trusted very many people," said Sasha, very quietly. "And I don't think he expected to die."

They walked farther, from the wide main walks, to the narrower crooks and crannies. She circled the courtyard and nodded to the guards at each door.

"Aren't you going to ask what we're doing?" said Sasha.

Elijah blinked innocently at her. "Going for a walk, aren't we?" He added, a little more seriously, "What I don't hear, I don't have to tell my captain."

Craftsmen and their shops permeated each corner of the castle. Willow Tree had to trade for most of its food with tapestries and carpets, carvings and metalwork. The rest of the castle was dedicated to living quarters, the kitchens, the comfort of the visiting royal party, and dust.

Sasha stopped, having passed it three times, in front of a short corridor beside the library. The loom's clacking gave a measured rhythm. "I like this one," she said, and walked down the corridor to the end. The end was not more than ten paces from the corridor's opening. A single torch flickered on the back wall, lighting the narrow door-less space. "There's no reason at all for it to exist, don't you think?"

Sasha tapped the pads of her fingers on the chill stone.

"Hm," said Elijah.

"I think it's interesting," she said, and went about kicking the stones and stepping on them, feeling them under her fingers. Nothing out of the ordinary happened. Finally, she huffed and crossed her arms, glaring at the corridor.

"If you miss lunch, Lia's going to take it upon herself to hunt you down, or Brown will," said Elijah. "We can come back."

"Fine," said Sasha and followed him out.

"I was afraid you might start taking it apart with your fingernails," said Elijah.

"I might still."

Sasha heard something creak behind her. Sasha glanced over her shoulder and saw a boy about her own age racing out of her irritating corridor. He wore a red messenger's cap. His dark skin wouldn't've been an uncommon sight on the bustling streets of the capital city, but this far into these isolated mountains it was rather surprising.

Sasha yanked up her skirts to scurry over and called out, "You there, messenger!" Elijah followed behind her with more dignity.

The messenger stopped, but looked anxiously over his shoulder. "Aye, miss—your highness," he amended quickly. "I'm running a bit late. Can I get yours later, p'raps?" He was slightly out of breath, jumping nervously from foot to foot.

84

"I don't need you to deliver a message," Sasha told him. "What were you doing down that corridor? It's got a dead end."

The boy froze. "Got lost."

"I was in there maybe half a minute ago," she said, stepping closer. "I think I would've seen you."

"That's an oddity, your highness," the boy agreed warily. "Now, if you haven't a message for me, I'd best be off." He bowed clumsily. "G'day, your highness."

As the boy started to turn away she said quickly, gambling, "If you call secret passages *oddities*, messenger."

She got a single glimpse of his wide, surprised, dark brown eyes before he was gone, disappearing around the corner. She crossed her arms, satisfied. It oughtn't to be too hard to find him again. She glanced back at Elijah.

"I didn't hear a thing," Elijah said.

The nobles' gathering room rippled with chatter and tinkling laughter. Will glanced idly.

As ordered by the chamberlain, he stood at the ready with a pitcher of water and commands to fetch anything their noblenesses required.

As ordered by the minister of Intelligence, Westel, Will kept an eye out for unrest and signs of plotting. He would poke through their correspondences, later, and keep track of the whereabouts and whispers of these six young nobles—the princess heir, her three closest ladies, and the two men vying for her hand.

This was far from the job Will wanted, but his master had sent him *here*, to this drudge work: following around silly court ornaments in the middle of nowhere; looked down on by an annoying fool of an ex-vice-captain; and having to sneak around behind people's backs to actually do anything useful.

Of course, sneaking behind people's backs was one of his specialties.

"Oh, come out and play, Dereck," said the laughing voice of the wiry-haired duchess, the princess Lia's closest confidante. Her dark locks were tied back, except for a single curl bobbing next to a small ear. The blonde count Dereck had pulled up a chair at the side of the room and was making notes on the stack of papers he was reading. "You have all winter to sit with papers," said the duchess. "Those long winter nights—"

"It's not like he'll have anything *else* to do," said the duke, and the baroness gave him a severe look. The baroness was a few years older than the rest and wreathed in a kind of stately, stodgy dignity, while the wiry-haired duchess circled the count with manic, mischievous cheer in her eyes.

The count had been too busy with a study of iron imports to notice the duchess coming until she stopped with a smile in front of him. The count Dereck looked up, startled, at the duchess who took this moment of distraction to snatch the papers from his hands and skip away, twitching her hips to her best advantage.

Will grinned. It was interesting, watching these de-clawed nobles use what tools they had.

The count stood with an accustomed sigh and followed the duchess to the center of the room, where the dark-haired duke, the grinning duchess, and the two other ladies stood around the princess heir of the Nerian Alliance. Lia had a pretty oval face with long, dark hair that fell straightly beside each cheek and down her back. Will hid a yawn and leaned against the wall.

"We're really here for three months?" said the baroness to the group at large. The baroness, a wide-eyed younger lady, and the wiry-haired duchess were the three ladies Lia had brought to keep her company in the hinterlands.

"Oh, come now, loves," said the duchess. "All those long cold nights to cuddle up and stay warm…"

"*Marie*," the baroness said and made a face that was at once severe and blushing. The younger lady tittered like she wasn't sure she was supposed to.

The duchess laughed and held the count's papers against her chest gleefully, ignoring his subtle glare.

"I'm going to want those back, you know," said the count.

"No you don't," said the duchess. The duchess twitched a finger at Will, who trotted obediently over. She handed him the papers and smiled. "Keep an eye on those," she said with another wag of the finger and Will withdrew.

In the corner, Gabrielle turned a page in a book. The six nobles talked of friends left at the capital and their real or reputed pursuits, fruit ices and Lia's new parasol, and the spring festival they would hopefully make it back for when the snows melted.

"Oh we had better," said the youngest lady. "What happens if we miss the firedancers? There was a very handsome one last year and I..."

Will shuffled his feet along the floor, a little unprofessionally. The younger lady, according to the files he had flicked through (even if this wasn't the job he wanted, that didn't mean he wasn't going to do his research), was a new addition to the eldest princess's inner circle and eager to prove herself with tales. He was less than interested in her hyperbole.

"I'll make a royal mandate for the snow to melt on time," said Lia.

The youngest lady said, "Can you *do* that?" while the wiry-haired duchess and the duke—*drinking buddies,* said the part of Will's brain that paid attention to files, *perhaps more, never monogamous*—laughed and laughed.

Will went and refilled a water glass, to shift the monotony a little.

According to Will's files, back at the capital the count dabbled in the ministry of Domestic Affairs, one of the seven Nerian state departments (none of the other six were nearly as fun as Will's ministry of Intelligence), and according to reports did it well. The count looked more interested in the reports the duchess had stolen than anything, thought Will, but that he was abandoning his chance for advancement in the ministry to spend the winter in Willow Tree meant the count saw and was interested in a chance for a higher advancement here. Will set the water pitcher back down on a low table.

The youngest lady giggled nervously, stepping in closer to the group to stage-whisper a raunchy joke she'd probably heard from one of her chambermaids. Her cheeks colored, as did the count's, while the duke laughed and the baroness shook her head.

Will noticed that when the youngest lady had drawn forward with her joke, the group had closed into a circle of four instead of six.

Lia and the wiry-haired duchess had drawn away from the others, who were now talking about an older noblewoman with a seemingly *very* interesting social life. Will was listening with amused interest to their gossip, until he realized how very quietly and naturally the princess and her duchess had faded out of the group at the touch of Lia's hand on the duchess's sleeve, like old familiar ghosts.

Will moved forward to refill the baroness's cup with water, and then went to stand at the wall again, in a slightly different position.

"You have a crease," the duchess said to Lia and the princess smoothed out her brow. They stood quietly away from the other four.

"Do you know what's going on, Marie?" Lia said, keeping her voice light.

The duchess shrugged. "I don't."

"But you know *everything*," said Lia with a sly smile and the duchess rolled her eyes. Lia brushed softly at her skirts and confessed quietly, as though it were something to be ashamed of, "I'm worried."

The duchess tapped the crease between Lia's carefully plucked brows, which had returned. "I can tell. But don't be." She waved a loose hand at the guards at the door. "We're wrapped up like a miser's riches, love. No one's touching us."

Lia's eyes strayed to Gabrielle, reading in the corner. "They better not."

The duchess laughed. "They don't want to mess with you!" she said and she drew Lia back to the circle.

The baroness had heard the last part of the conversation and said, "John and Dereck will take care of any malcontents."

The duchess glanced at her, the smile fading off her face.

"Oh yes," said the third, youngest lady, pale. "I hope so."

The duke slung an arm around the count's shoulders. "Dereck here will give them some fearsome paper cuts, I'm sure."

"Ha," said the count.

Will filled a few more water glasses and waited for his shift to end, so he could go wander around the castle and do the *real* work he was here for—defend the royals, find the assassins, save the kingdom, and prove to Westel that he *could*.

Will's attention flicked to the dark-haired princess heir and to the little royal curled up oblivious in the corner. Where was the third?

Elijah stood in parade ground rest in front of the new captain of the Guard. Some extra insignia on Brown's uniform did not improve his cold-eyed stare or disdainful smirk; if anything, it made them worse.

Knowing who should be sitting in that chair, wearing a captain's rank on his shoulder— it was hard for Elijah to resist disliking Harston's replacement.

"Sir," he said. Brown looked up from his papers as though he had just noticed Elijah was in the room.

"Hm," said Brown, his eyes flicking over Elijah without interest. He glanced down at a paper on his desk. "Guardsman Elijah. From, eh, Second Squad." His lips twisted with barely veiled disdain. "Common-born, I trust?"

"Yes, sir."

What, thought Eli, do you think it's contagious?

"Mm," Brown said. "I was reviewing the duty schedule and found some inconsistencies. It seems that you have been assigned an unfair number of shifts looking after, eh—" he glanced down but couldn't seem to find a paper that would tell him what he wanted. "The second princess," Brown finished.

"I don't mind the duty, sir," said Elijah.

And her name is Sasha.

"I do," said Brown. "I'm removing you."

Elijah's head lifted slowly at that, his focus narrowing in on the man in front of him, like the cold tunnel vision of the middle of a fight.

The captain had a city accent, almost, hidden under those soft noble consonants—he was from the edge of the noble residences, then, where the houses of the noble and wealthy that surrounded the palace began to melt into the lower city chaos.

Brown was almost one of them, then, a city boy with grime under his nails, words with sharp, rolling edges. Elijah might have expected more kindness from someone who knew what it was like to be a boy of unscrubbed cobblestones who was stranded and uncomfortable on the polished mosaic walks of the palace, except— Elijah watched the captain's nose twist with superior disgust and thought, ah, yes, you are afraid it's contagious.

Brown went on. "We can't have one guard get all the easy duties, strolling after princesses. I'm assigning you to the main door station for now. You may review your squad's duty roster for the rest of your schedule."

What the man meant was that he thought the second-eldest princess was an annoyance, and he was taking away what allies he could from her.

Elijah kept his hands clasped loosely behind his back and said, "Yes, sir."

It was his duty to plan for disasters, after all. He could handle this.

Gregory hurried down the hall. He hadn't meant to lie to Will when his friend asked if he could find the princess for him; and really, he hadn't lied. He had said he'd try to find her—he just didn't mention that he already had, and that Princess Sasha was trying to find their passages.

It felt so odd, lying to Will. A year ago (two years ago), he would have told his friend without the slightest thought. But a year ago (*two* years ago), Will hadn't left for greener pastures and they had still been as close as blood brothers.

It wasn't like they weren't close now. They were—but they were both different. A year was a long time (two years was even longer). Had Will really expected to come back after a year (two) away and to find Willow Tree and Gregory the same as he had left them?

But of course, Gregory thought, Will hadn't been expecting to come back at all.

The real question was: what was he to do about this? Should he to go back and tell Will now? Or maybe find the princess and make sure that was what she was really doing?

Gregory had no time to make a decision.

"Messenger," the princess said quietly behind him. Gregory whirled around, startled. "You know about the secret passages," she said.

Gregory stared. Her hemline looked like it might have some precious metal sown into it. "I don't know what you're talking about, your highness."

"Yes, you do. And you need to show them to me. That's how the assassins are probably getting in. It's a danger to everybody here."

That stung him a bit. But if the assassins were using the passages, Will would've figured it out. "Why would a lad like me know any secrets as important as all that?"

"I don't know," said the princess Sasha. "But I saw you leaving the corridor, the corridor that *doesn't have another entrance*." She glared at him. "I swear, if you don't tell me now, I'm going to hound you until you do, Gregory." At his startled look, she added, "I asked around."

"Your highness, believe me, I don't know what you're talking about." There was a shake in his voice and he hated it.

Princess Sasha put her hands in the pockets of her skirt with a sigh—skirts had *pockets*?—seeming oddly like a normal person. "You're a terrible liar, you know that?" she asked. "Just tell me. People could die if you don't."

Gregory looked nervously down the hall, eager to get away from this nosy princess and her demands, demands he couldn't obey, because, long ago, Gregory and Will had promised each other they'd keep this secret.

Years ago, Will had also promised that they would be brothers always, the two little orphan boys of Willow Tree. He'd promised to take care of Gregory, to watch out for him, to be there for him.

How can you watch out for someone when you're not even in the same mountain range?

Will didn't keep his promises.

Gregory looked at Sasha, who was watching him seriously, like the words he was going to say next truly mattered.

"Alright," he said. "I'll help you."

Her face brightened with a smile. She looked over her shoulder at a scowling, dark haired guard who stood far enough away not to hear them. "Tomorrow, at midday?" she said. "I'll meet you by the library."

"They took me off Sasha's duty," Elijah told Nathaniel. The two brothers pushed their way inside Willow Tree's kitchen, swamped by firelight and noise. Eli shook his head. "I haven't gone more than a week without being on her duty, not since I made first rank."

Nathaniel gave Elijah a sidelong glance. "They? Brown, you mean, that bureaucratic tick. He's got it for us, I swear."

Elijah questioned, while Nathaniel gave a serving girl a grin and a wink, "Us two, or all of Second?"

Nathaniel shrugged and snagged a half-loaf of bread. "Any pansy inbred is going to hate a group of well-trained peasants like our squad." He tossed him the bread and a rind of cheese and then grabbed a jug of cider. "But he might well have it in for the two of us personally," Nate added as they left the warmth of the kitchen. "We do stand out a touch."

"You do," Eli said. "I don't sleep during my watches. And I hold my tongue."

"Well, you're always watching Sasha, anyway, and you can't sleep during hers, unless you want to wake up without a charge," said Nathaniel. "I don't understand why you try to behave though. The only reason you've hung around so long after our four years were up is because of Harston and Sasha, and now the captain's gone and his rutting replacement's taken you off the princess's duty." Nate took a swig of cider. "This family of ours isn't made to produce good soldiers."

"What does that have to do with anything?" demanded Elijah. Eli tore off a hunk of bread and began to shred it absently. "What if something happens and I'm not there, Nate?"

"Come on, it's Sasha. She'll be fine."

Elijah looked down. "They got *Harston*."

"I know," his brother said. Nate sipped his cider, leaning against the wall, a relaxed off-duty guardsman with something dark in the set of his chin. He said, almost too quiet for Elijah to hear, "And we'll get them." He chewed a bit of bread and then grinned at Elijah, talking with his mouth full. "So what's Brown like? We've never had to deal with management before that wasn't Harston—I think he was afraid we'd scare them."

"That's an interesting way to look at it, Nate," said Elijah. "You've got an appropriate dose of humility there."

"So?" said Nathaniel. "What's he like? Come on, Eli, I know you did your research the moment you got out of his office."

Elijah sighed. "Youngest son, local fiefdom—that Aryen fief that's been selling their ancestral silver all over the black market over the past five years or so. Brown was officially second in command, but mostly did the administrative stuff, interacted with the nobility. You know Harston handled most of the field work and training himself, or left it to one of the squad leaders."

"Which might explain why Brown doesn't know such on-the-ground-level details as where Harston might have kept an accurate map of this castle and its passages." Nathaniel rubbed his eyes. "Well, that's fantastic."

First-born sons didn't join the Guard. (Well, Nathaniel had, but he was hardly noble-born, and it wasn't as though he had entirely abandoned the family business either). It made the Guard a troop of younger noble sons looking for glory, royal proximity, or a pension; or in the case of Second, commoners whose only other ways to legally touch a sword were to either join the army or become a smith.

Personally, Elijah had been more interested in knives and sneak attacks than swords when he'd first joined up, eleven years old and with scrapes on his elbows. Sometime in the past eight years, he'd become accustomed to the change.

Eli felt unbalanced without a sword on his side. That was dangerous.

Nate whistled. "But no money, no connections. How'd he end up vice captain?"

Elijah shrugged. "Scrambled, flattered. He's efficient, uncompromising; curries favor with those higher than him well enough, doesn't care about the rest."

"Good toady quality, bad leadership," said Nate. "Well, we're stuck in the mud, aren't we? What was the old man thinking, leaving us to him?"

"Like you said, he's excellent second in command material." Elijah brushed the last of the bread off his hands. "And Harston wasn't expecting to need a successor."

Nathaniel pushed a hand through his hair. "Well, that was right stupid of the old man, wasn't it?"

"Why are we doing nothing?" Andrea demanded of Doulings. "We're just sitting and *waiting.*"

"I get the feeling you're not very patient," Doulings commented dryly.

Yohan shook his head. "I agree with Andrea. So far we've killed one knight and you didn't even want us to do that. How is this helping the plan?"

Doulings fixed them both with a glare. "This isn't just about killing people. It's a," he searched for the best word, "*political* maneuver. It's a power struggle: a revolution primarily and an assassination secondly. Haven't you lot been rebels long enough to understand that? Keep your ears open and your daggers hidden. Everything and everyone must be in position before we strike. Your elders sent you here to be my eyes and ears, not my knives." He smiled at Andrea. "Patience, Miss Andrea, is a virtue."

"I didn't know virtues were so highly respected in your kind of work," she said.

"You'd be surprised." He eyed Yohan. "You keep an eye on Brown," Doulings said. "I want to know what he does and why he does it."

"What about me?" Andrea asked when he didn't go on.

"You work on being quiet," he said.

Yohan nodded and left the room with a respectful Ceren salute. Andrea turned to walk out as well, but Doulings called her back. Yohan looked as though he wanted to stop as well, but Andrea waved him on.

"You need to give me a little more respect," Doulings said. "This isn't going to work if you question all of my decisions. You're the one who cares about this, so I would expect a little more cooperation. If this fails, I'm just out of a bit of coin."

Andrea crossed slim arms across her chest. "You're just a paid murderer that the elders hired because they have no faith in our own power."

Doulings chuckled shortly. "I'm glad I'm not the only authority you have contempt for." He took a step toward her, his expression darkening. She had to look up to see his face, looming above her. "But trust me, my dear, I am far more powerful than your elders. I *am* someone to be feared."

Andrea stepped forward, smirking. "What? Now you going to tell me to watch my back?" Her voice fell to a cutting whisper. "That you got a knife somewhere with my name on it?" Her gaze didn't waver from his face. She spoke again, her voice back to its normal level, her tone unconcerned and confident. "You don't frighten me, Doulings." She looked him slowly up and down. "I've dealt with market toughs before. I've got four brothers. I could take you."

Doulings stepped back and leaned on a flour barrel. "Could you? Doesn't much matter. I'm not so petty as to want to cross daggers with you, especially not before I'm paid. Don't want to be short handed."

Andrea rolled her eyes and perched on the edge of a crate.

Doulings smirked. "I wouldn't be too eager to stick a knife in my chest, though, chit. You little rebels need me. You couldn't have done any of this without me. You may be good with holding your little secret meetings and grumbling about the Nerian Alliance, but you're infants in the real world."

"This was *our* plan," Andrea said, "to rid Ceren of the usurper's children, and place someone we can control on the throne so Ceren can finally secede from this burned Alliance. It was *our* contacts who found out the royals would be sent here during times of danger. You've got experience, sure, but we could have done without you. You just make it a little simpler."

He laughed. "I would've liked to see that, your little conspiracy trying to do this alone. It would have been quite amusing."

"We would've done it," she said, chin lifting. "We could've done all of this alone. We swore we would, and in Ceren oaths are holy."

Doulings snorted. "Gods? Destiny? That kind of idiocy isn't my cup of tea, chit. My future's my business and no one else's."

Andrea laughed. "You really aren't one of us, are you? We don't believe some higher power is going to win this war for us. *We're* the ones who swore the oaths. We have a duty."

Doulings smiled. "Well, I don't believe in duty, either."

"I wouldn't expect you to."

The next day, Gregory made his way toward the corridor the princess had been exploring when he'd first run into her. She was waiting inside, tapping her foot with impatience.

Gregory eyed her with uncertainty. This girl didn't seem the least bit suspicious: he supposed princesses just expected everyone to be trustworthy. One would think she'd know better, at this point.

"Where's your guard?" Gregory asked.

"Faithfully guarding my empty room, I trust." It hadn't been Elijah this time. Elijah would have been harder to fool.

Sasha hadn't seen Elijah in days and it was getting under her skin.

She eyed the unknown boy in front of her. "So how do you get in?" she asked. "I assume there's one here, right?"

Gregory nodded, uncomfortable. Sharing these was like confessing to the steward after Will and he had pulled some spectacular prank. He walked to the end of the corridor, gesturing for Sasha to follow.

Once there, he lifted the sputtering torch out of its bracket. "Here," Gregory said, offering it to her. The princess took it as though she'd never held a torch before.

He grasped the sooty bracket on the wall, twisted, and pulled. As he tugged, an entire section of the wall slid out towards him, turning on creaky hinges. It left a dark gap where a person could just slip through.

"Bring the torch, highness," he told her.

She followed him. Gregory closed the passage door behind her, wincing at the loud squeal it made. He needed to filch some oil to grease those hinges. Without Will here he hadn't used the passages much, except when he needed a short cut for a late message. At the thought of Will, Gregory winced again.

The princess lifted the torch nearly to the ceiling. In truth, that wasn't very high. The passage roof was barely a foot over her head. Sasha stared.

Gregory laid a hand on the cool brick wall, looking fondly at his surroundings. He remembered first finding these passages, remembered standing in the entrance, too shocked to enter; that amazed feeling at such discovery—that *he* had found these. The passages hadn't changed much since then. Motes of dust were caught in the torchlight, spiraling slowly.

The corridor was dark, the torch casting deep shadows all about them. The red-brown bricks had a light coat of dust and frail cobwebs gathered in abundance.

"Why brick walls?" Sasha asked finally. "Why didn't the builders use stones?"

"Bricks are thinner than the big stones they built Willow Tree with," Gregory said. "Most of these passages are inside walls. Right now we're in one of the walls behind the library. It'd be a trifle conspicuous if the walls were three times as thick wherever a passage was. They're conspicuous enough as it is."

The princess laid a hand on the porous brick, and then turned back to him, her mind elsewhere, already jumping ahead to how to tell this to Brown, just what the ugly man's shocked face would look like, and what the captain should do to make these catacombs safe. "Thank you," she said absently to Gregory. "I'd best be off."

Gregory blinked, to startled to frown. "What? We're not even halfway down it."

"There's something I need to do," she explained.

"I thought these were important," Gregory said. She watched, a little wide-eyed, as his eyebrows gathered in confused hurt. She thought maybe she'd insulted him. That happened sometimes when Sasha opened her mouth, especially around people her own age.

"They are," she said. "But I just needed to know how to get in. And, anyway, it's dangerous to stay here too long. The assassins use these."

"Not much," said Gregory. "I mean, I haven't run into them." Now that the idea had been brought up, it gave him the shivers.

"Well," said Sasha, uncomfortable, and Gregory realized what else the princess was not saying.

"Wait—you think I might be—be working with them? I—"

Sasha said defensively, "I happen to run into a boy who obviously just came out of the passages—which *nobody* knows about—who later offers to take me to them without even a bribe to spur him on? I'd have to be stupid not to smell something suspicious about *that*."

"Well, I'm not," he said. "I found these, just like you probably would've after awhiles—s'not that hard. And I didn't ask for a bribe just *because*. Not everybody demands something for something."

Sasha flinched back. "You could be lying. I don't know you; how can I trust you?" She turned to leave.

Trust *him*? Here he was, betraying his best secret to a stranger, and she— "If you don't trust me, not even a little, why'd you come in here at all? Why'd you even leave that little room of yours? If you're too scared that people are bad, why don't you go hide in your bed?"

She whirled back on him. "I'm *not* scared. I'm being sensible. I know where the passage is now. I'm going to Brown right now and I'll be done with it." She whirled around again.

"There's more than one passage," Gregory said to her retreating back.

Sasha didn't turn back, just kept walking. "I only need one to prove to Brown they're here. As soon as I've done that, he'll set men to actually look for them."

"Wait, wait." Gregory hurried after her. "You're telling the captain about them?"

"I already *said* that," Sasha snapped without turning around. "Thank you for your help to the Crown, Gregory!"

"What are you telling him for?" He grabbed her sleeve. She shook his hand off and turned angrily around once more. They were at the very mouth of the passage.

"The assassins are using them—or they could at least. It's a threat to everyone, especially me and my sisters. I'm not going to let some killers run freely around this castle if I can stop them. And I'm not going to walk right into one of their traps either," she added, fixing him with a glare. "I'm telling Brown about these passages as soon as I can and showing him this one as proof."

Gregory looked appalled. "You're just going to tell this secret," he demanded, the sweep of his hand encompassing all of the passages. *My* secret. "And to some pompous guardsman? Will he even listen?"

The princess wavered. Enough of Will had worn off on him that Gregory caught it.

"He won't, will he? He might just post a guard on this one, but he's not going to take some guards off the doors to come look for any others. And he'll stick you back wherever you're supposed to be and not let you out for anything. And you know it."

Sasha said, "I've got to try. If I don't tell him, if I don't gamble on the chance that he *will* listen to me, what else can I do?"

Gregory hesitated, then said, "*You* can stop them."

"*What*?"

"What does getting Brown to shut off these passages do for you?" Gregory said, letting the idea slowly unfold in his mind.

"It keeps the assassins from using them," she said.

"For the winter," Gregory said, his momentum building as more words tumbled out of his mouth. "But they'll just get you when you lot are riding home. Or back at your fancy palace, p'raps. What you got to do is find them out whilst there's just three of them, instead of waiting 'til hordes are chasing you around come spring."

Sasha opened her mouth, then shook her head. "That's not my job. That's what spies and soldiers are for. I'm only looking for passages because no one else will."

Gregory shook his head. "You want to keep you and your sisters safe," he said. "That's why you're looking. If you use these passages to find out who these killers are, 'stead of telling some captain about them, then you're keeping your sisters safe from them forever, not just for the winter."

She was hesitating, he could *tell*.

"Just do as you're doing now," Gregory went on, eager. "Find them out, and when you think you've got enough to prove to Brown who they are, *then* you tell him." He stepped forward, and encouragingly, she didn't back away. "Trust me, alright? I can help you. I know all the passages here like the back of my hand."

"You really think that we could do this? You're right about Brown; he won't listen to me." She eyed Gregory cautiously. "Maybe I should gamble on you instead."

Gregory grinned at her. Was this how Will felt whenever he connived them out of trouble, or talked them into someplace they weren't supposed to be? "We can do this," he said. "We'll find them and we'll save your sisters. Trust me."

She was quiet for a moment. "Can you find me again?"

Gregory nodded and watched as she made her way out of the passages, a thoughtful look on her face. A frown suddenly creased his forehead. What was he going to tell Will?

"Bastards," said a guardsman staring into his cup of ale.

Andrea was familiar with the various levels of drunk. She'd worked the tavern on the first floor of her stepfather's inn since she was old enough to fill a mug. Some you let cry into your shoulder and some you called Koen in to firmly escort home—even at twelve that brother of hers had had a man's height.

This one she would have called in her largest foster brother for.

"If those pox-begotten devils show their faces again, we won't stand for it. The Guard watches out for its own."

Andrea chopped a potato into careful chunks as she listened to exactly what her fate might be if anyone in black and silver ever knew what she was.

The stews were becoming more and more root vegetable and less and less meat as winter wore on, but the nobles' spices were a saving grace. Andrea thought maybe she should mention the idea to Charlie when she got home, which seemed like a very long time from now.

She jerked the potatoes off the board, almost splashing herself with the boiling soup.

Nik wouldn't be homesick, if he was here. Nik wouldn't homesick, if he hadn't been in bed with a racking cough the week the royal caravan had left. Nik would have got the old loyalist *and* a few of his bloody-fisted guardsmen minions.

Andrea glanced sideways at the cluster of guardsmen guzzling Cook's best ale and lifted her chin as she reached for another potato.

Nik probably would've listened to what Doulings told them to do, though, so he wouldn't have gotten Harston at all.

Will glanced through some papers he had filched from Brown's desk as he sat cross-legged on the lumpy mattress in the visiting servants' barracks. It was empty now, at barely past midday, the other servants all performing their respective duties.

The documents held little of importance, but he felt he ought to keep an eye on the captain's activities. With assassins after their highnesses and traitors loose in the castle, everyone was under suspicion.

A quiet knock sounded on the door. Will hurriedly stuffed the papers under his mattress and opened the door—he'd locked it, to keep anyone from barging in on him.

He found Gregory standing outside. "Did you find her?" he asked once he'd let him in.

"She found our passages."

It took Will a moment to process this. "She found them?" He dropped onto his mattress, shaking his head. "I have to say I'm surprised. I thought only a mouse like you could sniff them out." Will rested his chin on one knee, calculating the complications this might raise.

Gregory looked uncomfortable as he intensely examined a spot on the floor. "Yeah, well, anyways, I found her." Will glanced over his way. If it was anyone but Gregory, Will would think there was something he wasn't saying—but it *was* Gregory.

Gregory hurried on. "She said she wanted to show them to that captain fellow, Brown or whoever."

Will sat bolt upright. "She's going to let *Brown* into them?" What would that pompous fool do if he found them? If he found out that Will knew they were there and hadn't told anyone about it—

"She said the assassins are probably coming through that way."

Will pursed his lips, his mind still on the problem of explaining himself to Brown, or at least hiding that he knew of them beforehand. "I thought of that," he said absently. "But how would they know about them? I think it's unlikely."

"I convinced her not to tell," Gregory went quickly on with his story. "I told her she ought to use the passages, to spy with them, not have the captain block them. Why block the assassins now if they're just going to wait outside until their highnesses start back toward the palace?"

"You convinced her?" Will grinned at him; as startled by praise as Will remembered, Gregory grinned shyly back. "Nice work. Don't look so surprised, Gregory; haven't you realized by now you're brilliant?" Will sat back, considering. "It'll be useful, having an extra hand. Even if she is royalty." Will nodded,

111

drumming his fingers on his mattress. Through the lumpy material he could just feel the hidden seal that he'd been given to confirm to people that he was with the ministry of Intelligence. "Well," Will said. "If she finds anything out, could you pass it on to me? Don't tell her about me, though. I don't know how well a princess can keep a secret."

"I'll take this shift," a familiar voice drawled below her, the sound leaking up through the hay and wooden floor.

Sasha's guard protested, "But, Nathaniel—"

Sasha, sitting in the stable loft, looked down, listening.

"You're off duty, friend," Elijah's elder brother continued from below. "Go relax."

Sasha pulled up her legs—she'd been swinging them through the trap door of the loft—so that Nate could clamber up the ladder and join her, which he did.

He tossed her a thick wooden plank with a series of keyholes onto the hay beside her. "This the only place you could think of where Lia couldn't find you?"

She grinned at him and let her feet dangle again. "You have to admit my sister'd be unlikely to risk stepping in something."

"I wouldn't get too comfortable," said Nathaniel. "She visits the palace stables every day."

112

Sasha yanked her feet up through the trapdoor, in case critical sisterly eyes might be hiding below. "She does? What for?"

Nathaniel shrugged. "To ride her horse, I imagine."

"Not *every* day," said Sasha. "She wouldn't have time to do her hair, or put her face on." She twisted her nose.

Nathaniel said, "My buddy in Fourth says that they stand in the muck once a day when she stops by to brush the creature, at least. Sometimes she has the grooms exercise him instead." He tapped his chin. "Maybe it's a *her*. I think he might have said *mare*." He shrugged again. "Horse."

Below, one of the draft beasts exhaled loudly as though in disparaging response.

"Well, she didn't bring her mare," said Sasha, "I think," and she let her feet dangle again, Nathaniel's board of locks on her lap.

"Don't tell me you didn't bring your picks," Nate said with disapproval.

Sasha put her hand to the back of her neck sheepishly. Nate sighed and tossed her a set. "Practice," he said sternly.

"Yes, sir," she muttered and kicked at him with a dangling foot. She avoided his return swing and grabbed the lock board. Her picks scratched against the inside of the first. She hesitated, then said, "I haven't seen Eli around lately."

113

Nate leaned back in the scratchy hay, one straw poking out of the corner of his mouth. "Brown's keeping him off your shift."

"What?" Sasha demanded. "But Eli's always—"

"Well, Brown's not Harston." Sasha shut her mouth. Nate added, "And he's an ass besides." He plucked the straw from his mouth. "That's why I'm on your shift," he said. He grinned up at her. "Eli made me, and Brown's not got anything solid against me."

"Yet," said Sasha.

"Yet," Nathaniel agreed amiably.

The first lock popped open. "How's Gideon dealing? And the rest of the boys?"

"They miss you," he said. "Practice feels off balance."

"Well, you've got even numbers for the first time in years." Sasha frowned at the second lock. "Where do you find space to spar?" The snow had fallen thick and frigid, feet high all around the castle.

"We push the tables back in the dining hall, before the nobles break fast." He grinned and tapped her knee with his straw. "Gideon made another square—oh, and I *creamed* Stearns the other day," he crowed. "The look on that blond menace's face was priceless."

"I'd've liked to see that."

"I'd've liked you to, too," he said. "Why don't you?"

114

Her pick slipped in the lock. "It doesn't *work* like that, Nate. It's not that easy." She bent over the pick. "And I have things to do."

Nate hummed and chewed on the piece of straw.

Soft tapestries stood sentinel against drafts on the walls of a nobleman's room. The nobleman himself sat at a small writing desk, penning a letter that Will Rocole would glance over, later that evening, and dub innocuous if not strictly boring. He would not note the splatter of blue ink on the corner as anything more than noble clumsiness.

Andrea, who would slip into the room, later, with a bored sigh and flick of the eyes, would however note the splatter. She would pick up the letter and slip outside again and take it down to the basements where she would hand it to Doulings.

Chapter Four
Winter's Boys

Gregory was dreaming.

In his dream, he was ten again, and Will was twelve and a beanstalk, something he'd never really grown out of, now that Gregory thought about it.

It was summer, in the dream, because the peddlers were braving the mountains to reach the hungry little settlements in their creases. Gregory was full of wide-eyed glee at the bags of flour and actual *fruit* (not so gleeful about the vegetables); Will drank up every story he could convince the weather-worn men to share about the outside world.

Even then, Will was good at convincing.

A short man with a grumpy donkey told tales about the cliff-caves of the Ahar coast, where a whole city was built deep in the pink-ish sandstone. He'd traveled with a caravan through the desert country, he said, stopping at palm tree oases as they went from the high cliffs by the sea through sandy, arid dunes all the way to the old home of the empire on the strip of green land at the edge of the continent's great inland lake.

He taught the boys a few words in the oddly fluid language.

A pair of cousins had been sailors, once, and they talked about the sea, the rolling immensity of it. The Willow Tree boys were convinced they were exaggerating (nothing could be as big as their mountains) but Will thought they ought to go see it someday just in case.

The pair of cousins had been to Sylia, the rocky northern islets with their grand university and snowy winters. Gregory knew, at least, about frozen winters and nodded when they talked about ice.

Sometimes a whole caravan came through: grizzled and heroic caravan leaders, lithe horsemasters, sharp-eyed merchants and scrawny apprentices. There were bandits on the road, they said. There were beautiful women in the towns, they said, which made Gregory blush hard enough for the heat in his cheeks to be visible and which made Will ask about the bandits again.

The great cities could fit hundreds of Willow Trees, they said. Vast ships came in and out of the ports; merchants set up markets in the city streets and you couldn't hear yourself think over the sound of them hawking their goods. In the capital, the palace sat on a green hill and looked out over the roofs of the city and out over the golden hills and out to the great river that went all the way to the sea.

In Gregory's dream, Will was talking. "Here," Will said. "I'll be a merchant and you can be a grand prince." A peddler with two donkeys (one was sleepy and nice; the other not so much) had told them about the markets of Tinyej, down south, with hundreds of stalls lining roads that went up and down hills as steep as their mountains. "Or—or you be the City Guard and I'll be a pickpocket and we—"

The ten-year-old Gregory stood up. "I want to show you something."

"You're right!" said Will. "The kitchen would be a great marketplace—there's enough folk to dodge around, don't you think?"

Gregory didn't go to the kitchen, but Will followed along happily behind him anyway. Gregory went to a hall, hung with faded old tapestries they hid behind sometimes, if it was that sort of game.

"A Kainen carpet maker's stall!" said Will.

Gregory slipped behind one, holding a finger to his lips. He reached into an inconspicuous gap between two stones, and pulled a lever that felt like a bit of mortar. To the dreamer, the feel of the mortar was familiar. To the ten year old, it was rough and huge in his hand.

The wall opened like a door and Gregory turned around. "See?" said Gregory, smiling at his wide-eyed friend. "We can have adventures *here*."

Gregory woke up. His eyes flicked open and he stared up into the invisible dark ceiling, placing himself in the world, the well-known rumbles and wheezes of the other castle servants snoring around him. After a moment, Gregory rolled over and went back to sleep and didn't wake until someone stepped on him at dawn.

Sasha's latest guard was not pleased with escorting the princess back to her chambers. He had been winning his game of cards until royalty had come and called him away. What did her highness have to go and get sick for anyways? At least she could've had the dignity of waiting until after he'd won a few coins.

Sasha entered her room with a weak thanks to her guard. She heard him latch the door behind her and settle into his post just outside. Playing sick was one of her favorite games; she'd done it often enough before to get out of

Court.

Now she strode to her untidy clothes box and dug to the bottom. Sturdy Guard-issue practice wear was folded neatly next to commoners' clothes of various degrees of cleanliness—the best way to be called out as a fake in the lower city was to be well-scrubbed.

Sasha slipped off her dress and pulled on a pair of breeches and a worn shirt, after binding her chest tight with a long cloth. She crammed her brown hair under a faded cap and pulled on her soft leather boots.

Sasha had the luxury of having a room with a small window that overlooked a central courtyard—she suspected this is why the five comforters on her bed were not enough to keep her feet from freezing solid in the night. Now she slid open the wooden shutters, shivering as a draft of frigid air blew around her. A few rows of shrubbery, some benches, and a small pine were blanketed in snow.

Sasha grinned, feeding on the thrill of a good sneak. She eyed the snowy ground, now much higher than it had been before winter's onset, and quickly vaulted out of the window to land knee-deep in white powder. Outside the partially-protected courtyard, the snow was piled even higher.

She shut the shutters behind her and made her way through the small courtyard. The air was bitingly cold and she began to shiver as snow seeped into her boots and leggings, melting into her pants up to above her knees.

Two doors led off from the courtyard. She pushed through the snow towards the left. She tried to slow the clattering of her teeth and put her ear to the door, listening for movement on the other side. She screwed up her face and sighed. Well, it was an experiment. If this didn't work, she'd find another way.

She wrapped numb fingers around the door handle and shoved it open, into something rather solid. There was a thump and then a clatter.

Sasha shut the thick door behind her while Elijah jumped hurriedly to his feet. "Ow," he said. He brushed off his uniform and eyed her attire. "Sasha, you know the capitol's a three days ride away, don't you?"

"Three days in a carriage—a two day's *ride*," she disagreed. "And I'm not running off to play, Eli." She eyed his uniform. "You've got dirt on your front."

"That would be your fault," he said, adjusting his scabbard. "What are you doing, Sash?" He looked pointedly behind her. "I don't see a guard."

"Just passing through," she said. "Going to let me by, Elijah?"

"Do I ever? That's not how the game's played," he said. "And Sasha, maybe you didn't notice, but there are assassins in this castle and they're after *you*."

"I noticed, Eli," she said with a shove. "But the Guard's not going to catch them, Eli, and no guardsman's going to let me try. Brown's not doing anything—you know it's true," she said. "He's just letting Harston's killers walk. I'm not going to let him do that."

"He's trying to keep you safe, instead of running after specters," said Elijah. "Don't be an idiot, Sash."

"I can take care of myself."

He pushed his hands through his short red hair. "Blessed *bones*, Sasha. I don't care if you're trained; they know how to fight, too, and there's more of them than there are of you."

"Elijah, they killed Harston." She shook her head. "They tried to kill me and Gabrielle. I'm not going to sit and wait for them to try again."

He looked down the hall, fingering his sword hilt. "I'm going with you, then," he said.

"Don't you be stupid," she said.

Elijah said, "Why shouldn't I? I'm supposed to protect you, aren't I?"

She shoved him again. "No, you're supposed to protect this doorway, remember?" He made a face. "I'll protect myself just fine. You'd get yourself kicked out of the Guard if you leave your post."

"Sash," he said, "I'm not going to let you go assassin-hunting by yourself. Looking for secret passages or whatever in dead end corridors, with me waiting in the hall—fine. But I can't let you put yourself in danger." She looked up at him and Elijah added, "Harston asked me to take care of you."

"Information gathering is all I'm doing," Sasha said. "Not planning on any armed battles to the death."

"And your plans *always* work, highness." Elijah grinned at her. "Busting through a door *into* a royal guard; that was clever."

She stuck her tongue out at him.

"I see the years of etiquette tutors have done you a world of good. Did you skip them all to run about the city?"

"If I didn't go to lessons, Mother would have just locked me in my room. I can compromise." She took a breath. "Whether you want me to or not, Eli, I'm going to find them and I'm going to make Brown stop them. I'll find another road out if I have to, but I'll do it."

"And I'll find that road and block it, too. You're not getting past me, Sash. We've played this game before."

"It's not a game this time. They *killed* Harston."

"You're right it's not a game," he said. "You could get killed, too."

"I won't. Elijah, you have to trust me."

Elijah looked at her for a long moment and then he sighed. "Be careful, Sash," he said, shaking a finger at her. "Don't be stupid. Keep your dagger with you—and within easy grasp—and your eyes open. No dark alleys. You know."

He said, "If you get yourself killed, I will be very angry with you."

Sasha leapt at him and hugged him tightly around the neck. "I knew you'd come around."

He patted her on the back and looked at her wryly. "You checked when I'd be on duty here, didn't you?"

"Maybe." She winked at him as she scurried away. "I'll see you on your next shift, buddy."

On her way to the passage, Sasha passed some servants, more guards, and a noble—Duke John, the brunet of Lia's pair of suitors. She touched her cap, bowing her head slightly when she passed the duke. It was a proper way for someone to show their respect to someone of higher rank, when a bow was too time consuming, but mostly she did it to hide her face in case he recognized her. Sasha doubted it—when she was playing princess, her face was cleaner—but it never hurt to be careful.

Sasha reached the corridor that held the entrance to the passage without mishap. Remembering what the messenger had done yesterday, she tugged the torch out of its holder, handling it gingerly. With the other hand she twisted the bracket and pulled, grinning as the hidden door opened on newly-oiled hinges.

She slipped inside, pulled the door shut and settled herself to wait for the messenger's arrival.

Sasha didn't have to wait long. Gregory entered the passage and eyed her curiously. "How'd you get out? You nobles seem like you're near locked up in there. I half expected you not to show up."

She folded her arms over her chest, suspicious. "I'm not going to tell you where I've found a loop-hole in my protections. I'm not idiotic enough to *invite* assassins in."

Gregory looked bewildered. "What do I have to do with assassins?"

"You—" Sasha bit her lip, then spit it out. "You could easily be part of the conspiracy."

"I thought you decided to trust me."

Feeling a little harsh—her suspicions felt mean rather than righteous as she spoke them, looking at Gregory's wide eyed face instead of sitting in the nobles' room and envisioning what would happen if the assassins got to her, or her sisters—Sasha said, "All I decided was that I couldn't risk not using these passages. If I'm wrong, my mistake stops with me. It doesn't get to Gabrielle." She paused uncomfortably. "Did you want something in payment? Money?"

Gregory shook his head. "I just want to help stop these assassins, your highness. But I suppose you don't believe me."

Sasha rubbed her eyes tiredly. "I'm sorry, Gregory, I am, but I can't trust you. Trusting you would not be very intelligent. I'm only doing this because there's no other way to use these passages."

Gregory crossed his arms over his chest. "I'm *not* one of the assassins. I want to help you!"

"I said I'm sorry," Sasha said, reddening at the heat in his voice. "But it's complicated!"

Gregory looked at her for a long moment then turned and made his way down the passage, gesturing for her to follow.

A touch of guilt stirred in the base of Sasha's stomach as she twisted the torch in her hand. This boy—young man, really—was trying to help her and she was treating him like a suspect.

But he *is* a suspect, she protested silently to herself. Everyone is, until we find the assassins and whoever is paying them.

Sasha broke the silence. "Where does this one lead?"

Gregory looked back at her, considering. It was easy, even in the flickering torchlight, to see the stubborn jut of his chin. Perhaps he was wondering whether he even ought to help this ungrateful little princess. "Outside," he answered finally. "And there's a door that leads to the armory."

"Why do you think these were built?"

"I couldn't say for certain," Gregory answered. After a moment, he went on. "But most of them head outside, so I'd guess for escape, or maybe for entrance. There's some smuggling through the mountains…" His eyes flicked over familiar bricks, enthusiasm growing in his voice. "This castle's not very old. It was built right after your great-grandfather took the throne. I'm thinking maybe the soldier-king feared for his family's safety. These passages are planned." His voice slowed as he glanced sideways at her, remembering he was sort of angry with her, and wondering if he was boring her to death. "The castle is built around them, not them around the castle, if you get my meaning."

"So you know your history, then?" Sasha asked.

"Aye, I suppose. Will knows it better."

"Will?"

Gregory glanced quickly at her. "He's a friend." He looked up at the cobwebs nestled in the corner of the ceiling and said, "Everyone knows about the Nerian Alliance, and how the three provinces Ceren and Birnel and Panet made the Alliance to protect themselves from the old Ahar Empire to the west and the Kainen raiders in the south."

Gregory recited it, rote, from the lessons a tired servant woman would sometimes give the castle children (even the two unclaimed orphan boys, when someone felt generous) in exchange for an extra couple rabbits for her stew pot.

"Then, your great-grandfather, the head general of the Alliance's armies, declared the Alliance a kingdom and himself the king. The

128

soldier-king called it Neria because that was the city where the alliance treaties had been made. That's the basic story at least." Gregory shrugged. "Others call him a savior, banding the kingdoms together, or a usurper, doing away with the true kings."

"What do you think?"

Gregory surveyed her gravely. "I think, your highness, that it's getting late and I ought to show you what I need to show you before I have to get back to my deliveries."

Sasha tucked her hands in her breeches pockets and nodded. "So what's for today?" she asked. She followed him, holding the torch, as he scurried nimbly through the passage.

"Something useful," he answered. Suddenly, Gregory dropped down out of her torchlight. Sasha hurried forward to see that he was only descending a short flight of stairs.

"I was afraid you'd fallen."

Gregory laughed. "I know every brick and stone in these passages. You won't see me stumble down steps, your highness. Up ahead, there are some peep-holes," he went on. "Places where the mortar between the bricks has cracked. The walls were made very thin here, I don't know why. Some of its natural and some me and—some I did."

Sasha said nothing but she noted his words quietly to herself. There was someone else who knew these passages were here. She reminded herself for the umpteenth time to be wary; the reminder sounded a lot like Elijah.

"You can listen through those if you want. Not really my fancy."

Sasha said, "That would be useful. You can hear all sorts of things when people think no one can hear them." She paused. "If this isn't your fancy, why make the holes?"

Gregory froze. She eyed him critically. He really needed to learn how to lie. "I dunno," he answered finally. "Was bored, I guess."

They had reached another flight of stairs, these leading up. "Why so many stairs?" Sasha asked, gesturing at them.

Gregory glanced back at her. "Most of the passages are built inside hollow walls," he said. "Stairs are put in when we have to pass a hall or corridor. No walls to hide in, see?" He shook his head with admiration. "Imagine how much work went into making these." He patted the brick with an affectionate hand.

They had reached the spy-holes, little pinpricks of lights brightening the murky dark of the passage. A babble of voices and sounds of hissing and clanging met her ears. Gregory lowered his voice. "The kitchen's through there," he murmured. "The dining hall's up ahead."

Sasha bent over to peer through one of the holes. She could see little except fragments of figures and the flicker of torchlight and cook fires off tarnished pots and pans. The voices all melted together forming an incomprehensible blur. She closed her eyes and focused on weaning a single voice from the meaningless low roar of the kitchen help. She caught a few individual words and phrases before Gregory tapped her on the shoulder. It would take some practice to get that right, but she thought she could manage it.

"Highness? There's more peep-holes down further and a door to the armory as well. C'mon."

Sasha could still taste the edge of bitterness in his voice. She rose and followed her grumpy guide through the darkness.

"You're not having *doubts*, are you?" a thin man asked a nobleman, in a Willow Tree room hung with tapestries to keep in the warmth. Doulings smiled. "Because our mutual friend in the city doesn't like it when people have doubts." He had come to answer the blue-splattered letter.

"Of course not," said the noble. "I pay my debts."

Doulings laughed. "The reason you're here, my boy, is because you *don't*."

The noble laughed weakly along with him,

"No, wait," said Doulings, "you do. You just thought you could afford to pay in favors better than in coin, after your father cut you off." The noble's face was going bleaker and more nauseated as the thin man spoke. Doulings

smiled. "And the favors just kept getting darker and darker, until one day you couldn't say no to the next, because if the last few favors came out into the light you wouldn't just be cut off entirely from daddy's coin purse, you'd be banished, at the very *least*. Funny how that works, isn't it? I've always admired Lukas's skills in that arena."

"He's very impressive," said the noble sullenly.

"I don't like that tone," said Doulings. "Should I tell my friend in the city?"

"No," said the noble quickly. "Please, you don't need to say anything to Lukas. I just meant—"

"I know what you *meant*," said Doulings. "Now, what was it you wanted?"

The noble took a long breath. "You said—you won't hurt Lia?"

"Is *that* what's bothering your little head?"

"You won't hurt her?" The noble swallowed convulsively, but kept his gaze level with all of a gambler's fine skill.

"I won't touch a hair on her highness's head," said Doulings and smiled.

He might watch someone else kill her, though, or just have someone else hold the princess's hair back while he did his work.

They hadn't talked about it anymore after that first conversation, but every now and then Will would see that sullen look on Gregory's face.

132

Alright, so Will had left.

But it wasn't like Will had snuck off in the dead of night. He'd *asked* Gregory to come with him. It wasn't his fault that Gregory didn't want to come.

Will shoved his hands in his pockets. He wore the drab clothes that were the uniform for the servant's part he was playing. It was an easy act: until a year ago he *was* a servant.

Will couldn't resist the small smile that flitted across his face at the thought. He'd always told them he wouldn't stay down for long.

He had had to leave. Couldn't Gregory see that? How could his best friend begrudge him his chance at—at something *more* than this, more than being the orphaned charity case of an isolated castle? After all, Gregory could've come along. He was the one who had chosen to stay behind in this dusty little castle. He couldn't blame Will for trying to be something more.

The first time Will had met Gregory, they hadn't been orphans, yet. Will had had no idea that that was something they would soon have in common. In later years, he had realized that Gregory probably had known, even then. Gregory said he liked to hide from bad things, but even when he hid it was because he *knew*.

They had known each other before then, vaguely, in the way the eight-year-old bastard son of a maidservant might know the six-year-

old son of two respectable craftspeople. Even in a small castle, class boundaries matter; even in a small castle, the gap of two years matters to children.

Ruddy light spilled out the door to the kitchens to pool in the torch-lit hallway. Will closed his eyes for a moment, sinking into his chosen character. People here were obviously going to recognize him, so he'd shaped his act around that. He'd missed home, Will would say, so he'd joined the footmen and servants the nobles brought with them. A homesick young servant was much less likely to cause suspicion than a prying stranger.

Will stepped inside the kitchen, eyeing the newcomers, of which there were many. Normally the kitchen was staffed by only the cook and her two underlings. The nobles, expecting lavish meals of more than just baked bread and winter roots, had provided an army of extra helpers. (The servants would continue to feast on baked bread and winter roots).

Will would mingle with the servants, both old and new, sniffing for spies and traitors. Also, since Brown would tell him next to nothing, he planned to steal information from off-duty guards about the captain and his preparations. Everyone came to the kitchen sooner or later.

The cook spotted him. He'd reacquainted himself with her earlier. Her eyes narrowed suspiciously but her mouth crinkled in

a smile. "You mischievous wretch," Cook said. "Come to steal my pasties, I s'pect. Keep your hands to yourself." She tossed him a chunk of bread and turned back to her pots.

Will grinned at her back and positioned himself on a stool by a gossiping bunch of kitchen girls. Will eyed them appreciatively and they responded to his interest with giggles and flirtatious glances. One girl did not participate in the giggling, glancing once at him and then turning back to her chopping, shaking her head with an amused smile.

He pulled his stool over to her. Will always appreciated a challenge. "Those are some mighty fine carrots you got there, miss."

She didn't say anything, just smiled.

"You're new here, aren't you?"

She glanced at him. "So are you," she said, glancing at his clothing. "That's palace livery."

"Aye, it is, but I'm from here originally."

"You do have that mountain accent," she commented. Some thought flashed across her face suddenly and she leaned closer. "You're from *this* castle?" she asked.

"Born and bred."

She smiled, brushing her blond braid over her shoulder. "The girls were telling me some… stories. I think they may be making them up, to make fun with the new girl, see? But if you know them too? Some myths about this

castle?"

"Oh, aye, you mean the secret passages? Sure, I know the stories." Will flashed briefly on Gregory again.

Her face darkened—with worry? Then abruptly she smiled at him. Will didn't see why myths—even though the passages *were* real— should have any importance at all, since only he and Gregory—and now the princess—knew of them. But the look he'd seen on her face spoke differently. Who was this new girl and what did Gregory's passages matter to her?

If the assassins were using the passages, did this mean she might be involved?

The girl was looking down at her chopping, her blade glinting in the torchlight. She glanced up to flash him a smile. "Everyone knows these stories then?"

"Aye. At least the ones who live here. Living here and not knowing it, it'd be like living in Neria and not knowing the story of the Alliance."

The blonde looked down at her vegetables. Amusement in her voice, she commented lightly, "And it took me this long to hear of it! Perhaps I ought to get out more."

Still in his character, Will gave her a rascal's grin. "Well, beautiful, I'd be happy to oblige that wish. What's your name?"

She smiled up at him. "Andrea."

"It's been terribly nice to meet you, miz Andrea, but my masters might get a bit snappish if I stay any longer." Will nodded to her, winked at the other scullery maids, and left.

136

Andrea turned to the brunette maid on her left, pulling a new handful of carrots to her. "Who was he?" She kept her voice light and easy.

The brunette looked up, a laugh woven into her words. "He's a flirt, ain't he? Name's Will Rocole; I knew him as a kid. Little scamp, he was." She glanced at him approvingly as he disappeared out the door. "My, his year away has sure improved him." She grinned at Andrea and turned back to her task.

As for Andrea, her face had paled and her hand tightened on her chopping knife. She knew that name. Idiot, she thought to herself. Next time don't settle for knowing the spy's name, find out what he looks like!

That little flirt was the Crown's spy and she'd just betrayed a little too much interest in the passages. Andrea'd seen that suspicion on his face. Maybe he would pass her mistake off as simple curiosity from a newcomer.

But what if he didn't?

What if Rocole asked around— wondering why a kitchen wench thought the legends were so important—and found someone who knew that the passage myth was true? What if there *was* someone other than Harston who knew about the passages, even if she had done

away with his map? What if the spy *found* them? Next time she went delving for information, she better make sure that the one she was getting it from wasn't getting any from her.

Andrea itched to race after him, chopping knife in hand, but restrained herself. That would be even riskier than letting him find the passages. What harm could he do? They were in the castle now. It would be more difficult, certainly, but they could find more conventional ways to get around.

There was no reason to chase after him, no reason to tell Doulings. She blanched at the thought of the hired killer laughing at her mistake. No, no reason to tell him at all. Andrea continued chopping her carrots.

She would, however, keep an eye on Will Rocole.

Lia felt her baroness's horrified stare was a bit more than the revelation had warranted. "It snowed the winter before Gabrielle was born," said Lia, "but it melted before it touched ground."

The baroness fluttered a hand above her chest. "How can you not have been in snow before? A third of your country's snow-locked all winter!"

"Not a third," said the count. "Just the northern and southern mountains, and the coastal range on particularly cold winters." He'd bribed

the footman to give him his papers back and the

duchess was watching the stack beside him with greedy, malicious intent.

The baroness fixed them each with a steely look. "Have *you* seen snow?"

"It's wet," said the wiry-haired duchess with a shrug. The duke nodded agreement.

The youngest lady shook her head and the count said dryly, "I was raised on the edge of a desert."

"Well, you're going to," said the baroness. She crooked a finger at the footman, who was not at present a young man named Will Rocole. "I need the chamberlain." The footman bowed and left. "None of you know what winter is," said the baroness, with a horrified lift of her chest.

"It comes after autumn," said the duke.

"And it's *cold*," said the youngest lady.

"It's good to be cold, now and then," said the baroness. She settled back into her chair and when the chamberlain arrived, looking harried, she questioned him about snowshoes while the others exchanged uncertain looks.

When Sasha returned to her room after her excursion with Gregory, she found it had an occupant.

She hadn't checked the room before jumping in through the window, because she was running late and she was afraid her guard might

glance in to check on her. Sasha didn't even see

the person at first, as she took off her cap and boots and slid the shutters closed behind her.

She jumped about three feet in the air when a quiet, amused voice spoke out behind her.

"Well, that answers a few questions."

Sasha whirled around and said, "Gabrielle! What are you doing here?"

Her little sister smiled. "This is my room, too. You're the one who needs to be explaining things. Where have you been?" Gabrielle smiled sweetly. "Lia's been a little upset."

Sasha scowled.

Gabrielle grinned wider. "Well, she hasn't really. But she would if she knew what you were doing. I covered for you. So now you owe me, sister. What have you been doing, Sasha?"

Sasha shook her head. "You won't believe me."

"I'm young and naïve. I'll believe anything."

When Sasha was done, Gabrielle pulled her knees to her chest and rested her chin upon them. "You're going to need a better excuse than sickness," Gabrielle said. "Even Lia will see through that eventually—or she'll decide you're dying and come in to weep over you. I'll talk to her."

"You can get me out of her little Court? How? And if you can do that, why haven't you gotten yourself out of Court back home? I would've."

Gabrielle shrugged. "I like Court."

"You are an odd twelve year old."

"I'm twelve and a half. And one of us should stay in the nobles' room, if we want to catch these bad men."

"What do you mean by that?"

"The assassins have got sources. They have to, to have known we were coming here. They've got to have some sort of benefactor. Since it involves the throne, I'm guessing it's a noble. Some of the wealthy merchants might be able to finance this, but it much more likely to be coming from the nobility. And it would make sense they'd come to keep an eye on their work, don't you think?"

"Our own nobles are paying people to kill us? Those are Lia's friends. That's terrible."

"It's also very common. Don't you ever read history, Sasha?" Gabrielle frowned. "You know who it probably is, behind it all? Those revolutionaries, the ones who are clamoring to get rid of the Alliance."

Sasha looked blank.

"You know how minor officers of the government kept coming up missing? And all the thefts from the army supply stock? That was the Cerens."

"Why do you know this when I don't?"

Gabrielle sighed. "I *listen*, Sasha. I go to Court and hear what they have to say. I talk with the ministers and read Papa's reports. I pay attention."

"And I learn sword fight and run off to play in town. Or I did before we came here." Sasha glared at the coverlet on her bed.

"Basically."

Sasha looked at Gabrielle. "You'll help, won't you?"

Gabrielle laughed. "Of course. It's about me, too. I'll talk to Lia about getting you out of her little Court. She knows she's not Mother. And I'll keep an eye out for the benefactor—or whatever minion he's sent along, more likely." She fixed Sasha with a demanding gaze. "But you have to promise me one thing."

"What?"

"Be careful. Do not get yourself killed, Sasha."

Sasha grinned at her. "And leave you alone with Lia? Don't worry about me, Gabrielle. I can take care of myself."

Gregory didn't hear the door open, because he was asleep, drooling slightly into his threadbare pillow. He didn't hear footsteps threading his way, or the rustle of thick bundled fabric. He woke to the surprise of a thick, heavy horse blanket dropped on him. Gregory shoved himself to a sitting position, thought blearily about assassins, and blinked up at Will, who was standing over him and grinning.

Gregory wrapped his hands around the blanket with recognition and tumbled off his sleeping mat, eyes lighting up. He pulled on every hand-me-down scrap of clothing he had, wrapped his sleeping blanket around his shoulders, and followed Will who, equally bulkily-attired, toted the horse blanket. It was the only material they'd found that gave them a decent amount of time on the snow.

They opened the nearest passage entrance, Gregory doing the honors because they were his, and anyway Will's hands were full with the horse blanket and a flickering candle he'd left on the floor outside the room before he'd woken Gregory up.

The candle lit up the red brick inside. At the end of the passage, a thick door was set in the wall. It opened inward, and unlocked only from the inside. Gregory slid the bolt and creaked it open—it squealed, rarely used—and got a face full of frigid air.

Will reached up high to set the candle down on top of the snow bank, and then scrambled up the half-packed slope he'd spent the afternoon making. Will had used the side of an old crate to beat back the high snow and flatten it into something the two boys could climb up and over.

At the top of the slope, sinking in the cold, Will flung out the thick, stiff horse blanket and then he and Gregory crawled and slipped and rolled out onto it. The blanket buckled around them, sinking through the stiff, crumbling snow bank, but if they stayed on top of it the snow would take a few minutes to soak through the thick fabric.

A foot or so of sheer white wall rose around them as they lay on their backs and stared up at the sky. Every time they moved, they sank a few more inches, but this was a moment for stillness, so that was alright.

The sky was darkness and clear sharp light. Gregory's cheeks were rosy with cold, the bones in his fingers and toes starting to ache with the chill of it. He could hear the wind whistling through the high valley, but sunken down in the snow as they were, it didn't touch them.

If this had been a time for words, Will would have said *I missed the snow last winter*, and meant *I missed you*, but it was not a time for words, it never had been. They had been friends as long as they had been orphans and as long as that they had been coming out on winter's midnights to watch the stars.

It had been a tradition of Will's mother, every winter Will had had with her until her last (though she'd had to sneak out through other means than secret passages). He'd brought a young, mourning Gregory out here, eight years ago, and told him with his mother's drawl still tingeing the cadence of his speech, "The best stars are winter's."

Gregory felt a freezing dampness begin to soak at his pants leg. The blanket was failing. He shifted, the blanket sinking another inch with the creak of snow rubbing on snow, and looked over his shoulder at Will. There were several traditions for this night; Will's mother had loved traditions. Here was the next: he tackled Will sideways into the snow bank.

Will gave a gasping splutter, half his face stuck with white powder, and he yanked up the blanket, sending Gregory rolling into the packed snow under it. Will tossed the blanket to the side and the two boys went tumbling and crashing into the snow, tossing flying handfuls of it, chasing each other as they sank thigh-deep in powder, falling and tripping and face-planting, leaving Will-and-Gregory-shaped holes.

Their shoulders shook with laughter and cold. When the shaking became more from cold than laughter, they scrambled back through the snow to the passage's entrance and slid and stumbled back inside.

Will laid the wet blanket out in the passage to dry and they squelched through the castle by the light of Will's candle, shivering and dripping melted snow and bumping each other for warmth.

In the kitchens, Gregory fed the cook's guard pup dried strips of beef he had been saving for such a need while Will scrambled up onto the wide stone ledge that edged the hearth and worked at waking the night's embers into a crackling fire. Their clothes, their skin, and their hair began to steam and thaw as they grinned at each other sleepily. The dog yanked too hard on the strip of beef and Gregory tumbled off the ledge laughing.

The fire had fallen back to embers again when Cook found them there in the morning, Gregory's head pillowed on Will's stomach, the black pup snoring on his feet. She woke them with a rap on each skull, said, "Three overgrown pups is a bit too much," and gave them both a little warm cider before sending them back to bed.

"I feel useless," said Sasha. "All the time." She was sitting cross-legged on the floor of an old storage room. A redheaded young man sat across from her, his black and silver jacket folded carefully on top of a barrel.

"Don't be silly," said Elijah. He drew a card from the deck, looked at it with his blandest face, and added it to his hand. He discarded another. "Your turn."

She drew a card and made an impressively grotesque face; Eli played cards by going bland and unreadable, Nathaniel by being cunningly deceiving. Sasha knew she couldn't keep anything from her face, so she just exaggerated every twist of the nose until the specifics became unreadable in their own right.

"It's not silly," she said. "Either I'm a princess too blunt for diplomacy and not clever enough to rule, or I'm a guard trainee who's never going to be a guard. The most useful I've ever felt is this sneaking about in passages, listening to whispers, and we've yet to find anything!"

"I'm not going to ask about the 'we,'" murmured Elijah.

"The most useful I've ever felt, and still I'm failing miserably." She laid down her hand, face-up. "Full-palace, by the way," she added and grinned at Elijah's damped look of chagrin (he had a few good cards in his hand, but nothing to beat that).

The next day, Sasha waited in a corridor near the visiting servants' quarters and waited for the footman named Rocole to leave it.

She had been using Gregory's listening-holes, in the kitchen. This Rocole, a palace servant who switched between wearing the castle's accent or using lowland colloquial depending on who he talked to, had been making dangerous small talk with everything that walked within his radius. Rocole dragged information out of conversation, from the kitchen help, the hostlers, asking about the attack, about castle sentiments. From her maids and even off-duty guardsmen she listened to him slowly piece together a frighteningly thorough picture of Brown's protections around them.

This Will Rocole was a rebel spy, clearly.

Following him here, to his quarters, Sasha had seen him give a chunk of bread to a guard on duty, chat awhile; Rocole'd spoken with a girl hauling water and a noble's manservant. He'd visited some of the tiny craft workshops that huddled in one corner of Willow Tree.

Rocole'd strolled through the covered walkway that led to the stables; it had been difficult for Sasha to follow him there, down that narrow, straight corridor, with nothing to hide behind. She had had to wait until he was already in the stables before she could traverse it. She'd lurked in the hayloft then, watching him chatting with the hostlers.

Now, Sasha lurked out of sight of the door, wiping her palms on her trousers, unsure about what she was planning to do about this spy who asked too many questions and knew too much. She was certain she had to do *something*.

A few moments later the door of the visiting servants' quarters swung open and Rocole left. Sasha caught a glimpse of the room—it was empty. Once Rocole was out of sight, she crossed the narrow hall and tried the door, praying that he had not locked it. There were plenty of witnesses in the hall who would definitely notice a scruffy looking youth picking a lock in broad daylight—well, torchlight.

Sasha suppressed a sigh of relief as the doorknob turned easily under her hand. She slipped inside, her soft boots whispering over the stones in the floor.

It was a small room, very small. A couple of mattresses were stuffed inside and a shared, small chest for the servants' belongings. A torch spluttered in a bracket on the wall, but an oil lamp, which was lit, flickered on the floor next to one of the beds.

Sasha's eyes narrowed in suspicion. She would bet anything that that bed was Rocole's—an oil lamp was an oddity; it was needed for reading and writing—such as a rebels' spy writing reports to his masters.

Sasha opened the drawers of the chest, which were filled with clothes and knick-knacks. She had expected nothing more—why would Rocole leave evidence in a place he shared with other servants? Still, she checked the drawers for false bottoms and the chest for a false back.

Sasha tried his bed next—that was a place all his own. And, indeed, she found more than enough to prove her suspicions. Hidden in the bottom side of the mattress were documents. Her stomach tightened. They were government papers, like the ones she would find on her father's desk. Had the spy stolen them? What information did they hold? What secrets were being sold?

Sasha was reaching for them to find out when she heard the door open. She looked up sharply, grabbing panicked for the little knife in her boot.

Of course, she thought, you idiot. Why would he have left the lamp lit if he wasn't planning on coming back?

Rocole stepped through the door and shut it behind him. "Who are you working for?"

Her sleeve had fallen down to cover her knife. Sasha knelt on the floor, one hand on the

149

papers, the other holding her knife. She could hear her heart thudding in her ears, so loud she thought she might burst.

She almost laughed at him for not recognizing her except she was too fixed on figuring out if she could make it if she dashed for the door.

"You should really hide your stolen government documents better," Sasha said glibly, stalling for time. There was a quaver in her voice she could just barely contain.

He saw her eyes dart to the door as he moved forward, so he took a step back and locked it, without turning around or taking his eyes off of her. "Mind explaining how you found me out?" he asked. "I'm curious. I thought I'd been rather careful."

Sasha stood slowly, keeping her sleeve over her knife, though she was fairly certain using it was probably the only way she was going to be able to get out of here. Her legs trembled weakly. "You ask too many questions to be anything but a spy." She kept her back to the wall, scooting slowly toward the door, as he moved to block her.

"Or just a very curious lad," he offered cheerily. Rocole frowned, his brows curving together. "But how would you know what I do? I haven't seen you around the kitchen or anywhere, just following me in the halls. You do look familiar, though—"

Sasha let her sleeve fall back, revealing

her glinting dagger. Her jaw tightened, quivering, her eyes flat. "Now, sir, if you would move to the side a bit? There's somewhere I have to be going now." She hoped he would not try to put up a fight. She didn't want to hurt him.

Then it occurred to her to wonder what exactly she was going to do once she left the room. Tell Brown? If he believed her—should she grab some papers as proof?—he would probably arrest this young man as a traitor. Sasha knew what her country did to traitors.

Still, they had murdered Harston. Didn't they deserve the same fate? And if she didn't leave quickly, he might call his friends. She only had the one knife and she wasn't as sure of herself as she let Eli think.

Will Rocole had drawn in a breath when he saw the knife, and now his eyes darted around, looking for something with which to defend himself. Not seeing anything, he brought his gaze back to her face as he took a few slow steps back.

Then he darted forward again, hands up, eyes widened in recognition. "Wait—you're the princess."

"Clever of you to figure that out," Sasha said. "Now, if you would please—?"

"But why are you after me?" he asked. His face lit as he realized. "You think I'm a spy for the rebels?" He held up his hands and stepped toward his mattress. His eyes flashed toward her knife, held steadily in front of her. "I'm a spy, but not for them—I've got proof of identification, just let me get it."

The surprise in his voice convinced her more than any of his words. Sasha nodded slowly. "If I see even the glint of a blade," she warned.

He bent down and ruffled through the papers that had been under his mattress. Sasha watched him warily. He lifted the bottom of the mattress and felt for a slit in the bedding. From it he drew a stout wooden cylinder, one base carved and capped with the crest of the intelligence ministry of Neria, of her father. Such things were used for impressing wax seals.

"Oh," said Sasha.

He stood again, slowly, but she did not lower her knife.

"How do I know that's real? That you didn't just steal it or forge it? I'm no expert—I could be fooled by a fake emblem."

"There's not just that," Rocole said quickly. "I also know about the passages—"

"The assassins know about them," Sasha interrupted, "so it's a moot point."

"But they obviously don't know that *you* know," he said. "I know that you're using them, because I know the person who found them first. Gregory will vouch for me."

Sasha opened her mouth to say that she wasn't sure if she trusted Gregory, either—which was starting to feel more like a lie every time she said it, thinking about the earnest, painfully honest brown-eyed boy. But something else occurred to her. "Wait. Rocole. *Will* Rocole. You're *that* Will?"

"Gregory's talked about me?" Will asked, taken aback, his eyes on her face, not on the blade. "What did he say?"

"I think that's his business," Sasha said. She raised the knife a little and added, "He didn't say you were a spy."

"Well, that's good, I suppose, as I asked him not to," Will said. "Though it might've made this a little easier."

Sasha eyed him over the blade. Will said, "I couldn't hurt you if I tried. I don't even know what side of a knife to *hold*."

Sasha thought about the earnest, honest boy who had called this young man a friend. Gregory was such a terrible liar. She lowered her blade slowly.

Will grinned with delight and bowed a little at her. "Well, your highness, it's nice to meet you."

"Please don't call me highness," said Sasha. She knelt beside the mattress, tucking her knife in her boot once more, but still leaving it loose in its hilt. "Do you have—uh—sources here?"

Will grimaced. "No. My only assignment is to keep an eye on the nobles, check correspondence and such—routine work."

Sasha frowned. "But you're always asking questions—of the servants and the guards. You're looking for the assassins, just like me."

"Aye, but that's off the books, you see," said Will. He grinned. "I didn't join the ministry because I *like* to follow orders."

A small smile forced itself onto her face. "So how did you get these?" she asked, ruffling through the papers.

"Swiped 'em off Brown's desk," Will said nonchalantly, looking at her from the corner of his eye. "That man's lock is pitiful."

Braggart, Sasha thought. Her fingers itched to try her own skills on Brown's door, to see if she could. "We're after the same goal," Sasha said. "Let's help each other."

Will checked the lock on the door behind him and then sat cross-legged on his lumpy mattress, gesturing for Sasha to do the same. She slid off her knees into a more comfortable position. "So," he said. "What have you gathered?"

"You first," said Sasha.

Will laughed and complied.

Lia resisted the urge to shift uncomfortably in her seat—a princess heir had to be stately, even just among friends like these.

They were gathered in Lia's dressing room: the princess heir, the wiry-haired duchess, the dignified baroness, and the youngest lady. At home, this would be a room of its own, but here it was her bedroom and reading room as well.

Lia had not slept well the night before, but the shadows under her eyes were hidden with face paint and any exhaustion behind the gentle, queenly smile she'd learned from watching her mother administer Court. She watched curiously over the maid's shoulders as the girl sorted through her wardrobe.

"Silk," said the baroness, seated grandly on a chair. "Silk, or wool, if it's thick." She turned to the rest of them. "Now, you're going to get wet," said the baroness severely. Her barony was so far south that it was past the flat, fertile inland valley that made up most of southern Neria and instead was nestled high in the snowy mountains that were the border to the southern country of Kainen. "You should be prepared for that." The baroness's mother managed the estate while they waited for her brother, the five-year-old baron, to grow up.

Lia had been a witness for the little baron's swearing in when the baroness's father, the old baron, had passed away three years ago. They'd let him wobble after pigeons and peacocks on the green palace walks after the ceremony until he had collapsed onto Lia's lap and slobbered all over her gown while he slept.

The baroness gathered the pile of cloth from the maid and then dumped it in Lia's lap. "Layers," she said. "Leggings under shifts under wool petticoats under heavy skirts. Here, try this first—" The baroness thrust fabric at Lia. The maid moved the pile of clothing to the bed and then helped Lia remove her overdress when she'd stood up.

The baroness watched critically as the maid fastened the first skirt around the princess heir. She passed the maid another skirt and said, "Dereck and John are being quite attentive."

The duchess laughed. "So are we," she said. "It's not like we all don't have our own advantages to gain—though there are a few advantages the boys are after that we aren't." She grinned at Lia, who bit the inside of her lip to hide a return laugh. Sometimes being friends with Marie was more challenging to Lia's deportment than all of Court.

The young lady chewed over what the duchess had said, then gasped comprehension of the first part. "We aren't here for status or land. We're here because we like Lia."

"Don't be crude, Marie," the baroness agreed, who had understood the second part as well, and was referring to both.

"I'm not crude, I'm honest," said the duchess.

Lia smiled. "You're crude, *and* you're lying," she said.

The baroness made a dissatisfied noise in the back of her throat and returned to her subject. "I saw you walked out with John yesterday afternoon."

"Yes," said Lia, "Us and a guardsman strolling the battlements."

"His idea, I imagine," said the wiry-haired duchess. "Did he keep you warm?" she asked sweetly.

"So," said the baroness, "Which one?"

Lia put her hands on the thick skirts gathering at her waist. "What kind of question is that?"

The baroness tutted impatiently. "Which one will you say yes to? Anyone with eyes knows their majesties want you to choose, soon."

"Why?" said the youngest lady. "Wooing is the best part of marriage, my mother says."

"The royal line needs an heir," said Lia. "What if something happened to Father? Who would be king?"

"How can you think of something like that?" said the youngest lady. She knocked on the wood bedpost and the duchess looked at her curiously.

"What are you doing?" said the baroness.

"The noise scares bad luck away," said the youngest lady. "My nurse taught me."

"A peasant superstition," said the baroness. She wrinkled her nose. "And a northerner one, too, by the sound of it."

"We can't all grow up in the south," said the duchess. "And you're the one who left your precious mountains."

"One of my family had to be a

representative at the court," said the baroness. She turned to Lia, who was beginning to sweat in her layers. "Well?"

"I'm thinking about it," said Lia, wading a thick scarf in her hands. "There are a lot of questions to answer."

"Which one is handsomer?" offered the youngest lady.

"Who's richer?" disagreed the duchess, grinning.

"Who will make a better king?" said the baroness.

"A better husband?"

"Who your mother likes better?"

The baroness stood in a rustle of skirts and kissed Lia on top of the head. "Who you like better," she said and hooked her arm through the youngest lady's. "Come. You, too, Marie. Let's get the rest of us dressed."

"I can dress myself," said the duchess, waving lazily from the bed. "Go on ahead."

The baroness and the younger lady swished from the room, the door clicking shut behind them.

"The question is," said the duchess sagely, "which one do you want to put your hands all over?"

Bright red, Lia flung the wad of her woolen scarf at the duchess's head. "Marie!"

Lia dropped onto the bed, keeping her back fire-poker straight with the ease of long practice. "Dereck's no good at *people*," she said quietly to the duchess, and sighed. "He's no good at numbers, either," Lia said. "I did his sums for him once and they were easy, so how good can he be?"

The duchess quirked an eyebrow at her and Lia blushed. "He couldn't get things to line up and I—"

"I think that *was* him flirting," said the duchess.

Lia shook her head, smiling. "I just do sums with Dereck, sometimes," said Lia. "He tries to explain taxes and revenues and things." She waved a lazy hand in the air. "There are patterns in the numbers, and they have to match up. Once we got a map and wrote all over it and stuck it with colored pins…"

"Sums," said the duchess, tasting the word. "Is that what you young pups call it now?"

Lia smirked at the duchess, who was two years her senior. "Don't fret; you're not getting that old, Marie. I still call it *walking out* with John."

"Rose garden?" said the duchess with a slow smile. "He does like to walk there."

"Half the bushes high enough to make a maze," said Lia. She hesitated, and said, "Have you…"

The duchess took her hand and laid her cheek on the princess's shoulder. "Not for a year," she said. "Not since he kissed you at midwinter—he's not stupid."

"And you're a good friend," said Lia.

The duchess made a face. "Eh. It was nothing. He's not *that* pretty."

The red-brown bricks of the passageway were lit up by the flickering light of the torch. Sasha held it again while Gregory scampered along in front of her. The silence was complete but for the sound of Gregory's feet and the crackle of the torch.

Sasha's steps were silent; it was difficult to get past a half-asleep guard if your footsteps were loud enough to wake them.

She hadn't yet told Gregory of her encounter with Will; she wondered briefly if Will had told him, but decided that if he had, Gregory would've said something. Concealing knowledge was not one of his strong points.

Sasha adjusted her grip on the torch and, eyeing the ground in front of her, asked mildly, "When were you going to tell me your friend Will knew about the passages, and that he was a spy for the Crown?"

Gregory jumped and whirled around, staring at her. "How—how did you find that out?"

"I, ehm, ran into him," she said. "We swapped stories; it was interesting. He said he's trying to find the assassins, too."

"Aye, he is," said Gregory, his voice a little shaky still from shock.

"Knowing there's someone else on this, a professional, makes me feel a little better," confided Sasha.

"Decided to trust me after all?" Gregory asked, a little sullenly. "Since you're trusting my friends and all. I suppose Will does have that effect on people."

"Gregory, don't take it personally," Sasha said in a tone that could almost be apologetic. "There are assassins out to kill me and my sisters. I can't trust *anybody,* not entirely. And I must trust you somewhat to even be here at all."

There was a pause as Gregory digested this. "Tell me about Will," said Sasha, trying to change the subject.

"Will," Gregory said. He shrugged. "He's a friend. My best friend in the world, I suppose. We grew up together, here at Willow Tree."

"You two found the passages?"

"No. *I* found them." Gregory shrugged. "Will's better at everything else. He could always talk us out of trouble, or into it." His voice sank, barely audible. "But these passages, they're *mine.* I found them. My one skill, eh? Finding dusty little pathways to nowhere."

"If you hadn't found them, I'd still be pacing in that corridor, staring at the walls."

Gregory brightened a bit. "That's true, isn't it? I'm helping rescue some damsels in distress."

"Why did you tell me about these passages, Gregory?"

He looked down. "Because Will and I promised that we wouldn't ever tell. And I needed to break some promises."

"I thought you said that you two were the best of friends."

"We were. And we are, I suppose. But he left. A year ago. He only just came back."

"What did he leave for?" Sasha switched her torch to her other hand. The fabric of her breeches was rough as she wiped her hand on the cloth.

Gregory shrugged. "To see the world, I guess. He doesn't want to just be another person. He wants to be *somebody* and he can't do that here. So he left."

"And he didn't ask you to go along?"

Gregory shook his head. "He asked, but how can he expect me to have gone with him? This is *home*. I have a life here, and so did he." He snorted. "But it wasn't *grand* enough for Will," he said, dragging the word out. Gregory sighed and slid down to sit at the base of the brick wall.

"It's been a year," he said. "People *change* in a year. I've grown up, and I don't think he's noticed. I don't think *I* noticed until he came back." Gregory lifted his head and his voice gained strength, but not volume. "I'm not just the little brother anymore."

He stopped and added, "I don't mean it like he's a bad fellow. It's just, well, he did the thinking for both of us and I was okay with that. When he left I had to learn to do some thinking for myself. Now that he's back—I want to be me; I want to be *Gregory*. I don't want to be Will's echo."

"And so you told me."

Gregory opened his mouth to speak again but Sasha shushed him. "Listen," she hissed. Footsteps sounded and voices echoed towards them, jarring in the bricked darkness of the passageways. Her eyes grew wide. "It's them; it's got to be!" She jumped to her feet and so did Gregory beside her.

Sasha turned to race back towards the entrance they had come in through. The footsteps came from the other direction. They were faint, but growing louder—too loud. The passage was long and straight; she and Gregory wouldn't make it beyond the corner before the assassins came into view.

Gregory grabbed her arm. "This way," he whispered.

"That's where the assassins are!"

He grabbed her hand, insistent. Her gaze flicked anxiously from him to the darkness beyond him, her ears filled with the sound of footsteps. Gregory's hand tightened on her arm and she let him pull her along.

He was off in an instant and she hurried behind him. Gregory skidded to a stop before a stretch of wall that looked just like all the others.

Sasha could hear the assassins' feet slapping on the floor, their voices rising and falling. They hadn't noticed them yet, but if they came around the corner they would. There was nowhere to go, nothing to hide behind.

In front of her, Gregory suppressed a cry of triumph and a door swung open from the wall. The pair darted in and shut it behind them.

"What is this?" Sasha whispered.

Gregory shushed her, the footsteps nearing.

Sasha saw torchlight flickering through a crack in the door they had just passed through and put out her own torch against the brick wall. The flame died, hissing as it threw them into darkness.

Sasha pressed her forehead against the chill stone, screwing up her eyes, holding her breath. There were two sets of footsteps, one heavy, one soft. "Carrot and turnip stew for dinner," one commented, and then they moved past the hidden pair, their voices fading with their steps.

When Sasha could hear nothing but Gregory's soft breathing and her own, she began to feel the walls around her.

"What did you have to put the torch out for?" Gregory complained.

"They would've seen it! We could see the light from theirs. Besides, I thought you knew every stone in these passages. Not afraid you'll lose your way, are you?"

"I'm only worried you'll trip and break your neck. What would I say then?"

Sasha laughed, more out of relief than anything. "What is this place? It's not a passage, more like a little hole in the wall. I can barely stand up without hitting my head."

"I don't know. It's almost like they're a secret within a secret. I guessed the assassins wouldn't know about them. They've probably only got a *map* or something," Gregory said, deep scorn in his voice at the word. "If we had run for the entrance they would've heard us and caught us."

"Why do you think these holes in the walls are secret, not planned?"

"Their entrances are as hidden as the ones to the main passages. For this one, there's a hollow brick. You pry it out of its place and there's a doorknob behind. I took a dagger and scratched the brick up, years ago, so I could find it again easily."

Sasha looked down. "Thank you, Gregory."

"You're welcome, I suppose." But she could almost hear him smiling in the dark.

Chapter Five
In the Dark

Gabrielle positioned herself in a small alcove of the noble's gathering room, where she could survey the whole room with ease.

Lia and her friends were stumbling around in far too many layers of clothing and bulky boots stuffed with old silk shifts meant to keep their feet warm. They looked ridiculous, preparing for a jaunt in the frozen outside world. Gabrielle turned another page in her book, watching them over the rim of it.

It was good that Sasha had confided in her, and that she had decided to find the assassins' benefactor. Gabrielle had been chafing in this small pool of little fish. She missed the real Court, alight in splendor and power.

While the power-play between these petty juveniles had kept her interest for awhile, it was not nearly as fascinating as the struggles between the great nobles at home, or between the ministers who were her father's advisors. They *mattered*.

"I see you're plotting, princess." Nathaniel the guardsman leaned on the wall beside her, hands tucked idly in his pockets.

"Aren't you supposed to be over there?" The rest of the guards swarmed, black and silver bees, by the door. Gabrielle sank back into her little alcove, looking at the lanky man out of the corner of her eye. She was used to the black and silver uniforms and even perhaps to this particular tall redheaded figure, but not to *speaking* to them. Gabrielle hugged her book to her chest.

Nathaniel squinted across the room. "Probably. I'm sure Gideon will tell me about it later. So who're you giving the evil eye, there, little one?"

"No one," she said. *Little* one? "I'm just watching."

"That's watching? Remind me not to make you angry, kid." Nathaniel scratched the inside of his calf with the other foot. He nodded at the dark haired duke. "Who's that one, who's caught your eye?" Nathaniel grinned at her. "Got a crush?"

Gabrielle gave him her best cold glare.

"Impressive," he said. "It's easy to tell you're Sasha's sister when you muck up your face like that." Nathaniel nodded toward a second nobleman, the count, this one light haired and square-shouldered. "Him, too." He tilted his head. "Princess Lia's suitors, aren't they?"

"Yes," Gabrielle said, looking away from him.

"*So* what're you staring at them for?" Nathaniel circled over to her other side.

"I've got to learn how to flirt from somewhere," Gabrielle said dryly.

"Uh huh. Sure," he said. "Sasha's up to something." Gabrielle glanced over at him slowly. "Now you are, too."

"I'm not up to anything at all," said Gabrielle. "I'm just watching."

"I wouldn't want you watching me like that," said Nate. "So you think one of them was behind the attack?" He crossed his arms. "Why would they have done that? You'd think they of all people—future kings, for moonlight's sake— would want your family to stay in power."

"You think they're trying to take down the monarchy?" Gabrielle asked. She slid out of her alcove to get a better look at him.

"They attacked the royal family." Nathaniel shrugged.

"They attacked the two younger daughters of the royal family, and poorly, too," she corrected. Nathaniel looked at her. "The only time they aimed well was when they killed your captain."

Nathaniel leaned his head back against the wall. Now he was not looking at her. "Hard to miss a big man charging with a sword."

"I wouldn't know," she said quietly. Gabrielle wouldn't have mentioned Harston to Sasha. She probably should've known better than to mention him to one of his guardsmen.

Nathaniel shook his head to clear it and then turned to grin at her—why did he keep doing that? "Me either." He stretched lazily. "So why would Lia's suitors be behind this all?"

"What do you know about our inheritance system?"

"Ah," he said. "Do you and Sasha inherit the throne before Lia's husband would?"

"In the event of my parents and Lia's death," said Gabrielle, "yes."

Nathaniel looked at the two suitors; the dark-haired duke flirted with Lia; the count watched them while he talked with the princess's ladies. "The men who would be king," he said.

"His name is John," Gabrielle said. "The one with the black hair and the smile. He's got a duchy down south, one of the oldest holdings. He'd give us excellent connections with the old nobility, which would be useful the next time they get grumpy about my great-grandfather's father being a merchant. The blonde one is Count Dereck. His lands are more extensive, but they're on the Ahar border."

"Which is why he holds himself like a fighting man."

"Does he?" Gabrielle peered at the count.

Nathaniel smiled and said, "Look at the slope of his shoulders and the distance between

170

his feet. His knees are a little bent, for balance, like. Don't let the ink spots on his hands fool you."

"*You* don't stand like that."

Nathaniel shrugged again. "I'm not a fighting man."

"You're a guard," said Gabrielle. "And stop *doing* that."

"What?"

"Grinning at me like that. You smile too much, you know."

"You don't smile enough." Nathaniel looked at the two suitors. "Going to keep an eye on them, my little highness?"

She wrinkled her nose at the title. "You think you're clever, don't you?"

"I *am* clever, kid."

It had been hard to find a place where a nobles' servingman, a Willow Tree messenger, and a royal princess in scruffy boy's clothing could meet and talk in peace, without notice.

What could be more secret than a secret passageway?

Will stood, leaning against the brick wall. Gregory sat at his feet, playing with his red messenger's cap. Sasha sat with her knees pulled to her chest while light from Will's oil lamp glittered in the murky darkness.

"How are we going to do this?" Sasha asked. Gregory glanced at her then turned to

Will, the closest thing they had to an authority on the matter.

"If it was easy, Brown would've had 'em in the bag weeks ago." Will drummed his fingers on his thigh. "My ministry is pretty certain the Cerens are behind this all," he said. "I have to agree—everything makes sense that way." His lips quirked. "You know how the assassins probably know of the passages? When your revered relative," Will nodded to Sasha, "built this place, all of the designers and such were loyal to him. But for the actual workers, he probably just picked some commoners—Cerens. These passages have been anything but secret."

Gregory chuckled and crammed his hat on his head. "And they didn't hide them particularly well, either," he said.

"They hid them pretty well," said Will. "Who else has found them but you? And your highness, of course," he added with a courteous nod to Sasha.

"You don't have to call me highness," said Sasha. She looked at Gregory questioningly but didn't rebut Will's statement.

Gregory met her eyes and shrugged, blushing not quite hard enough for it to be obvious, and then he turned to Will. "So, how *are* we going to find the assassins?"

Will nodded, bringing himself back to business. "I'm going through the servants and the Guard," he said. "Looking for suspicious folk."

"Have you found any?" asked Sasha, leaning forward eagerly. She and Will had discussed matters before, after she raided his room, but had spoken only briefly and in generalities.

"There was a girl in the kitchens," Will said. "She asked some questions that could've been innocent, but I'm not sure. But I'm almost certain there's one in the stables. I talked to some of the overseers about who was off shift or just didn't come into work. I'm trying to place all their whereabouts, on the morning of the attack." Will grimaced. "I'm working at it—but it'll be awhile before I have anything worthwhile."

Sasha nodded. "I think I should try to listen for what they say when one of the nobles' servants isn't questioning them."

"The peepholes in the kitchen wall?" asked Gregory.

"Perfect," said Will. "That may be very helpful indeed."

"My little sister will be helping as well," said Sasha.

Will frowned. "She's twelve, right?"

Sasha shrugged. "She's investigating the nobility. Gabrielle thinks that one of them is probably funding the rebels, or working for whoever is."

Will nodded thoughtfully. "Very possible. Well, good, that covers another hole."

Sasha pushed herself to her feet. "Come on, Gregory, let's go."

Will stooped and hooked the wire handle of his oil lamp with a couple fingers. He offered it to Sasha with a bow. "For your highness," he said. "I can make it out of here without a light."

"Don't call me highness," Sasha said, but she took the lamp.

At the main doors of the castle, the baroness was giving a stern lecture to the other nobles. Gabrielle, officially another member of this miniature Court, had declined the adventure and was curled up in her room with a book, perhaps with the window open for a chill breeze.

Piled beside the door were flat, light wood-and-leather structures that were wider than a man's foot and much longer. The baroness had beamed proudly at the pile, called them "snowshoes" and circled her friends like an army officer as they worked to strap the contraptions to their feet.

The youngest lady used the footman as a balancing post while the two men elbowed each other.

Lia knelt by the wiry-haired duchess, tugging at the laces as she tied her foot down, continuing an earlier argument.

"You care a lot more than you pretend to," Lia told her quietly.

The duchess laughed. "It's sweet that you think so, but no. I'm not applying to anything more than heartless, beautiful, dashingly clever court ornament."

Lia might have said more, but the doors opened and the baroness ushered them out into a gust of wind that chilled her to her trembling core.

The footmen had packed the snow around the door down so that the princess's court could crunch their way up a mostly-solid, icy ramp.

Lia let the boys clamber up before her and she followed, the wood of her shoes creaking on the ice.

They reached the top of the snow, more than a man's height above where the floor of the meadow would be in summertime. Lia balanced on the steep, icy ramp, hovering at the line between the stamped-down ice turned greyish-brown by the footmen's efforts and the untouched glistening plain that spread outwards, white and unbroken.

The youngest lady was squeaking about something, and the baroness was instructing them, but Lia had never smelt air this cold and she wasn't listening.

Color rose into her cheeks and Lia stepped off the packed surface of the ramp and into the open snow. She sank a handswidth with a startled squeak—before either the duke or the count could rush to her aid, she wrenched the shoe from the ice, shook it uncertainly, and kept going, a little more slowly.

With every step, Lia broke the surface of the snow, but she never sank very far so she figured that was probably how it was supposed to work. The plain spread out around her, rising into the hills and she let the noise of the others fade behind her. When Lia was far enough to hear the wind, she stopped.

The world was cold and white. The green bristles of the gathered pines were hidden with thick heaps of snow, standing stately and wise in the frozen day. The white slopes spread upwards and out to the grey sky, and Lia watched their stillness and tried to let it seep into her self like the wet snow was seeping into her boots.

Lia turned slowly, snowshoes creaking, to see the whole white hemisphere around her. The cold peace was broken only by the footsteps behind her that led to the squat castle and figures of the bundled nobles and guards.

"They're still here, aren't they?" said Lia, stopping with her face towards the castle and the guards, and the wiry-haired duchess who had hopped from footstep to footstep, following her.

The duchess knelt down, thrusting her mittened hands into the clean white powder. "Hm?"

"The guard was doubled, after the—" Lia's voice fell "—*incident*. The captain hasn't decreased it. Whoever they were, they're still here."

The duchess rocked back on her heels, balanced while she patted the snow nestled in her gloves. "Where else would they go?" she asked.

"I don't know," said Lia. She watched the others of her court spread out and come closer as they stepped gingerly in the snow. "But—why haven't they done anything? I'm worried."

"You'll get wrinkles," said the duchess.

"But I *am* worried," said Lia. "I can't help it."

The duchess hesitated. "I think they have other plans, otherwise they would have tried for you again." Lia opened her mouth and the duchess added, "I don't know what they are. But maybe I'm a little worried, too." She tossed a tightly packed snowball into one hand and grabbed a loose handful of powder with the other.

"What're you doing?" said Lia, curious.

The corner of the duchess's mouth quirked a mischievous warning. "I *have* seen snowy winters before," she said as she rose to her feet.

"Marie—" There was a shriek as the duchess dropped the snow from her left hand down the back of Lia's jacket, and then the duchess was bounding away with flying snow shoes, hurling the snow ball in her right hand square into the back of the duke's head.

Lia swept anxiously at the back of her jacket, snow seeping down her spine. The duchess turned around, shaping another snowball and grinned widely at her. "Something caught your tongue, your highness?"

Lia set her shoulders and grabbed at the snow, leaping into the fray. The day dissolved into breathless, dripping laughter.

His sword was cleaned and secure, his buttons and buckles polished, his eyes alert, his stance impeccable, his dagger sharp, but Elijah felt distinctly as though he had been caught napping on duty.

Because this wasn't his duty. Standing here at the castle entrance, looking stern and dangerous but for his fire-top of hair, was not why Elijah was a guard. It wasn't to rise through the ranks and secure more shiny metal badges for his shoulders and chest. It wasn't to serve under idiots like Brown. It was because of a captain who had given him a chance once upon a time, and because there was a princess he needed to protect.

This was not his duty.

When Brown entered the nobles' gathering room, Will knew the captain couldn't possibly be there for him. Brown was far too proud to go to an amateur spy he didn't respect. Nonetheless, as Will shifted the drinks on his tray and watched idly though his eyelashes, Brown made a beeline straight for him.

"Rocole, we need to talk. Just come with me," he said, and stalked out of the room.

Will glanced at the nobles—none of them had seemed to notice the encounter. With a sigh, he followed Brown out of the room.

Once they reached Brown's study, the door shut securely behind them, Will said, "That was a long way from subtle. You want to blow my cover?"

"Which one?" said Brown curtly.

"What?" said Will.

Brown sat stiffly in his chair. "I was looking through some of my predecessor's old papers," said Brown. "And I discovered something surprising." He leaned forward and said ominously. "No spies were sent along to help guard the princesses. Westel wrote Harston explicitly to apologize."

Will's heart leapt to his throat, thudding wildly.

A cool part of his mind wondered quietly: if they were Harston's papers, had the old captain known as well?

Somehow it wouldn't have surprised Will at all if he had.

Brown continued, "Which means you, Rocole, have lied to me. Who are you working for? Tell me the truth, lad. I can call in the guards with one shout and you won't like what they do to traitors."

Will stared at him, then caught his voice, and said quickly, "I *am* working for the Crown, sir."

"According to this," Brown said, tapping a paper in front of him, "you are not."

"Do you think Westel tells everyone *everything* he does?" asked Will.

The expression on Brown's face soured further, if that was possible, and Will quickly changed his tact. "It's true, there is no spy assigned to watch for the assassins," Will said, his expression as sincere as he could make it. "But I *am* working for the Crown. My assignment was to keep an eye on the nobles. I may have overstepped my boundaries a touch," he amended apologetically.

"That is an understatement," said Brown.

"You saw the seal," said Will. "It was authentic."

Brown made a noncommittal grunt.

Will leaned forward. "My only crime is attempting to aid and protect the royal family, when I was not *specifically* ordered to. I am overeager perhaps, but no traitor." He tried his best to look trustworthy.

Brown scowled. "In the Guard, disobedience is punished heavily, Rocole," he said darkly.

With a pounding heart, Will reflected that Captain Brown and Minister Westel probably got along famously. It was no wonder that neither liked Will.

"As glorious as discipline is," tried Will, "how could I just sit by and *watch* as assassins hunted down our royal family?"

"You should have obeyed your orders and done nothing more nor less. That is how the system works. You can't simply do as you please, or our entire society would fall down around our ears." Brown glared at him. "What are you, lad, an apprentice?"

"A journeyman," said Will.

"First-rank, too, I'd wager," said Brown.

Will didn't say anything. His cheeks started to burn and he quashed the urge to look at his feet—he wasn't Gregory for goodness's sake!

Brown continued, "I should've known when I saw you that such a little sprite as you could never be assigned to *this*. Just a journeyman," Brown said, shaking his head. His expression darkened. "Rocole, I will make sure the minister of Intelligence hears of this when we return to the capitol. Until then, if I see your nose sniffing around where you oughtn't to be, I will personally make sure you are removed from any position of influence and returned to the civilian status you deserve."

"Sir, yes, sir," Will said. He bowed sharply to the captain and left the room.

The door swung shut quietly and anticlimactically. Will didn't see the point of annoying the authorities on the *little* things.

Will walked down the hallway, digesting this unsettling new turn of events. Obedience had never been his highest quality, and that was something he was not planning on changing. Brown would not *see* his nose sniffing anywhere he oughtn't to be—but Will knew he wouldn't stop. He would find the assassins. He wouldn't let anyone stop him.

Just a journeyman? Will had never been *just* anything in his life. And, if he had anything to say about it, he never would be.

When the three of them met again, they settled in near one of Gregory's hidden alcoves, in case they heard footsteps. Will had been combing through the dossiers of every servant, while Sasha used Eli and Nate to comb through each of the guards (Eli had an unexpected amount of previously collected intel on each one, which made it easier to start with the more suspicious individuals).

They had stumbled across some dark pasts, some embarrassing affairs, and a few petty and ambitious plots to rise to junior chef or chief hostler, but nothing yet screamed *rebel* or *assassin*. Sasha was worried nothing would ever scream at all, not loud enough to be heard by a princess, a street-shy messenger, or an amateur spy. That was hardly enough to make her stop trying.

Sasha wondered sometimes why these two strange boys were helping at all. She felt like she owed them something, and thought it might be an explanation.

"This isn't the first attack on my family, you know," Sasha said softly as she poured over one of Will's chicken-scratch reports.

Soft for Sasha, anyway. Even quiet and withdrawn she was obviously made of nicked sword steel, well-balanced with a rough leather grip.

Will looked up from his own papers; Gregory shivered, beside their lamp. She paused momentarily under their stares, then went on.

"When I was nine, a group of men snuck into the palace. They hid in the back of a greengrocer's wagon, in bags of potatoes." Sasha smiled faintly. "I asked around about the details of it, later, and then snuck around to find out the things they didn't want to tell me. It was the first time I figured out that sneaking was important, that people would keep things from me if I didn't go looking for answers."

Will smoothed out their papers with long-fingered hands, though they didn't need smoothing. He was used to ferreting out secrets, but always other people's. He was not used at all to the idea of people keeping your own secrets from you. "People have tried to kill your father a lot more recently than eight years ago."

"Yes," she said, and Gregory shuddered at how easy and commonplace that answer was in her mouth. The only things that people died from in Willow Tree were sickness, old age, and accidents. He wondered what he and Will would be like, if they had something to blame for their orphanhood other than a violent winter flu.

Sasha said, "But they got the closest."

While Will ran the pads of his fingers over the dried ink of names, Sasha fiddled with the hilt of her dagger.

"Gabrielle was four, already starting to read. He hid us both in the closet of his study—we'd been painting on the floor while Father worked." They had made an awful mess, often, but the king cared more about his daughters than his carpet.

"He threw them all in the fire, our wet drawings, so maybe they wouldn't realize we were still there. They killed the two guards outside the door. I found out their names, later, but I've forgotten them since." She drew her dagger and started cleaning it unnecessarily.

"Just a door," she said. "I listened to them pick it while I hid behind one of our father's winter cloaks in the closet. Just a door between men with knives and people I cared about and I couldn't do anything but hold Gabrielle and whisper things to keep her quiet. It was the most helpless I've ever felt in my life, until I watched someone kill Harston right in front of me."

Sasha sheathed her dagger. Her mother's daughters didn't cry in public. It wasn't seemly. Guards didn't cry at all. She wiped roughly at her cheeks, knowing she wasn't controlled enough for the first title and not brave enough to deserve the latter. "It was the first time I realized I was helpless," she said.

"But you're not," said Will, nodding toward the dagger in her boot, the calluses on her hands.

"Not as helpless," Sasha agreed. "But that's why. That's when it happened. That's why I'm here."

Soft tapestries hung heavy and thick in the nobleman's suite. He sat at a small writing desk and tossed a sealed ink pot back and forth between his palms.

"Evening, m' boy," said Doulings and the noble leapt up from his seat. The assassin was standing in the back of the room. "I hear you've been pining for me." There had been another blue-spattered letter.

"I—I wanted to apologize for my tardiness," said the noble. The first word was a stammer, but for the rest he drew himself up to stand straight, resting on propriety. "To report on the present circumstances of our—arrangement."

"You have competition," said Doulings. "This isn't so easy as you thought—or at least so easy as you promised. You're the gossip of the whole castle. I know." He took five precise steps forward, passed the noble, and draped himself in the abandoned chair. "Well?" Doulings said, beginning pleasantly. "You told me it was a sure thing. If that has changed, we may have to renegotiate our," he smiled, "arrangement."

The noble stepped backwards. "She just likes Dereck more than I thought. But it's a pitied sort of affection, like a lame pup she's taken in. In the end, she *will* choose me," said Duke John.

"Would you bet on that?"

"I would," he said. The duke looked relieved.

"Hm," said Doulings, leaning back in his chair. "Better kill him just in case. We know what *your* skills at gambling lead to."

The duke was both red and pale. "That isn't necessary," he said stiffly.

"You're the one who brought it up," said Doulings.

"I don't want him *dead*," said the duke. "I just wanted to explain. I didn't want you telling Lukas I wasn't holding up my side of the deal."

Doulings laughed. "Don't lie to me, boy. I don't care what you tell yourself, but if you didn't want him dead, you wouldn't have called *me*."

Now the duke was faintly green. "I wanted to explain."

"And you have. Excellent job," said Doulings. "I can't get any news to Lukas anyway, so you'll have to wait for spring for me to decide whether or not to tell him you've paid your debts to our society. A springtime engagement would be heartening for the spirit, don't you think?" He stood up.

"I am doing my best," said the duke, following him to the door.

"Are you now?"

"My word of honor."

Doulings snorted. "What is that worth? You also swore loyalty to the king." Doulings paused as he turned the doorknob. He had heard something—a squeak? The swish of skirts and the patter of feet on stone. He flung the door open.

A small shape hurried in the opposite direction, skirts hiked up to allow her to run. It was easy for Doulings to catch up, as his legs were much longer.

A few moments later, Doulings returned to the duke's room, dragging the squirming girl behind him. John quickly shut the door behind him, panic in his gaze. "Do you know who she *is*? You can't just drag her in here!"

"What are you worried about? We were planning on killing her anyway."

The duke's eyes were wide as he waved his hands about. "Someone will have seen you!"

"There was no one in the hall, elsewise she would not have been standing with her ear to our door. It's if she runs off that we'll have the issue." Doulings gave the girl a shake. She squirmed against his grasp. "What did you hear?" She bit him and he let her go with a yelp.

The girl ran toward the door, but quick with fear the duke grabbed her and knocked her off her feet. John twisted the front of her dress in his hands. "Tell us. What did you hear?"

She spat at him. "Traitor."

The duke threw her to the ground and her black curls spread out around her pale face like a halo. "Do with her as you want, Doulings." He wiped the spittle from his cheek and left the room.

"Gabrielle! Are you in here?" Lia rapped on the door to Sasha and Gabrielle's shared room. Sasha quickly slipped out of her worn boy's clothes and into a loose dress. It wouldn't do for Lia to see her in trousers.

"Gabe's not here," Sasha called, opening the door. Lia's face was taut and worried. Lia's guard hovered uncertainly behind her.

Sasha's latest guard and Elijah—though he'd been kept from looking after Sasha, he had traded his way into guarding Gabrielle occasionally—flanked the doorway, looking bewildered. Sasha frowned and asked her friend quietly, "Eli, you're guarding the door; you thought Gabe was in here?"

"She *was*," Eli said.

Lia, who had been pacing the hall nervously, clenched her hands in her dark gown. "Have you seen Gabrielle? I can't find her."

"Wasn't she with you, in the nobles' room?"

"No," Lia said. "The guards said she went into your room here, but she must've gone somewhere else because she's not here!"

Sasha sat down on her bed, two cold hands clenched in her lap. "Maybe she went to the library or something," she offered.

"I haven't checked there." Lia turned to whirl out the door and charge down to the library.

Sasha stood and grabbed her sister's shoulder. "Lia, calm down, alright?" Sasha turned the older girl around so they faced each other. "We need to think this through," she said. "We can't just run off in separate directions. You go to the library and—" Sasha bit her lip, mind racing. "And then the mess hall and check for her there. Then I need you to go back to the nobles' room. She might just have gone for a walk and will be heading back there. Don't panic."

Lia smiled tremblingly at her. "You and your cool head, Sasha." She hurried quickly out the door.

Sasha didn't watch her go, burying her face in her hands, letting the cold of her fingers cut through the fearful blur in her head.

Don't panic.

No, of course not. It's just that a duo of assassins—or maybe more—are trying to kill us and our youngest sibling has mysteriously disappeared, she thought, a little hysterically. There's no reason to panic at all.

If Sasha closed her eyes hard enough, she could smell something acrid and smoky, like someone had thrown wet, clumsy paintings into a hearth fire to burn.

Elijah looked through the door. "Sash?"

Sasha blinked rapidly, surfacing with a thudding heart. She gave Eli a smile she hoped was reassuring, then stood up and went over to the door. She told the other guard. "Please tell the captain that Gabrielle is missing, and then, if you could find squad leader Gideon and tell him as well?"

The guard bowed shortly and ran off.

"Eli, can you stay here?" Sasha asked, her eyes tracking the other guard as he moved down the hall. "She might come back." He nodded and she turned to go back into her room.

"Sasha," said Elijah. She paused in the doorway, but didn't look back, knowing what he would say. It was what Harston would have said. "You should stay here, too."

"I'm just going back into my room," she said, flashing him her most innocent smile.

Elijah grabbed her shoulders. "Don't take me for an idiot, Sasha," he said. "I of all people know that front doors don't mean a thing to you."

Sasha glared. "She's my *sister*, Eli."

His hands tightened on her shoulders. "And you're my—*charge*. And so is she. I'm coming with you." Elijah quirked the corner of his mouth. "You won't admit it, but you know you need the backup."

Sasha swept his hands off her shoulder. "Let's go then," she said, already halfway down the hall. He ran to catch up.

"Where?" Elijah asked.

"Since you were outside the door, I think she used my route through the courtyard—

maybe she bribed the guard? She's looking for the man who's funding the assassins."

"Your twelve year old sister?"

"She's—" Sasha began defensively.

"I know she's smart, Sash, but this is serious stuff. She's a kid, still, and she's tiny besides."

"I didn't ask her to go do anything!" Sasha said, furious and not at Eli. "She was just supposed to keep her eyes open in the nobles' room and maybe ask some innocent questions."

"The whole Guard is scouring the halls. So where are *we* going?" Elijah asked. Sasha looked over her shoulder at him. He said, "You found them, didn't you? The passages?"

"So did they," Sasha said. "If they've got her, that's where she is. The Guard would never find her there."

"Lucky for her, her sister likes to stick her nose in places it doesn't belong."

"Why don't we just kill her?" Yohan eyed the bound figure with unease. "That's the whole reason we're here in the first place. We've been trying to get to those princesses all this time and now that we've kidnapped one you don't want to?"

Doulings gave the man a disdainful glare. "Do you remember how I caught her? She was listening to a conversation between me and our noble friend."

191

Yohan shrugged. "All the more reason. We can't have her repeating those things she heard. The longer we leave her alive, the more likely she'll find some way to escape."

The scorn in Doulings' eyes was unmasked. "She's twelve, Yohan." There was an indignant squeak. "Beyond that, no one can find us here. Of the people here, only Harston knew of these passages and the secret died with him."

"And, so, why isn't *she* dead yet?" Yohan said.

"She was listening at the door of our noble's room. Do you *understand*? She knew he was one of us, that he was a part of this. I need to know how she found out. I need to know who else knows, so we can get rid of them as well. If someone finds out who's behind all this, we're ruined. They must not suspect our noble—even if he wins back their trust, even if her highness does love him, they might look in to his duchy's financial records. And, well, we can't have that."

Yohan nodded, accepting his reasoning, and stepped over to where Andrea stood guard over the princess. Gabrielle was gagged and blindfolded, her hands tied behind her and her feet hobbled. She shivered fearfully as she cowered on the floor of the passage, and it was easy to make out wet tracks of tears rolling down her small face.

"She's so small," Andrea said. Doulings was out of hearing range, standing with a torch a little ways down the passage.

"You're not going soft, are you?" Yohan gave her a worried look.

Andrea glared at him. "I'm not losing my nerve if that's what you mean. It just caught me a little by surprise. I'm not used to thinking of *them* as—anything, you know?"

"All she is, little one, is a target," he said gently. "Keep that in mind. This is for Ceren—"

"Don't preach at me, Yohan," Andrea snapped. "I know that spiel as well as any. I'm *not* losing my nerve," she repeated.

Andrea walked away from him, towards Doulings. "Do we all need to be here? Folk will notice if we all stay away for this long. And if they connect that with the princess being missing, we're all in deep trouble."

Doulings nodded curtly. "You should all leave. I'll take care of the prisoner. There are a few things I need to ask her." His smirk was chilling.

It was odd, that the thought of death did not make Andrea's stomach churn and yet the idea of torturing the princess did. She banished any distaste. Andrea knew her father had done such things before, when they had managed to get their hands on someone more important than the local tax collector. Her father knew, as he had taught her to know, that some things were more important than right and wrong. Her father had died for that belief.

Andrea's attention turned to the princess once more. A child. But among the

193

Cerens that the Nerians had killed there had been children as well. An eye for an eye. She turned her back on the girl. "Come on, Yohan, let's go."

He walked in the direction of the stables; Andrea took the other passage, heading toward the doorway in the corridor by the library, torch spluttering in her hand.

Sasha was certain her heart was going to beat itself out of her chest. She stepped as quietly as she could into the passage.

Elijah carefully closed the door behind them, staring around at the small space. Sasha winced as the bolt clunked in the lock. They hadn't taken a torch inside, deciding instead to feel their way through the darkness.

Placing her feet as carefully and silently as possible, Sasha started down the passage with a redheaded shadow behind her.

She pointed down a different path, tapping Elijah's shoulder and turning him—there was no light. "If we split up, we'll cover more ground. Don't engage any assassins alone, alright?"

"Hey, at least I'm trained for this." Eli glanced around at the dark walls. "You've been running around back here all winter, haven't you?"

She glared at him, even if he couldn't see it.

"Fine," Elijah said. "You're trained too. I rephrase: at least I'm *supposed* to be trained, highness." He pointed a finger at her, which she could barely see in the dark. "No one-on-one fights to the death for you either."

"What if there are two of them? Then can I?"

They separated. She didn't realize Elijah could walk so quietly. She didn't wait to watch him fade into darkness, but instead just moved on.

Sasha heard someone's footsteps approaching—not Elijah's. The light of a torch was flicking past the corner, getting brighter. Sasha scrambled to find Gregory's hidden gap in the wall, searching by feel for that one brick that he had marked.

The footsteps—only one pair, Sasha thought, but still, that would be enough—came closer and it took all of her nerve to keep searching for the brick and not to go running back down the passage to the exit.

Perhaps Sasha should have run. The assassin turned the corner before she could find it.

Sasha drew a sharp breath as the assassin froze, a mere ten feet away, both taking in the situation as fast as their minds would allow. The assassin's appearance surprised Sasha more than anything: it was a young woman, not much older than Sasha, and pretty, with blond hair and the greenest eyes Sasha had ever seen.

The assassin dropped her torch—it fell to the ground, the dancing flame still lighting the scene—and yanked a knife from her belt, hurling it at Sasha. With a squeak, Sasha ducked swiftly, falling to her knees on the rough floor. She heard the knife whistle above her head and clatter to the floor somewhere behind her.

Elijah was just going to have to be mad at her.

When Sasha stumbled to her feet, her own boot knife in her hand, the assassin was almost on her. Sasha sprung at her, but the assassin dodged easily and swung a second blade at Sasha.

She missed as Sasha darted to the side, her back to the wall, ducking under the assassin's outstretched arm. Sparks flew as the knife skidded along the brick wall.

As the assassin tried to recover her balance from the miss, Sasha's foot slammed into her gut, sending her flying backwards into the other wall of the narrow passage. Torchlight gleamed in their two blades as the assassin rose grimly and leaped at Sasha.

Sasha dodged to the side again, though not as quick, and earned a slash along her cheek from the assassin's knife. The assassin hurtled past Sasha with the force of her own spring and Sasha helped her along with a well-placed shove, sending the assassin toppling into the opposite wall.

The assassin turned swiftly, and shoved herself off the wall, her face bloodied from the rough brick. Her knife made a bright arc in a backhanded slash at Sasha, who jumped backwards and out of the way. Sasha stumbled on the uneven floor and put out a hand, catching her balance on the wall behind her.

The assassin pressed her advantage, stabbing her knife downward toward Sasha's head. Sasha's hands shot up and blocked the assassin's descending hand. Her knife hand was trapped, too, holding the assassin's blade away from her. Sasha twisted her lower body swiftly and sent a vicious sidekick into the assassin's chest.

The wind went of the assassin's lungs and she choked. Sasha let go of the assassin's knife hand with one of her hands, though still holding it firmly away from her with the other. Sasha'd gotten the wind knocked out of her before; she knew she had at least a few seconds before she would need two hands to keep the knife under control.

Sasha stepped towards the assassin and put all of her strength into striking the hilt of her blade under and up into the assassin's chin.

The assassin's eyes rolled back, then fluttered shut, and she collapsed to the floor, unconscious. Sasha fell back against the cool brick of the wall, chest heaving, her blood simmering with adrenalin.

Sasha took one deep, steadying breath and then opened her eyes, which she hadn't realized she had shut. The assassin wouldn't be out for long, and she still needed to find Gabrielle.

Sasha turned her knife in her hand. It was clean, the only red on it the reflection from the torch which crackled dimly in the corner where the assassin had dropped it. She hadn't even nicked the other girl with her blade.

There was a scrape and a scramble around the corner. She raised her knife. Elijah tumbled around the corner, into the firelight. "I heard—" He spotted the assassin, unconscious on the floor.

"Well," said Sasha, only slightly apologetic. "It wasn't to the death."

Stepping over the unconscious assassin, Sasha started down the passage the way the girl had come, heart thudding frantically. "I think this way's probably a good direction," she said. Elijah stepped over the girl as well and hurried to catch up with her.

Sasha didn't know how many assassins were guarding Gabrielle—just because all she had seen was two didn't mean that there *were* only two. There could be a hundred bloodthirsty knife fighters at the end of the passage for all she knew. But it was her little sister who needed saving; and she had Elijah to back her up.

Sasha moved quickly, and as silently as she could manage. Drawing on all her years of tiptoeing past guards and sneaking into places where she oughtn't to have been, Sasha's feet didn't even whisper.

Elijah, beside her, ghosted over the floor just as quietly. She glanced sideways at him. Maybe it was a warrior thing, too.

They had left the assassin's torch behind to splutter on the floor, not wanting it to herald their coming, and had to make their way through the dark passage by Sasha's memory, and one hand held out before them to feel their way through the black.

In Sasha's other hand, she still grasped the knife Harston had given her years ago. She could feel it shake.

At each corner and turn they stopped and listened for any sound that would foretell that someone stood around the bend: the light sound of breathing, the whisper of fabric, the scrape of shoe on stone.

Finally, on the third turn, they found them, with no need for cautious listening; light from a torch flickered on the dull bricks.

Sasha pressed herself against the brick wall, the rough material grasping at her loose garments and closed her eyes, trying to listen for the assassins.

"One," breathed Elijah. "But he walks soft." She nodded.

Surprise being the only advantage she could hope for—the man sounded bigger than her—but, then, who wasn't?—Sasha adjusted her grip on her knife and whirled around the corner.

One man stood in the corridor, facing away from her, standing over a gagged and bound Gabrielle. He turned quickly, a wicked-looking blade in his hand, a curse on his lips.

Sasha's gaze darted to Gabrielle's wide blue eyes, the one freckle below the left one, and then back to the man as he ran at her, knife extended in front of him.

She waited as though frozen until he was almost upon her, and at the last moment darted to the side, his knife missing her by inches; she turned as she moved, throwing one leg behind her so she faced the way she had come.

The man couldn't stop himself in time to turn and stab her. His blade went harmlessly past her side. Sasha grabbed his knife arm and trapped it between her arm and her side. With the other hand, she grabbed his finger and yanked it viciously to the side.

A dull crack sounded, echoed a heartbeat later by the man's howl. His grip on the blade slackened and Sasha knocked it to the floor then kicked it, sending it skittering away from them.

The man reached for her face with his far hand, fingers clawing for her eyes. Sasha darted behind him and shoved her foot down and into the back of his knee, meanwhile shoving with all her weight down on his shoulders.

He collapsed to his knees, but as he did so he grabbed the collar of her shirt and kicked Sasha's feet back from under her, throwing her over his shoulder and upside down into the far wall.

Sasha slammed into the wall and slid down it, landing painfully on her shoulder. She gasped for breath as she sagged to the ground.

Her shoulder and back throbbed hot and cold with pain, shooting down her sword arm.

Please let nothing be broken—

Sasha rolled herself over as quickly as she could and put her back to the wall—everything seemed intact, even if she could feel her heartbeat in every aching muscle.

Elijah was fighting the thin man. Eli had been disarmed, his sword on the passage floor, but he'd drawn a dagger from somewhere. So had the man. They circled, slicing and retreating.

Sasha slipped off a boot and threw it at the man's head. Expecting a dagger, he ducked. Elijah slipped in and struck his hand, sending the dagger skittering across the floor. The man leapt forward and grabbed Elijah's knife hand. Elijah tried to sweep the man's feet from under him, but the man tangled their ankles together, trying a sweep of his own. Gabrielle squeaked. The man tried to peel Eli's fingers from the dagger with one hand while he tried to claw Elijah's eyes out with the other.

Elijah ducked backwards, keeping a hold on the knife, and tried to knee the man, who blocked the blow. The man punched Elijah straight on and Eli's head snapped back with a sharp sound.

Then the man's head snapped forward. His hand slipped off and he collapsed to the floor.

Sasha stood behind him, the hilt of her knife wet and red where she'd slammed it into the assassin's skull. Elijah felt his cheekbone and winced, breathing hard.

Sasha knelt and cut Gabrielle's bonds, pulling her to her feet. Gabrielle wrapped her arms around her sister's middle and patted Elijah's hand, too, without letting go of Sasha. The split in the thin man's scalp bled sluggishly on the floor. He inhaled shallowly.

"What's the point of bringing backup if you don't even wait to say *charge*?" Elijah demanded.

"We managed, didn't we?" Sasha said, grinning. She tried to shrug and winced massively. "Fine," she said. "Next time we'll do better."

The torchlight flickered, casting shadows.

"We need to get out of here, before someone else comes or he wakes up," said Sasha, starting to move for the exit, as fast as the human corset around her middle would allow. "Gabrielle, are you alright?"

Gabrielle nodded, her head bobbing somewhere around Sasha's midsection.

"*Next* time?" said Elijah.

Chapter Six
Knowing the Way Home

It took two corridors in warm torchlight before Gabrielle would release her death grip around Sasha's waist in exchange for clinging to her hand.

Elijah kept a step behind them, not out of courtesy. He guarded their flank while he trusted Sasha to keep an eye on point.

They entered their room by the front door because there wasn't any reason not to. Sasha's skirts twisted around her ankles as though after that whole adventure they were going to betray and trip her *now*. Gabrielle was pressed close against her, her fingers squeezed white, which probably was not helping.

Sasha eased herself out of Gabrielle's hold, pressing her little sister softly onto the soft couch. Across the floor, the carpets were barely tweaked from her morning practice, laid in careful lines by little hands.

"Hey, hey there, it's alright now." One hand still trapped in Gabrielle's grip, Sasha brushed back Gabrielle's hair with the other, ghosting over the bruised cut that bled over one temple.

Gabrielle gulped in a breath. "I don't—I don't remember, Sash."

"Does it hurt?" Sasha looked over her shoulder. Elijah stood at the open door, looking out—he wanted to see them coming, whoever did come, but he wasn't putting even so much as a door between him and his princesses. "Eli, she's hurt. Her head's bleeding."

"Get something to stop the bleeding," he said.

"I *know*." Sasha was ripping underskirts as she spoke. "Gabe, are you dizzy at all? Is your vision okay?"

"A little dizzy," she said.

Pressing fabric to Gabrielle's head, Sasha digested her sister's earlier words. "What don't you remember?"

"Exactly why I'm bleeding," said Gabrielle, her eyes dark and damp, her breath settling slowly back from gasping as she tried to tuck panic away. "All I remember is waking up in the dark."

"You don't know who snatched you," said Sasha. She took a longer strip of cloth and wound it around black curls, securing the pad of makeshift bandage in place with shaking fingers. "We need to get you to the infirmary."

Gabrielle bit her slip, swallowed carefully, and shook her head. "But I," she began. "If I *think* maybe…"

"Sasha," Elijah called in quiet warning.

Captain Brown entered the room with a glance but not a nod at the redheaded guardsman at the door. "Your highnesses," Brown said. He stopped. "You're injured."

"The assassins got to her," said Sasha bluntly, waiting for a dismissive twist of the hooked nose, but something must have struck too close to home, seeing bandages wrapped around black curls.

Brown stared. "How?"

"She doesn't remember."

"I—" Gabrielle squeezed her eyes shut. "But I have to. I remember a little—I was looking for the assassin's benefactor, because, because they've got to have one, and…"

"Someone must have seen you," said Sasha, shaking a little with anger. She looked up and Brown had his nose pointed at her.

"Highness? A word, if you would."

Sasha stepped over to him, suspicious. "Captain Brown?"

"Your sister was hunting assassins?"

Sasha began to open her mouth to protest, then stopped. She swallowed.

"I don't care what antics you choose to embroil yourself in—Harston, bless his bones, made it *clear* you were too out of control to handle safely."

Sasha raised her head, staring at him. Brown had told her to *stop*.

Brown caught the glance and sneered. "How stupid did you think I was, highness? I didn't get to vice-captain rank by sheer good looks."

"You let me investigate?" she said.

"I didn't *let* you do anything. If I could have made you listen, I would have, believe me. I certainly *tried*," Brown said. He glanced pointedly at Elijah. "I condone nothing here; my *job* is your safety. But because royal safety is my job, actively pursuing criminals is often outside prudent allotment of my resources. I can't actively toss away help from overly stubborn forces."

"You've been anything but helpful!" she protested.

"If you couldn't get around *me*," Brown said, "then you should've have been doing anything but embroidery. Of course I tried to stop you." His face twisted. "I didn't think you *were* getting around me, but that much is clear now." He shook his head. "I may not approve—and I do *not* approve, don't mistake me—but I can't deny we are overmatched here. The criminals have to be stopped; and you seem as though if I *actually* locked you in the nobles' rooms you might set them all on *fire*."

"Thank you," she said primly.

"But to involve a *child* in your adrenaline-chasing?" Brown said. "Even of you, I would've thought better, your highness."

Sasha was pale. "I didn't ask her to do anything."

"You didn't stop her either. She is *twelve years old* and you're her older sister. You've got a responsibility not to let her follow you into a den of killers."

"She wasn't supposed to do anything but keep an eye open. It was *her* choice."

"She's not old enough to be making choices like that," Brown snapped. "Little girls are supposed to be protected. If you'd *let* anyone do that, I'd argue that for you, too."

"I don't need protection."

"You're bleeding," Brown drawled. "Hadn't you noticed?"

Sasha exhaled sharply and resisted the urge to touch her bleeding cheek. "This is my family," she said. "I have a right to try to protect them—I'm a big sister, like you said. That's my *job*."

Brown shook his head, turning away.

"Captain." The voice from the bed was sharp and steady, even if the face it came from was still streaked with tears. "I," said Gabrielle, "am twelve and a half."

"You're still a child," Brown said, though with a little less certainty as she lifted her chin and gave him her best icy stare.

"I don't follow anyone anywhere I don't believe I need to be," Gabrielle said.

"Do you remember where that was now?" Brown asked.

Gabrielle sniffed with Lia's best derision for a lesser Court flunky. "No. But I will."

"Not sure that's how concussions work," muttered Elijah from his guard post just inside the entryway.

"What do you remember?" Brown asked briskly. "The last thing?"

"Why would you care, if I'm just a child who should have stayed in the nursery?" Gabrielle said.

"Because I am supposed to catch these killers," Brown said. "I will, and I'll use whatever tools I have to in order to serve the Crown. You should never have been in that situation—but you were."

Gabrielle shivered, closing her eyes. "The last things—the nobles' room? I don't know."

There was a quiet creak by the door; Brown didn't notice. Elijah straightened and watched Sasha slip out to the corridor while Brown continued quizzing Gabrielle.

"Gregory?"

"I heard something happened," Gregory began, wobbly. "Is everything alright?"

Sasha whispered, "They had Gabrielle in the passages."

Gregory started, brown eyes wide.

"She's alright now; breathe, Gregory," she said; it was useful advice for her as well.

When Sasha blinked, she could still see the glare of torchlight on brick, flickering in green eyes and a keen knife, the dread of knowing danger stood between her and her little sister.

She hadn't *asked* Gabrielle to go hunting assassins. She hadn't put her into that danger—not on purpose. Her stomach was leaden, her heart in her throat.

"If you hadn't gone to look for her," said Gregory, slowly.

"But I did," said Sasha. She closed her eyes. "I'm not going to keep myself up nights wondering about ugly *ifs*."

"If you hadn't gone to look for her," said Gregory, quietly, "then no one would've found her. Because no one but the assassins, and us, know about the passages."

"Gregory?"

"It's not safe," he said to his shoes. Gregory raised his head and looked at her, shrugging a little. "The captain needs to know where they are."

"But they're yours," she said. "I know you don't want to give them up."

"They're not mine," said Gregory. "They're the castle's. They're just brick and darkness, and now they're not *safe*. You're my friend, Sasha. If I can make you and your sisters a little safer, I should. The captain needs to know where they are."

Gregory squeaked, swallowed in a sudden hug. "Thank you," she said. She pulled back. "I imagine you'd want to see his face when the wall opens up, but there's a chance he'd try to arrest you. I trust you—"

"But you didn't once," said Gregory. "He might not either."

She nodded. "So I'll tell him."

He nodded, swallowing, and turned to go. Two paces away, he faltered.

"Gregory?"

"I don't know where to go," he said. "I mean, it's always to the passages, when I'm scared, but it's what's in them that I'm scared of." He looked over his shoulder, bright-eyed.

"Find Will," she said.

Gregory moved down the hall. Sasha pulled back inside the room only to find Elijah standing stiff-shouldered in front of Brown. Gabrielle had wiped her cheeks, color slowly returning to them.

"I'm still on her duty, sir," said Elijah.

"You already lost her highness once today," Brown began dismissively.

"I already found her once today, also, sir," said Elijah. "I'm on her duty."

Brown looked at the black eye forming, the knuckle-shaped bruises, the stubborn set of the guardsman's jaw. "I suppose you are. I'm sending reinforcements to the infirmary in an hour, before that eye starts swelling shut."

"Understood, sir," said Elijah. Gabrielle hopped off the bed and tiptoed over to him. Eli took her hand in his and they left the room, brushing by Sasha. "I'll keep her safe," he said, in passing, too quiet for Brown to hear.

"I know." Sasha strode toward Brown. "At the beginning of the winter," she said, "I warned you about secret passages. Well, I found them, sir." It was a lie Gregory had already told Will, so she thought he wouldn't mind.

Brown blinked, raising his head to look at her—he'd been elsewhere in his head, making plans, schedules, finding ways to spin the event.

"It's where the assassins took her, sir. Come with me and I'll show you."

Sasha could tell half of Brown was off scripting event reports as he followed her down the hall; but there was also a part of him that wasn't simply placating her. There was a part of him that was looking sidelong at the blood on the hem of her skirt and eyeing the walls as though they might hide enemies.

Despite everything, Sasha had enough spare emotion to feel vaguely satisfied as the doubt was wiped off Brown's face. She could barely stop herself from rubbing his nose in an "I told you so" as his eyes widened, taking in the sight of a door opening mysteriously from the wall at the end of the little corridor by the library.

She stepped through the small doorway and looked back at him. "Coming?"

Brown ducked through the door after her. "What is this place?"

"I told you," Sasha said, lifting the torch she had taken from the bracket, and glancing over her shoulder at Brown. "There is a hidden passageway system in this castle. It was built to allow my family to escape through, for protection, but the assassins have discovered them and have been using them to infiltrate the castle." If he asked her how she had found them, she would lie. "This is where we found Gabrielle."

She turned to look him square in the face. "Do you believe me now? The passages, they're *real*, and the assassins have been using them."

Brown touched a brick wall softly and stared down the passage until it disappeared in darkness. "We will leave as soon as possible," he said. "I do not know the locations of these passages; they are a security hazard."

Sasha shook her head, wincing as her hair smacked her cheek and made it sting. She touched her hand to her cheek and it came away wet and red. "But I know where—" Sasha began.

Brown turned and strode out of the passage. She hurried to catch up with his long stride. "We cannot confirm that you know of them all," Brown interrupted. "We must leave. It is no longer safe here."

"But—"

When they reached her room, he held open the door for her. "It's not safe," he said. "We're leaving."

She took the door and he strode quickly away. "Neither is home," Sasha called after him, but she didn't think he heard her.

Second's squad leader Gideon, the squad leader of Fifth, and the second in command of Fourth Squad (the leader had been left with the queen, as was fit) stood in the office of Captain Brown.

The captain had moved to the office that the castle steward had given originally to Harston. Harston had held it short enough that Gideon could think of it as Brown's without much of a twinge.

Gideon had a feeling, however, that when they got back to the capital that the room in which Brown would sit and write letters and draw up schedules and contracts and deal with his officers would always be, in the head of the squad leader of Second, Harston's office.

There wasn't much Brown could do to change that, and Gideon didn't really want him to be able to.

"We are leaving in the morning," said Brown. "Tell your men to pack up. The snow has thawed, enough."

The snow was still several feet high in places, grey, brown and slushy everywhere else. But Gideon wasn't a mountain boy and the captain said that was thawed, so it was.

The three officers bowed and left the captain of the Royal Guard to his own packing.

"That was sudden," said Fifth.

Fourth shrugged. Even as a second-in-command of the queen's squad, Fourth was higher on the totem pole than Gideon, who was the leader of the commonborn Second, or the leader of Fifth Squad, which was reputably filled with the lazy, the drunk, and the guards who probably should have been flower sellers.

When Gideon got back to his room, he pulled off his boots and tugged the light armor of his Guard uniform over his head and hung it properly in its place. The rest of the makeshift barracks was quiet. His squad was all either on duty or enjoying their leave, but there was a girl with short brown hair sleeping, curled up on one of the cots.

Gideon was tired enough that it took him a moment to realize that this was no longer a regular occurrence in his world. "Sasha?"

She startled out of her sleep and cursed like she'd been raised by guardsmen since she was nine years old and they'd stopped holding their tongues around her years ago. "I fell asleep," she said. Sasha kneaded her eyes with the heels of her hands and said, "I need to talk to you, Gideon."

"What happened?" said Gideon. He stood stiffly above her, hands clasped behind him, unsure if he was questioning a subordinate or speaking to royalty. Sasha had been one of his charges for a long time. "I got your message and I sent Second out, but Brown recalled the alert an hour ago."

"I found her," said Sasha. "Eli and I did."

"You're here alone," said Gideon, just realizing. "Where's Elijah?"

She rolled her eyes at his knowing look. "I left him with Gabrielle and went out the back way. He can forgive me later." She sat up a little straighter. "Gabrielle was—hidden. It will take too long to explain. Gideon, she found something out about the assassins. They're not going to stop until they get to her."

"The Guard will protect her."

Sasha shifted her legs and let her feet fall to the floor. "Brown says he can't do anything on her information—and, curse it." She kneaded her eyes. "There isn't much information to go on; and he's *afraid* of pissing off nobles with more rank than he's got. Will you help?" said Sasha.

There were thoughts clanging and shouts going off in Gideon's head, like they had on the practice field, watching Sasha face down Brown, watching himself hold his tongue like a good guard.

"I need another pair of eyes on Gabrielle," said Sasha, a wary kind of hope in her eyes. "Please."

Gideon felt a headache coming on, but he knew what he had to say. He sighed, rubbing one temple. "If the captain is not assigning more watches to her—"

Sasha leapt to her feet. "I don't *care* what Brown thinks, Gideon. I don't care what he assigns or what you have to say to him. Gabrielle is my little sister. She's *seen* them. They are going to try and kill her and you *aren't going to let them*." She was on her tiptoes, in his face.

"If the captain is not assigning more watches to her," repeated Gideon over her, loudly, "then the boys and I will have to watch her off shift."

Sasha rocked back down onto her heels, blinking at him.

"I'll look after her, highness, me and any boy in the Guard who's willing."

"Thank you." She hugged him tightly around the middle. "Don't call me highness."

Gideon patted her on the back, then held her at arm's length. "I can't help that," he said. "What are you going to do?"

"I'm going to find them," said Sasha, sitting down on the bunk like everything had gone out of her legs. "And I'm going to stop them, however I can." She put her face in her cold hands. It had been a long day.

"You let us know if you need us," said Gideon.

Sasha looked up, startled, and smiled, tired and grateful. "Yes," she said. "I will."

The next morning, Gabrielle stood outside the door of the nobles' gathering room, rather sure the butterflies in her stomach had fangs and icicle feet.

Gabrielle wanted to hole up back in her and Sasha's suite with six blankets and two books—no, she wanted to be in her *own* room, curled up in her writing desk at home, with her familiar quills, her bookshelf, the familiar sight

216

of familiar bougainvillea blooms out of a familiar window. Gabrielle wanted the bright lamp-lit space of the ministers' council room, with its wide shining table, the scratch of scribes' quills on parchment. She wanted the deep leather chair in her father's study, the comfortable silence of two working minds, and the candlelit sight of him leaning over his papers.

She wanted to be home.

But Gabrielle had remembered a little of the day before; *danger*, there was someone in danger. She couldn't do much, but she could warn them. Gabrielle pushed open the door and stepped inside the noble's room.

The door didn't swing shut behind her right away; it stopped to let another figure through.

Gabrielle frowned at the tall redhead over her shoulder. "What are you doing?"

"You know how boring the front door is?" Nathaniel said.

Gabrielle spent the day holed up in an alcove, stone walls on three sides of her, reading a book on Aharian political systems. Nate spent it just outside the alcove, leaning against what he claimed was a "very pleasant piece of wall."

The day faded towards night. Gabrielle wove her fingers into the lacings of her coat, her stomach tight with uncertainty. As the nobles began to disperse for the evening, she tapped the shoulder of the two noblemen of the party and asked quietly for a word.

There were two guards at the door of the nobles' room, still, though others had left with Lia. Nathaniel was stopped halfway to the door. Three guards; *three guards, three guards*, Gabrielle repeated in her head like a magic spell. They'd keep her safe; they'd have to, because she had to say this. One of these men was innocent.

Count Dereck and Duke John looked down at her, wearing excellent expressions of perplexity. One of them had let a thin man named Doulings grab her; one of them had, unknown to them, been promised a knife in the back someday soon. She looked back steadily.

"One of you is in danger," said Gabrielle. "I'm not sure which." She raised her chin, eyeing the dark-haired duke and the count who walked like a fighter but hid behind the ink stains on his hands. "I don't remember much, but I remember the assassins wanted to kill one of Lia's suitors."

John glanced at Dereck, eyes wide with amiable concern. Dereck didn't remove his gaze from Gabrielle. "Is that so?" he said.

Gabrielle nodded. *Three guards.* "Be careful," she said. "There will be an attempt to murder one of you." She took her hands from where they had been weaving into her jacket's lacings and brushed them down her skirts, as calmly as she could manage.

"Thank you," said John. "You may have just saved our lives."

"I hope so," she said. "One of your lives." Dereck stood a little straighter, stiff, as the implications sank in. Gabrielle said, "One of you is a traitor, though. One of you tried to get me killed, and *he* can go rot."

She curtsied to them and left the room.

A day later, Andrea let her fingers brush the leather hilt of her dagger. It was her favorite, a throwing dagger that her father had given her when she finally managed to land a knife at the center of the target. The blade was keen and wicked sharp and she always kept it tucked into a boot or, like now, up a sleeve. It was the blade she had thrown at that wretched brat's head.

Andrea was alone for this mission, waiting in a dark alcove. Doulings had decided that to kill this count only one of them was needed. He had grinned at her when he'd told her the mission and said, "You see, things like this are why I keep you around."

It made her sick. They had both killed, but Doulings did it for money. Her people were fighting for their country and their freedom. They had sworn oaths. It was their duty. How could they take orders from a man like him? Still, as her father had told her when she was small and he was still alive, one must use what tools one has. It was better to be sickened than to be dead, or an oathbreaker. It was better to be dead than to be an oathbreaker.

The door across the hall opened and out walked the target, the count. The blond man was flanked by a guard who looked uncommonly alert. Most of the Nerian guards looked asleep on their feet. Asleep or not, she knew, they were quick at calling for help.

Andrea quickly took in the situation. She would take the guard first. He was wary and that scar on his face hinted that he had seen action—his colors weren't black and silver, but instead the livery of the count's lands, cloth drab as the desert they hailed from. A man-at-arms of the noble's border county had probably met at least bandits and skirmishes before.

The count should be no problem at all, once she had finished with his guard. Andrea drew her dagger, felt its familiar weight, and then hurled it at the guard. He didn't have a chance and crumpled to the floor, her knife buried in his chest.

Andrea drew a second, stouter knife— almost a short sword in its own right—and charged out toward the count. His reactions were quicker than she suspected: he turned to face her and drew a sword from his belt.

She tried to cut at him, but the count blocked her easily with his longer blade. Andrea pulled away and he swung his long length of steel down at her. She blocked his downward strike, wincing at the power behind the blow.

The count pushed down on her, using his height and power. Strength to strength, she would lose any competition of such and she knew it. Andrea kicked out at him, striking a blow to his stomach. The count disengaged their blades and dodged her second kick.

She stepped back and they circled each other. Andrea looked at the count with more respect, noticing the ease and familiarity with which he held his sword, and feeling the twinge in her arm where she had held off his blows. She hadn't known that any Nerian nobles knew how to handle any weapons more potent than a fork. She feinted to one side then lunged in, earning a long cut down his arm.

The count was stronger than her, and taller, but few of her opponents weren't (Quant was shorter, but at almost fifteen her littlest foster brother was too young to count).

Andrea darted in quickly again and again, but he was more wary now. Andrea relied on her speed and agility to win her fights. The count, apparently trained in swordcraft only, was unused to her swift knife-fighting jabs and darts. Of course, she was unused to his longer weapon, as commoners were not allowed to carry swords.

He struck again and she dodged. Her best chance was to keep him dancing and tire him out. But that would take time.

Footsteps sounded down the hall: someone had heard and called for guards. Frantic, Andrea thrust his sword to the side and kicked the noble in the gut.

She had no time for the killing stroke, and instead took off at a run, stopping only to yank her bloody throwing knife out of the guard. The guard groaned, his eyelids fluttering.

Andrea stumbled backwards in surprise. She had thought he was dead.

Behind her she heard the guards stop to check on the count and heard him, breathless, tell them to follow her, but she did not look back to see if they did. She rounded a corner, shoved open one of the doors to the passages, and slipped inside.

Andrea leaned against the cool brick. It was pitch black inside with no torch to light her path, but she would feel her way through the darkness. She closed her eyes, though it made no difference in the unlit passage. So the guard lived. One of Andrea's greatest prides was her aim, and she had aimed for his heart.

Hadn't she?

She heard voices outside the passage. They didn't know of the passages, of course, but it reminded her she had to hurry to get back to the kitchens before they had the sense to see which servants were unaccounted for. Andrea touched her hand to her face, pulling it away quickly once she felt its cold stickiness. She needed to clean up as well.

Andrea hurried through the passages, stumbling in the dark, feeling her way along the passage with her clean hand. The other hung at her side, loosely clutching her favorite knife with slippery, bloody fingers.

In the rush, and the hurry, and the darkness, the blade fell from her numb grasp and clattered to the floor.

Sasha woke to pale morning sunlight streaming through the window. When she stepped out into the sitting room, Gabrielle was sitting quietly on the couch, dressed like she'd been ready hours before, a book she wasn't reading open in her lap.

There was no time for her solitary morning practice. Sasha poked her head outside the door and relaxed. "Nate, I'm going for a walk. Can you come sit with Gabrielle?"

Nate pushed himself off his lazy slump against the wall, eyes flicking down the hallway. "How's her head?"

Sasha shrugged helplessly. "She can walk in a straight line. She still doesn't remember much of that whole day."

Nate shifted his hands in his pockets and said, "One of Lia's pet nobles was attacked last night—the blonde count."

Sasha scrunched her face, searching for names. "John? No, John's the duke… Dereck, then. Is he—?"

"Shaken up, but uninjured—one of his guardsman was not as lucky—knife to the shoulder—but lucky enough; the poor sop's breathing at least. I was on nobles' room duty— that's where I heard it. The whole gang was fluttering over the count," said Nathaniel. He

223

grinned. "His sheer discomfort at the attention carried me through the horrors of boredom."

Sasha chewed softly on her bottom lip. "If he's the villain—do you think the assassins are upset they lost Gabrielle? Or they're trying to make him seem innocent?"

"Or, it was an honest attempt on his life," said Nate, "and maybe Duke John's the one allied with the assassins. They are competitors, after all." At Sasha's blank look, he added, "For Lia's hand?"

"That's a depressing thought," said Sasha.

Nathaniel glanced over her shoulder at the pale little girl in the suite. "Isn't it all?"

The castle was active: servants dashed here and there, running last minute errands for their masters. A bored Fifth Squader in reluctant tow, Sasha ignored the bustle and scanned the scant crowds for the tell-tale red cap of a messenger. Instead, it was Gregory that found her.

"Morning, highness."

She turned. "Gregory, what's the highness for? You were calling me Sasha last time I checked."

Gregory grimaced. "It's just, with you all up in your dress and all, it's not the same." He glanced at the guard behind her, who wasn't paying them any attention.

Sasha glanced down at her dress. "I'm no different, silly. It's only a skirt."

"S'pose." He scuffed a foot on the ground. "I guess you're here to say good bye?" Gregory didn't meet her eyes.

"We're heading for home today." She smiled at him. "You could come with us."

Gregory shook his head, smiling wryly. "Good bye, Sasha."

"Maybe we'll see each other again someday," she said instead of saying farewell.

Now Gregory looked her in the eye, and gave her a doubtful smile. He had enough grace to say, with little audible sarcasm, "Maybe." Gregory bowed deeply to her, as proper for a lowly servant to a princess, and walked away.

When someone said his name, Gregory jumped. He turned around, startled, in the (previously) empty corridor he'd fled to after saying goodbye to Sasha, and then sagged against the wall.

"Hi, Will."

"Come with us," said Will. He leaned hesitantly against the wall next to Gregory, something cautious and very young about him.

"I can't." It was a squeak. It had been hard enough having this conversation with Sasha.

Will opened his mouth and shut it. "I left," said Will. "I left because I assumed you would come with me. I left this *place*, Gregory. I never thought it would mean leaving you, not forever."

"I told you I—"

"I know. But I can't imagine it, Gregory, I still can't. I can't imagine wanting to stay." Will took a breath. "But if you *do*," Will said. "If you want to live here for the rest of your life, if you don't want to come with me—then please don't come."

Gregory was gaping.

Will glanced at him. "But *I can't* is not a reason." He looked almost angry, for Will. "You're *brilliant*."

"What?"

"You're smart," said Will. "You're smarter than me, Gregory. You're the smartest person I know. You put things—real things—together like they're puzzle games and you don't know how to give up. You're kind; you help strange angry princesses for no reason. Don't you dare tell me you *can't*." Will rubbed his fist over his eyes. "I hate the idea of leaving you here, because you deserve more than just this castle. You deserve to see the rest of the world, and the rest of the world is missing out for not knowing you.

"So stay if you *want to stay*. I'll be behind you, Gregory, I'll cheer you on, I'll be on your side, because that's where I'm supposed to be. But if it's just because you're afraid you won't be able to *make* it out there, then I'll knock you out—I'll ask Sasha to knock you out—and then I'll drag you out of here."

Gregory took a shaky breath and Will gave a shaky smile back and finished.

"If it's what you want, if it will make you happiest to stay here, please stay. But never because you don't think you're good enough, or smart enough. You're more than enough, mate." Will took a long, trembling breath. "Do you *want* to stay?"

"Yes," said Gregory in a very small voice. "I don't want to leave."

There was a long silence. Will let his head fall back against the wall and thought about the rest of his life.

"Well, if you can't leave, then maybe, maybe I should stay." Will said it very quietly. Gregory raised his eyes from where they were staring at his feet. "Because you're right. There are things more important than glory, than the ministry, or than showing Westel that I'm worthwhile."

Gregory stared at him.

"You're more important, Gregory. I promised I'd take care of you, and I left."

Gregory shook his head. "But you can't change the world from a mountain castle. You don't *settle* for things, Will."

Will stuck his hands in his pockets. "Settle? Madness, my friend. No, just—change." He grinned. "I bet it'd be even harder to get the castle stewardship here than it would be to get Westel to make me his subminister."

"If they made you steward, the old steward would rise from his grave. The castle would burn down—the very *stones* would catch on fire." Gregory watched Will warily, trying to figure out what he was saying, not wanting to hope for impossibilities.

"What do you imagine Westel would do if I inherited his ministry?" Will shrugged. "But, you and me? We could take care of this castle spectacularly, if we decided to."

"Cook would be on our side, though I think she'd get better locks for the pantry." Gregory chewed his lip. "Will? You sound like you're actually considering this."

Will opened his mouth, then closed it. He looked at the bustling royal retinue, the brocade bright against the stone walls. "I don't intend on living my life without my best friend," said Will.

Gregory could hardly breathe. "You're really coming home?"

Will shrugged, almost blushing. "Here I am." He got the breath knocked out of him by Gregory's quick hug.

Words spilled out. "You can move back into the room, and I didn't get to show you my new route to the pantry—Oh! And Sasha will visit—it *is* her castle, after all."

Will ruffled his curls, biting his lip against a smile.

"But," said Gregory. He took a breath. He stepped back. "But you can't stay, Will."

"What?"

"Sasha needs someone to help her."

Will set his chin stubbornly. "I'm not going to leave you alone again. I made a promise once."

"I remember," said Gregory. "But Sasha needs you more than I do." He took a steadying breath. "Will, you don't belong here anymore."

Will stared.

"*I don't want you to stay*," said Gregory, biting his lip. "Go—go *home*, go back to the capital. Help Sasha. Fight some bloodthirsty assassins for me. Become—become minister of intelligence, become a royal general, become a playhouse actor who works for pennies. I'll be fine. I don't want you to abandon Sasha, and I don't want to watch you sit and rot and regret not leaving for the next thirty years."

"I can tell you're lying."

"Only about the first bit." Gregory took a breath. "Will, I'm not six years old anymore. I'm not crying myself to sleep in the infirmary. You don't need to take care of me anymore."

Now it was Gregory's turn to get seized and squeezed tight. Will buried his face into his shoulder and then pulled back, holding him at arm's length to fix him in memory—a smattering of brown freckles over his cheekbones, a smudge of torch soot, a unfamiliar stubborn tremble of his chin as he refused to let himself break.

"You'd better visit," said Gregory, and smiled.

When the carriages and wagons rolled unsteadily up the pass out of the valley, a small figure in a red hat stood on Willow Tree's battlements, gazing steadily between the stone crenellations. The wind was cold and heavy blankets of snow still coated patches of the meadow, but it was beginning to thaw.

A feeble sun shone in a chill blue sky and Gregory watched them go until they disappeared from sight.

On the second day of journey, they stopped in a low flat valley of brambles and yellow brush. The small farmhouse on its edge, whose goats nibbled the brambles and whose olive trees climbed the sides of the hills, was thrilled to provide a royal lunch, as the royals were paying. When they went next to market, they would be able to buy instead of barter. The groomsmen checked the horses' hooves and wiped dust from the sides of the carriages while their animals crunched through the grain in their feedbags.

Gabrielle had curled up in their carriage with a book and Nathaniel at the door. Sasha hopped out and wandered towards the circle of dismounted black-and-silver guardsmen. Elijah peeled away from the crowd. "Probably could get lost in these hills, too," Eli said, offering the beginning of a scrap of banter.

Sasha blinked up at him, wrapping her hands in her skirts. She hadn't even looked at the hills. "I'm an idiot," she said.

Elijah paused. "Well," he said.

"No, don't make a joke, I mean it," she said. "I should have told Brown right away. I screwed up."

Elijah stepped closer, drawing them further from other ears. "You didn't," he said. "Gabrielle's safe because of you. We found out more about the assassins—you know what two of them look like now, and we know one of the noblemen is crooked. We haven't won yet, but you didn't screw up."

"I should've told Brown from the start," Sasha disagreed, voice low.

"You did."

"No, *after* Gregory showed them to me. I should have gone straight to the captain and told him where the passages were."

"But you knew he wasn't going to do anything with them," said Elijah.

"I wasn't prepared to *do* anything either. It would have been different if I'd kept the passages secret because I had plans to—to, I don't know, to lay a trap for the assassins, say. I probably could have gotten at least half of Second Squad to back me up. But I didn't. I just wanted to feel like maybe I was doing something, instead of just handing things over to Brown and letting him fix it all. He's an idiot, but how was I any better, wandering around back there hoping an answer would jump out of the brickwork?"

"It's not your job to do anything," said Elijah, who had been looking more and more unsure of how to respond as she'd spoke.

"Then I should have just told Brown. It *is* his, no matter how irritating I might find him personally."

"Sasha, you can't blame yourself. You did the best you could."

"No, I didn't. That's the *point*, Elijah. I got in the way of the Guard doing what it needed to do, and I didn't even manage to get anything *done* with that information."

Elijah started to open his mouth again and she glared. "I'm not looking for comfort, Eli. I'm an idiot, and I'm angry about it, and I had to tell somebody."

"If you hadn't known about the passages, you couldn't have saved Gabrielle," he pointed out stubbornly.

"If I'd told the Guard about the passages, then they would have known and *they* could have saved her—and maybe got those assassins, too!"

"Sasha, calm down. It's not your job to do any of this. It's not your fault."

"Why isn't it my job? Why *isn't* it my job to keep my family safe? Or even just to not do stupid, selfish things without thinking them through?"

"Sash—"

"I just—" She put her head in her hands and squeezed. "When I do something, from now on, I mean to *do* it, not wander around feeling righteous."

"Don't forget the think-first part of it, too," said Elijah finally, slipping back into wryness to find his composure. "It might take a little practice."

Nearby, the count had climbed out into the brambles, thorns picking at the fabric of his trousers while the duke laughed and the youngest lady cheered him on. The baroness had stayed in the carriage; she sat looking out the open door, fanning herself with a lacey contraption.

Lia took her slice of crusty bread, topped with thick soft goat cheese, and walked to the edge of the clearing in the brambles, away from the noise. When she stopped, the duchess was at her elbow, nibbling an olive.

"I'm going to marry John," said Lia.

"Ah," said the duchess.

"I told him yes, yesterday." Lia tore off a crumb of bread and tossed it for a sparrow. "I think it's right," she said.

"Mm." The duchess flicked an olive pit into the brush. She looked sideways at Lia and said, "Are you going to eat that bread?"

"Please don't tell anyone," said Lia. "Not yet. I have to tell Mother first."

When they got back in the carriages, Lia offered the duke her elbow to help her in and he followed into the carriage after her. Watching, the count wrapped his fingers around the stem and then gave his tiny brambles rose to the youngest lady, who preened all the way home.

Chapter Seven
A World, Wide and Strange

Their carriages rolled up the slope to the palace on a day with a bright sky and no clouds in sight. The lowland heat—warm for a day in early spring—weighed heavily on Sasha and she shed her coat. Beside her, Lia smiled and Gabrielle stared up out the window, watching the grand arch of the royal gate rise above them. Sasha silently folded her coat and laid it in her lap.

The carriage rolled to a stop, the stamp of horses' hooves on cobblestones fading. The driver came around to open the carriage door and the three princesses exited the carriage. Their parents were waiting to greet them. Sasha noted a few new lines on her father's leathery face as he knelt to meet Gabrielle face-to-face.

Lia greeted her mother with a kiss and an embrace. Sasha stood clutching her jacket. Her father smiled at her. "Welcome home, Sasha, Lia," he said. She nodded.

Her mother gave her a smile, all teeth. "Give your coat to the footman, dear."

The king put a hand on Gabrielle's shoulder—she was far too short for him to put an arm around her—and the pair, jabbering happily, walked away, presumably to someplace where they could finish their discussion of overseas trade in peace. The queen blew Sasha a kiss and drew Lia away with an arm tucked in her daughter's and a pointed question about a certain pair of men.

This was, Sasha reflected, the moment where, in years past, she would feel a gentle pressure on her shoulder and look up to see Harston's square face and bushy eyebrows, laugh lines full of telltale creases.

Sasha turned to the carriage driver, who was removing the horses' harnesses. "Here," said Sasha, stepping forward as she tossed her coat over her shoulder. "Let me help you with that."

The air of the capital city was sticky and thick after cold, dry Willow Tree, but it was good to have noise again, and to walk in open air. Andrea had her long, plain coat slung over one arm, her hair pinned up to reveal her nape to the sun, and her sleeves rolled up as far as she could.

The scent of burnt nut rose off the chestnut roaster's stall. The crowds pressed close around her. As she stepped past a stall hung with dried bundles of herbs and flowers, a young man shoved past her; Andrea shifted her center of weight to keep from stumbling and gave the back of his head a firm glare. She was moving forward again—she'd forgotten how *rude* city people could be—when her hand flicked to her side, which was missing her coin purse.

Andrea scanned the crowd behind her, already moving back. There was the rude young man and his scrawny compatriot—the distraction who'd bumped her and the fingerer who'd snatched her purse.

Andrea ducked around a carthorse and a woman with a string of children and grabbed the fingerer's wrist, whipping him out of the crowd and into a side street.

Andrea twisted his wrist into a firm lock and shoved him against the wall, keeping an eye on his friend, who leapt to his aid, crying, "Fire and candlelight, what do you think you're—"

She snapped her head up to glare at him, keeping a steady hold on the boy. "I think I dropped my purse," she said, twisting the wristlock a little. The distraction's eyes widened—this was his buddy, but a broken wrist would also mean an end to the pair's livelihoods.

"*Thank* you for picking it up for me, gentlemen. You were just going to return it, weren't you?"

When Andrea returned to the street, she was humming a little and her purse was properly tucked inside her skirts. She moved off the wide market row and onto a smaller but still bustling street.

Charlie's inn was three generations old, built back in the days just after this city had gone from being a minor Ceren trading post to the capital of an empire spanning three kingdoms.

The inn was in a decent part of town. A missing cobblestone was rare and the streets moved quickly with artisans and housewives and wagons.

Andrea stopped in front of the two-story wooden inn and eyed the painted silhouette of a hound above the door, the scraggly line of flowers along the base of the wall, and the ruddy light spilling through the open door.

"Andie?"

She shifted a shoulder at the sound of the familiar voice, deep but not any older than hers. She knew without looking behind her or at the shadow overlapping hers against the inn wall that he was tall and broad-shouldered, about the weight of two of her. "Your flowers are looking rather feeble, Koen," she told her foster brother.

"Cold winter," Koen said. From the lumpiness of the shadow, she guessed he'd just come back from the mill, a bag of flour over each shoulder.

"You have no idea. The Dog needs a new paint coat," Andrea added. "And the door's crooked—what drunk banged into it?"

She could hear his face creaking, hiding a smile. "If you go inside, they won't eat you," Koen said. "Charlie does feed us."

"I'm not *afraid*," she said and marched inside.

Inside the inn, the first-floor tavern was smoky and warm. A long bar and heavy round tables made the room. Firelight flickered in the hearth and through the door to the kitchen, behind the bar. It was late afternoon, too late for the midday crowds, and too early for the evening ones. Koen creaked in behind her.

"Maybe I'll just go up to my room," Andrea said. "I'm very tired," she added defensively to his amused silence.

"Mm," Koen said.

A small blonde head poked its way around the corner from the kitchen. A sharper, thinner version of the same head poked itself out just above that. "Nik!" screeched the smaller blonde boy. "Get down here!"

"I'm busy!" shouted Nik down the stairs. "Stupid bed sheets won't tuck in!"

"Get down here anyway!" shouted the smaller blonde boy and then he launched himself across the room at his foster sister.

Three thumps—the little Quant, then Koen from behind, and then Nik had pounded down the stairs and joined the mass and he was laughing, "You lucky dog! How did it go? Did we win?"

"*I* should have gone," said Quant. "I'd have licked the whole bunch of them!"

"Only 'cause they'd be too busy wonderin' why a four year old was attacking them, you runt."

"I'm fifteen! You weasely, pig-sticking—"

"Andrea?"

Andrea looked over Quant's blonde curls at the short, round innkeeper who stood in the doorway, and the skinny blond young man behind him. It explained why there had been no fourth thump—Pieter, the taller blonde boy, had gone to get their foster father.

"Welcome home," the innkeeper said, only barely keeping from beaming.

Andrea would've said, *Charlie*, and then probably something else, but she couldn't think what else to say, and she was having trouble swallowing.

Charlie moved swiftly across the tavern floor, Pieter following, arms open. Andrea buried her face in Quant's curls. As Charlie and Pieter joined the circle, she reached out her hands to try to grasp each one of them, hold them tight and never let them go.

The hostlers let her help unharness the carriage horses and lead the big-hooved placid animals to the stables. Sasha finally tossed her winter coat over a fence to keep it from getting in her way while she unfastened buckles, heaved heavy packs off carriage tops, and patted the warm, rising and falling sides of the horses.

"Elijah, you lazy sword," Sasha said, taking the lead rein of a bay who blew at her apathetically. "Sooner we finish, sooner these boys can get off their feet." Elijah had helped her with a jammed buckle—or tried to, but she'd snarled at him until he laughed and backed off to let her wrench and curse at the blasted thing—but Eli hadn't moved to help the other hostlers.

Elijah hadn't moved a lunge's length from her.

"Oh," Sasha said. She twitched the reins and the horse followed along behind her amiably, flicking its tail at flies with enviable accuracy. "Relax, Eli. We're not in Willow Tree anymore."

"And that's supposed to make me feel better?" Elijah said. "At least then we had a good guess about how many there were."

"Thanks for the thought, lady, but we're on these feet until sundown," said a scrawny apprentice who was scrubbing down the side of a dusty carriage. "Soon as we get these shiny, and those all fed and watered and brushed down, it's mucking stalls or fixin' carriage wheels. Unless you want to grab a shovel—"

"That's her highness you're speaking to," said a footman, who had picked up Sasha's coat from where she'd flung it on the fence and was folding it over his arm. "Your highness, her majesty the queen requests your presence at the lily pond courtyard for afternoon tea."

"Mucking out stables?" said Sasha thoughtfully.

"Perhaps an improvement over miniature scones," said Elijah with a straight face.

The footman sniffed. "At the third bell," he said stiffly. "May I escort you to your rooms, to prepare yourself?"

"Gird myself for battle? I don't need an hour for *that*." said Sasha. The footman continued to stand there, looking stiff. "You may escort my coat, if you must. I *have* an escort."

Sasha stepped through the high door of the stables, leaving the footman behind and losing herself in the thick perfume of fresh hay and old manure, the creak of leather and the sigh of horses. Nate said Lia came to the stables every day. Did she need to lose herself sometimes, too?

"I've never mucked out stables before," said Sasha. When Nate said Lia took care of her mare herself, did he mean that part of it too? "Perhaps it will be an adventure."

"It will be an adventure, too, if you ignore your mother's wishes."

"Pah, you can go drink tea with that footman if you're so eager for it, Eli," she said. "I said hello to Mother, didn't I? I'm too exhausted to face society right now. I've had

Mother displeased with me before; I can deal with it." She opened the bay's stall and walked in, brushing his big, soft ears while she worked on taking off his harness all the way and hanging it up.

"It won't just be an adventure for you, though," said Elijah. She glanced sideways at him. The horse pushed at her chest with his nose. "If the queen hears the hostlers let you act like a stables apprentice all day, she'll have words with the horsemaster."

Sasha gave the horse one last pat, then stepped out and closed the stall door behind her. Someone else would have to brush him down and give him a hearty dinner. She sighed, "I hate tea."

"Not when Stearnes brews up a pot next to the practice yard on winters' mornings," said Elijah.

"While Gideon frets about the proper regulations for palace fires," said Sasha. "But I like old dingy battered mugs, and with Second I only have to smile if I feel like smiling."

The palace footman was still hovering outside, eyeing the coat in his hands. He was new, and according to his fellows the middle princess sometimes had a sense of humor and he wasn't sure if that had been it.

Sasha swept out. "To tea, then?" she said. "My room first, I think, though. Do you think you could help carry my bags?"

"Your highness," the footman said with

a bow, feeling much more comfortable with a more ordinary duty to complete, and rushed politely to the carriage, which was being unloaded by the servants who had gone with the royal party to Willow Tree. He lifted several of the cloth bags and one unwieldy trunk—but the last pile of bags was snatched from before his feet.

Sasha slung two over each shoulder and set off. "Keep up," she said.

"Your highness!"

Elijah followed behind, hands empty, trying not to snicker.

Gabrielle slipped into the wide leather chair tucked in one corner of her father's windowless study. Oil lamps lit the whole room, but most especially the area around the desk and the area around the chair, bright enough to read and write. The chair was smooth and cool, slippery against the silk of her dress, and Gabrielle fit perfectly into a familiar hollow in its seat.

The king of Neria dropped into his own chair behind his desk, the lamps lighting the crags in his face as he smiled. The king was tall, something none of his daughters but Lia had inherited, though both she and Gabrielle had claimed his hard, thick hair.

Gabrielle ran her hands along the chair

arms, took some long steadying breaths and then said as lightly and matter-of-factly as she could, "The Sylians sent a new trade delegation, then?"

"They did," the king said, the smiling creases in his weatherworn face deepening. "You know, I believe your mother has a welcome-home tea planned in her daughters' honor."

The king leaned forward and Gabrielle pulled her knees to her chest, trying to keep a smirk off her face as she looked over her skirts at him.

"How about," said the king, "we tell her you're indisposed?" He pushed the notes of the latest minister's council meeting at her and said, "I'll have the kitchens send up some supper."

Familiar walls, familiar smile, the familiar handwriting of her favorite court scribe—Gabrielle rubbed quickly at her eyes, pulling the notes to her with her other hand. Indisposed wasn't much of a lie at all.

"I think you made the little maid cry," said Elijah. "She rushed out of your suite like something nasty was after her. What did you do?"

"What did *I* do? *She* was trying to undress me," said Sasha. "And yanking out my hair trying to comb it—you just didn't hear *me* yelping through that door. I hate maids. I can dress myself just fine."

There was no sound from the space behind her shoulder.

Sasha made a disgruntled sound and elbowed him without looking back, trying to wipe the raised eyebrow and Harston-like disapproval off his face. "Fine, I don't hate maids. I hate *stockings*. And I hate hair ribbons."

The path they walked was curving along the edge of one of the wings that spiraled around the palace's center, the old stone city's keep. The lily pond courtyard was on the far eastern side. "Don't you have to report in?"

"I'm on caravan-guarding duty," Elijah said. "Until you're properly settled in, you're still part of the caravan. Gideon won't rat me out, I think."

"He won't," agreed Sasha. "Well. Not unless Brown asks him outright." Sasha took a steadying breath and smoothed her skirts as the lily pond came into view. A few dozen noble ladies gathered about in the sun with fans and parasols, wrapping elegant fingers around dainty teacups.

"On guard," murmured Elijah in her ear, and then stepped back to join the unobtrusive guardsmen who stood around the perimeter of the queen's tea party.

Sasha grabbed the hem of his sleeve and said, "She didn't really cry, did she?"

There was a shadow of amusement on the guardsman's face as he tried to keep a straight expression. "I exaggerated."

She tugged harder on his sleeve in vengeance, using the leverage to step up into the garden, her best pleasant Court expression on her face. "Hello, mother."

The queen swept over the colored tiles, white and green mosaic matching the patterned fall of her skirts and the stillness of the lilies on the nearby water. She kissed Sasha on the cheek and pressed a warm cup into her hands. "Welcome home. Lia said the trip was pleasant."

"I suppose," said Sasha. "A little less than exciting."

"Then it is good you are home again," said the queen.

"Yes," said Sasha, sipping her tea. "What could be more exciting?"

The minister of Intelligence squinted at the young man in front of him and Willard Rocole stared back, keeping his face decidedly amiable. "What was it that you wanted, Minister Westel, sir?"

Westel steepled his fingers on his desk. "I just had an interesting conversation with Captain Brown."

"Did you, sir? That's nice."

Westel's eyes narrowed. "Don't think me a fool, boy. You lied to an official of our government."

Will tried his best to look apologetic. "Sir—"

"You seem to forget your place, Rocole. You do not obey instructions; you do not listen to your superiors. You are a detriment to this department and I have an urge to demote you to apprentice."

Will jumped up out his chair. "*Apprentice*? Sir, I'm better than half of the second-level journeymen. You can't stick me back with the 'prentices."

Westel watched him, unblinking. He hadn't even twitched a finger when Will had risen from his chair. "Yes, I can, actually. And don't overestimate your skills, boy. You're adequate at code breaking. You've an admittedly uncanny ability to recite the files you have read. But you have no *discipline*."

Will shook his head. (He was the *best* journeyman at code breaking—well, maybe second best, but the *best* had no people skills, so really Will had the better deal here). "We have rebels and assassins on the loose. We need to catch them, not worry about marching order."

"Discipline is everything," Westel said. "Without it all we are is a horde of untrained animals. Without it, everything falls apart." He quieted down, running his ink-stained fingers through his short black hair, sprinkled with white. He glowered at Will for a moment, and then muttered, "Those rebels and assassins are why I'm *not* demoting you. You are arrogant and unruly, but I can't spare even one half-trained agent. I need you all, Neria needs you all, or we may well be at the mercy of these Ceren radicals."

Will suppressed a sigh of relief. "Thank you, sir."

Westel glared at him. "Don't get cocky, boy. The next time I send you on an assignment, do as you're told."

Will saluted him, grinning. "Yes, sir. You can trust me, sir."

The minister of Intelligence scowled. "I doubt it."

"I've lied to you, my friends, and I must apologize." The queen tapped a small spoon on the side of her tea cup, the ringing chime falling into sudden polite silence.

The young peacock ladies clustered around Lia, the queen's older, respected advisors and friends, and the visiting wives of ambassadors looked to her majesty. A thirteen-year-old countess newly come to Court twirled her pale orange sun parasol and watched with shy excitement.

There was a swift collective murmur that the queen could never voice an untruth. The queen smiled graciously.

"I've brought you together on a falsehood. We are not here only to enjoy the beautiful day. We are here to rejoice in my eldest daughter Lia's engagement to Duke John of the southern provinces."

The courtyard erupted into young squeals, voiced congratulations, and the rustle of fabric as the crowd converged on the queen and the princess heir.

The second eldest princess turned her head to meet the eyes of a redhaired guardsman who had been about to leave and report in to his proper authorities. Elijah stood back quietly against the wall and returned her stare.

On a small iron-wrought chair, Gabrielle sipped her tea very slowly, trying to keep the blood from draining from her cheeks.

"A summer wedding," said the queen. "The hills will be golden and the sky blue—the color scheme I think will have to be reflective of the season." The women around her nodded seriously. Some appeared to be taking notes.

The more brightly-colored ladies flurried around Lia. "You must be so excited!" squealed the younger lady who had accompanied the princesses to Willow Tree. She tugged on Lia's sleeve, bouncing. "He's so *handsome*."

"Smart, too," said the baroness firmly. "Confident, strong. Good traits in a prince."

"But handsome's the *important* part," said the youngest lady. Lia met the duchess's wry eyes over the youngest lady's head, sharing a hidden grin.

The other young peacocks of Court, Lia's extended circle of friends, rivals, and compatriots, swarmed on her as well, offering congratulations and advice, some well-meaning and some bawdy—or as bawdy as a smart woman would get in the presence of the queen.

They would say more, later, and watch to see if she blushed.

Sasha almost went to her as well, but instead stepped over the artfully mossy wall to where Elijah had stationed himself out of the way. "If he's the one who snatched Gabe—"

"We'll watch them both, you silly goose," he said. "Go drink your tea, and we'll figure this out."

"Now ladies," the queen said trillingly. "Let's keep our fans over our mouths when we're in less close company. I will be disappointed if I don't get to see the Court's surprise with my own eyes."

It was cold, but Gregory had expected that.

Rags wrapped around his hands were makeshift gloves, and he'd stuffed his threadbare boots with them as well. He had had to leave his red messenger's hat, and wore an oversized woolen cap, shapeless and colorless with age and too many washings. He wore his only suit of clothes, but had a blanket wrapped around his shoulders.

A bag dangled from his shoulder, a few shriveled winter apples and some bread and hard cheese bounced within, along with the knife, which he had found an oversize sheath for, in fear that it would slice through his bag.

The snow had mostly melted, though patches of it here and there were visible. If Will

251

had still been at home, he and Gregory would've disappeared for a day, risking sizable scoldings, and gone in search for a perfect patch of snow and the last snowball fight of the season. But Will wasn't here and Gregory eyed the remaining snow with trepidation instead of joy, knowing that there would be no warm hearth to return to once night fell.

Gregory adjusted the strap on his shoulder, the bag banging into his thigh, and tried not to think about cold nights or hard ground or the fact that it took a carriage three days to reach the capitol. He didn't want to know how long it took on foot. Gregory began to think longingly of home, but stopped himself.

He reached into his bag and took out the Ceren knife. It glinted in the weak winter sunlight as he unsheathed it.

Gregory'd found it in the passages, one of the assassins' knives, and thought that perhaps it could help Sasha prove something, or help the little princess remember.

It had taken him two days to come to the decision to get the knife out from where he had hidden it in the passage walls and pack his bags.

Gregory was a quiet mountain lad; he would be lost in the bustling city and he knew it well. Will could adapt. Gregory wasn't that kind of person. Well, he'd never tried it, but he doubted it. He wanted nothing more than to be back in his little valley, his little castle, his little passages. Why couldn't the rest of the world leave him alone? Why couldn't he leave *it* alone?

But if the knife could help Sasha and Will at all—and, Gregory thought, very very quietly, if *I* can help at all—then I can't stay here.

When the sky began to darken, Gregory stopped and took a good long look at the trees that covered the mountainous land around him. Dotted between his familiar evergreens were trees with reaching branches and wide smooth leaves that he had never seen before. He picked a big, flat leaf up and held it in his hand for a moment, something a little like wonder burbling through his fears. Then Gregory curled up in a bed of pine needles, shivering, and fell asleep with wind howling through the trees' crowns.

He huddled in his blankets while the world spread out around him, wide and far and strange.

Chapter Eight
A Return to Cobblestones

Four days later, Will lay on his back on the carpet of the baron of Aglebury's private sitting room, flicking a copper coin lazily across the backs of his fingers.

Sasha paced, keeping an eye on the window.

The baron was out on a long hunting trip—Sasha had asked Gabrielle which apartment closest to Duke John's would be reliably empty. Now Sasha lurked by the window, keeping an eye on the next door over while she filled Will in on recent developments.

Nathaniel had a watch on Count Dereck's afternoon duties at the ministry of Domestic Affairs.

"You know," said Will, "royal weddings mean free food?" He grinned up at her and got the roll of her eyes that he'd wanted, the tension draining from her shoulders in exchange for exasperation. Will tossed the coin up, caught it, and then tucked it up his sleeve for safekeeping.

"Get up and help me watch," said Sasha. "I want to keep an eye on him. Maybe we can find something out and prove to Brown, that either the duke or the count's gone bad."

"If we know more about whoever's behind this whole plot, that could help, too," said Will. "And you're perfectly capable of watching a door without my help." Will closed his eyes, settling down into the soft carpet. His hands were folded over his stomach, as he napped near the wall the noble apartment shared with the duke's.

"Humph," said Sasha. "You know, that's a *very* undefended position you're in."

Will grinned up at her winningly without opening his eyes. "That's why I keep you around, to fight off the angry men with swords."

Sasha tried not to touch the window's curtains as she peered through the slit between the hanging fabrics. A twitching curtain in an empty apartment might warn someone. Sasha had picked the lock on the servant's door in the back while Will watched for any approaching company. They'd had to do it late at night, and leave it unlocked for their entrance later. The servants' corridors were too crowded in the day.

"He's moving," said Will. He pushed himself to his feet and headed for the door.

"What?" said Sasha.

"I heard him open the servant's door while you were busy staring," Will said. "We're not the only ones who can use the back door."

"You're a headache, Will Rocole."

"Thank you," he said, grinning.

They slipped out the back. A dark-haired figure garbed in starched servant's clothes, the duke was hard to follow when he joined the purposeful stream of servants going back and forth between the apartments.

The duke turned out of the narrow servant's path. Sasha waited for a breath and then followed him out the corridor. She could hear Will creeping quietly behind her. Glancing out of the corner of her eye, she caught sight of the duke once more. They followed him until he slipped out of a small servants' gate in the outer wall, the gate's single guard barely glancing at one more palace servingman—or two off-duty servants heading back home to the city.

"You know what this looks like?" Will said.

"Yes," said Sasha grimly. "Lia's engaged to a traitor."

"Your sister's got terrible taste," said Will. "Or terrible options. The treasonous pretty boy, or the distracted bureaucrat? Though, one of them blushes and one of them smiles at you while your family gets murdered behind your back, so the choice shouldn't have been *that* difficult."

The duke headed down the narrow grassy slope that marked the border between the sprawling palace and the town surrounding it. The streets at the immediate base of the hill were quiet, clean, full of lower noble houses or rich merchants. To Sasha, the quiet was almost eerie.

As they reached the crowded streets of the true city, Sasha felt Will stiffen beside her, even as she happily drank in the ruckus, a familiar childhood lullaby. "What is it, Will?" she murmured.

"We're being followed."

Andrea slipped through a gap between two street stalls, their owners shouting prices and goods only to be drowned in the general clamor. Wanting to tie up loose ends, she'd gone looking for the spy from Willow Tree who had found her suspicious. To her surprise, she'd found that Will Rocole had more than suspicions—he was following the Cerens' own noble.

Rocole and the scruffy boy with him— his assistant, or some street lad Rocole was tearing information out of?—were up ahead; she could see from the tilt of their heads that they spoke quietly to each other. Andrea peered at them through the corner of her eye, strolling towards them through the crowd as though she had nothing but a walk on her mind.

A pair of the City Guard—their familiar white and brown a sharp contrast to the black and silver of the Royal Guard—trotted past her and Andrea quickly swerved out of the way and behind a booth selling brightly colored scarves, which were waving in the chill wind.

The blonde stepped from behind the scarf seller's booth, quickly scanning the crowd for a sign of the spy—how had Rocole managed to disappear so quickly? Her head whipped as she glared at the bright, moving mass of persons, her braid cutting through the air. With his damned plain brown hair, Rocole fit in easily with the crowd.

But, no, wait—there Rocole was, slithering between two rickety buildings, blending into the darkness like the sneak he was.

Andrea picked up her stride, darting past a matronly woman arguing fiercely with a farmer come to sell his goods in market. She barely dodged the woman's flailing carrot as the robust lady emphasized her demands with waves of the orange root vegetable. Andrea pushed past a heavily loaded donkey who swished his tail noncommittally at her, and then slipped between the two buildings, the sound of the street muted momentarily.

About to race out the other side of the alley between the houses and into the adjacent street, as bright and bustling as the one behind her, Andrea paused, one hand resting a breath above the wood of the wall beside her. There was no glimpse of Rocole within the jostling crowd. The young woman turned her head, looking behind her at the source of the faint sound that had stopped her.

A window shutter creaked, half-open, a few feet up the wall. The latch—it was locked from the inside—had been broken. A few wood splinters fell between the cracks of the cobblestone ground of the alley.

Andrea smiled and stepped toward the window.

After Will had left to play the decoy, Sasha followed the duke as he descended further into the city.

When the rough-garbed nobleman slipped into an inn, Sasha cautiously followed him in. The swinging sign hanging outside read "The Drunken Dog," which Sasha decided described the mood of this place accurately. The common room was rowdy and dim, heady with the stink of ale.

Sasha skirted the edge of the common room, flanking the piece of ground where the duke stood, conferring with a rotund and aproned man Sasha assumed to be the innkeeper. The innkeeper pointed the duke to a flight of stairs and said something Sasha could not hear over the noise of the common room. The duke nodded and ascended the narrow stairway. Sasha kept an eye on the innkeeper, and when he turned away, she strolled up the stairs, acting as though she had a perfect right to be doing so.

Luckily, no one pointed or asked what that ratty looking kid thought he was doing. Sasha slipped into the hallway that seemed to be the full scope of the second floor. Doors ran down it, numbers carved in the wood, and a single window at the end of the hall let in a feeble ray of sunlight. The door labeled number eight swung shut as she stepped off the stairs. Sasha hurried over and pressed her ear against it. She could barely hear anything through the door: everything in the inn was made of thick, sturdy timber. The beams that supported the house were clearly visible in the walls.

Sasha heard two voices inside, both male, speaking in low voices. She tried the doors beside the room number eight, thinking maybe she could hear the duke better if she was in one of them. Maybe she could open the window in there. The shutter of the window in the duke's room—she only guessed, but if these shutters were like the ones downstairs—would not be able to hold in their words nearly as well as this solid door. But the doors were all locked, and she hadn't brought lock picks.

Sasha paused, thinking quickly, and glanced over at the window at the end of the hall. A moment later, she was looking out of it, down at the protruding edge of wood that stuck out just where the bottom level of the inn met the upper.

It was, she noted, just about the width of the sill of a window on a carriage.

Will pressed himself against the wooden wall, an open doorway to his side, trying to breathe as silently as possible as he listened to the blonde's footsteps in the alley, a mere room and broken window shutter away from him. With straining ears Will heard the assassin—Andrea, she'd said her name was, though he knew of no reason to believe what she had said—pause and he sucked in a worried breath. He had hoped she would just pass him by.

Will quickly scanned the room he stood in, looking for something that could help him, hide him, that he could fight with. An old woman's advice rang nonsensically in his head—*fight with your words not with your fists*. He shook his head, brown hair falling over brown eyes.

Will was in some sort of carpenters' workshop, the benches around him stacked with wood and tools. There were plenty of weapons: half-carved table legs and staffs, as well as knives for whittling and carving, gleaming sharply in the half-light that fell through the broken shutter in the room behind him.

It wasn't very large, just made of three rooms: the one with the window and the one Will hid in, where the work was done, and then the front room, for customers. He could see the front door of the carpenters' shop in the next room, light glinting feebly under the doorframe. It opened outwards.

The room brightened sharply as Andrea pushed the shutter open, a slow creak echoing the frantic thud of Will's heart. As he heard Andrea vault through the window, her feet thumping softly on the floor inside, Will caught sight of a sturdy wedge resting on a nearby bench. He grinned.

Andrea was moving swiftly through the room behind him. Will quietly grabbed the wedge, and then took off at full speed toward the front door, making no care to hide himself. He did bend over as he ran, hoping that if she threw anything sharp at him that she would miss.

Will just heard Andrea rush after him through the blood pounding in his ears. Will skidded to a stop before the front door, hand scrambling to shove it open. A fresh breeze surrounded him as the door fell open and he threw himself out into daylight. Will slammed the door behind him.

He felt Andrea push at it, the force of her sprint behind her. Will staggered back a foot or so, then shoved the door back in place and pushed the wedge under it.

It held.

Andrea pounded on the door, cursing him, foul words squirming through the cracks. Will, ignoring the stares of the bustling street, took off at a run. Andrea's cursing was muted and he heard something heavy—a bench?—get kicked over as the young woman ran back to the window, now her only exit from the premises.

Will pushed himself into a sprint, dodging between oblivious townspeople, and grinned to himself as he turned a sharp corner. He'd be long gone before she got out onto the street.

Wind picked at her Sasha's garments, teasing the stray hairs that had escaped from beneath her cap, as she inched her way along the side of the building, balancing precariously on the thin protruding wooden beam.

An entire floor below her, the ground leered up at her.

Sasha moved as quickly as possible; she had to hurry along a short stretch of wall that edged the alley between the inn and the next building. Once she carefully pulled herself around the corner of the inn, she was on the backside of the building, which meant someone could only see her if they looked out the back window of the building behind the inn.

The duke's room was the second one down from the window, she thought to herself as she looked down the row of rickety shutters. Sasha inched along, checking to make sure the first room was empty before she whisked by the window—she'd fall off the narrow ledge if she tried ducking below the view of anyone in the room.

She heard the duke's obvious noble accent from the second window. It would be risky to duck by it, but, even then, what would she do? She couldn't just stand out here on the ledge all day. She glanced back to the window she had just passed, watching its rickety shutter flapping a little in the breeze. There had been no one in that room, she recalled.

She eased the first shutter open, willing it not to creak, and tumbled quietly inside. The princess sat down at the base of the window and listened hard to the words that were drifting on the wind to her straining ears.

"You'll let him know?" said the duke's voice on the wind. He was seeking reassurance. He had asked this question before.

"Of course I will, you idiot. I'll let him know you've been a good little boy. Was that all you wanted?"

This voice she knew, too. Sasha had heard it in the passages, right before she and Elijah had gotten into a fight that ended with her driving her hilt into this man's temple. She hoped it had scarred. She hoped he had constant headaches and bad dreams every night.

The voice belonged to the man from the passages. She had found which noble had kidnapped Gabrielle.

"When she said yes, Lia told me to keep the engagement a secret," said the duke. "They'll announce it soon, surely, but I wanted Lukas to know as soon as possible."

"He will," said the other man. There was a dull smack. "You're an idiot," he said. "You came all the way out here to tell me that? I'd have found out soon enough."

"You said if I didn't hurry, you were going to—"

"I did, didn't I?" said the man. He sighed. "I suppose when I try to frighten the wits out of you I shouldn't be surprised when it works."

"Uh?"

"Go back to the palace and enjoy your bride to be while you can," said the man dismissively.

"While I can?" said the duke almost too quietly for Sasha to catch. She could almost hear him working up his nerve. He said, "You *said* you wouldn't hurt her. Doulings? You promised."

Doulings, thought Sasha. That's his name.

"Would I lie to you?" said the man.

Yes, probably, thought Sasha.

"I won't hurt her," said Doulings. "But she won't be much fun for awhile, you see, as she'll be in mourning soon."

"Ah, yes," said the duke, faintly.

Sasha pressed the back of her skull to the edge of the window, listening to the creak of footsteps and the opening and shutting of the door in the next room over. The duke and Doulings had left the room.

Sasha stood up and stepped out the window again, splaying her fingers over the rough wood of the outer wall and inching along. Her toes scraped along the narrow ridge, her calves straining as she kept her balance.

The shutters of Doulings's room were not fastened, clacking slightly against the wood frame in the wind. A particularly good gust swept down the alley and she pressed herself against the wall, nails digging into the weatherworn walls. This was much higher up than a carriage roof. She listened hard for any sounds of movement in the room.

Sasha inched a little farther, and then reached over carefully to open the shutters. She dropped into the room on the balls of her feet, wishing she knew where all the creaky floorboards were. The room was a copy of the one she had just left—rough walls, simple bed (but this one was rumpled), a desk, and a chair competing for floor space. Sasha had only enough time to walk over to the desk and wince at the squeal of the wooden drawer before the door to the room clicked open.

She was too far from the window to leap for it. The man named Doulings walked into the room.

Gregory's feet were sore. He'd walked for a couple of days before he'd reached the main road and a kindly farmer had offered him a lift to the capital.

Gregory's eyes were sore as well, from watching the mountain range in which Willow Tree was cradled fade into a blue stain on the horizon, a faraway bruise the eye could barely distinguish from the sky.

It'd taken him longer than he'd thought to make it to the palace from where the farmer had dropped him—who knew a city could be so big? He felt smothered. The entire population of

Willow Tree was barely a single street. He stared around him. Here, the people's winters took place in wide, crowded streets and courtyards, not huddled in torch-lit castle corridors.

The crowds around him had plenty of pale blondes and brunets who would have fit in perfectly to Willow Tree's hall, but Gregory also saw people who looked like Will's brown-skinned Birnelese mother, others of a darker shade who spoke something that sounded like the Aharian tongue Gregory had once heard a few words of, and some people who even looked like Gregory. He pulled his coat in tighter around him and stared at a woman who looked almost as brown and beautiful as his mother had.

The palace reigned over the city from a grassy knoll; Gregory stood at the bottom of the green slope, eyeing the beautiful construction that crowned the hill. The palace was a complex of wings spiraling out from a central hub, which was a contrastingly grey and squat inner keep, ugly and worn when compared to the delicate architecture and smooth white stones of the outer, newer buildings. Even from here Gregory could glimpse the telltale glimmer of sunlight on high glass windows, and see green bows and colorful blooms from gardens and courtyards interspersing the stone and glass of the outlying wings.

Taking a deep breath of lowland air, and missing the sting of cold that Willow Tree's would still be carrying, Gregory started up the flat road which cut into the hill and led up to the palace's main entrance, feeling the weight of the knife in the small pack he'd slung over his shoulder. A high white wall circled the palace, broken by a handful of gates, the large and fabulous for the nobles, then a couple of decidedly smaller ones through which the servants and lesser merchants entered.

Gregory approached the smallest gate he could find. The guard who stood at it looked down at him, smiling a little. "I don't know who dared you to come here, sonny," the guard said. "But tell 'em to stop picking on boys who're littler than them."

"What do you mean?" Gregory asked, trying to look as innocent as he could.

The guard chuckled, mostly kindly. "We don't just let any street kid come wandering through for a fancy."

Gregory looked down at himself; he wore his single suit of clothes and worn shoes, passed down through the three sons of Willow Tree's blacksmith before they came to him. He looked up, smiling sheepishly at the guard. "Sorry, sir. I'll tell 'em so." Gregory trudged off on sore feet, walking along the white wall. The guard watched him go.

Gregory fumed silently to himself—it was either to fume or to despair. Now what was he to do? How could he get the knife to Sasha if he couldn't even get inside?

In front of him—he'd walked far enough around the palace now that the guard's gate was no long visible—a section of the wall was in deep shadow. A tall, thick-canopied tree leaned over it; it was planted in some sort of garden, on the inside of the wall. Gregory grinned.

Stepping into the shadow, he looked swiftly around him. The wall nearby him was not immediately interrupted by any gates, so no guards were there to see him. Any watching from the city were not in view. The streets that lined the noble residences—only the rich could afford homes near the palace—were empty and quiet. In any case, the shadow ought to hide him well enough from watchers who stood in the noonday sun. Slinging his small pack over one shoulder, Gregory turned to the wall.

Gregory examined the mortared cracks between the stones and then glanced at the height of the wall. He could do this, he assured himself. How many times had Will and he dared each other to race up the trees of Willow Tree's forest, in the spring and summer when snow wasn't piled six feet deep (or even then)?

He wriggled his toes between two stones and pulled himself up. Sliding his foot up, he found another foothold. He reached higher with his hand, searching for a place to insinuate his grasping fingers. Nervous, Gregory looked over his shoulder, but there was no one who could see him. He could only imagine what they would do if they found someone trying to sneak into the palace.

He found a handhold. He was halfway up the wall. A few more scrambling pulls and

Gregory was about to crest the top of the wall when he heard voices.

He froze; a pair of patrolling guards marched along the wall's broad top. Gregory's arms strained as he kept himself down, not daring to pull himself up on top of the wall. A small green bug crawled along the mortared crack his fingers dug into and he prayed no one would walk by and find him like this.

The voices faded. Gregory gratefully pulled himself up and onto the wall, raced across, and then let himself down into the limbs of the tree. His hands scraped over the rough bark as he scrambled down the trunk. He landed with a thud.

He was inside.

Sasha pressed herself against the hollow of the desk, the ridges of her spine hard against the wood. She had knocked the chair out of the way and dove for the empty space it left, hidden from the front of the room. She could hear Doulings breathing and tried to place him in the room with her eyes screwed shut with effort.

Doulings entered and shut the door behind him but did not latch it. He walked across the room and she lost track of him. She could only make out the faintest whisper of his shoes on wood; she listened hard for the sound of him coming toward the desk.

Sasha moved as quietly as she could in the hollow of the desk, twisting around so she crouched on the balls of her feet, instead of sitting with her legs propped up. If he came, she would not be caught with her chin on her knees, scrambling to twist herself into a defensive position. If he came, she had her knife in her boot, she had the element of surprise.

She did not have her father's cloaks hung around her, muffling her ability to move, however much her head was trying to convince her she was drowning in heavy wool.

She did not have a small Gabrielle in her lap, her toddler fingers exploring her cheeks and nose while Sasha tried not to grip her little sister too tight and frighten her into making a sound.

Sasha did not have the smooth palms of a nine-year-old who had never held a sword, who had never known the helplessness of hearing the cut-off cries and wet thumps of the two guards outside her father's study door.

The bed creaked under Doulings's weight.

Sasha screwed up her eyes again and listened hard, ignoring the smell of burning paint and paper rising in her mind. If he went to sleep, could she sneak out past him, out the window and to the streets and away?

Sasha would have to, or wait until he left and hope he didn't sit down to write a letter before then. She listened to him shift. Sasha ran her finger over the whorls of the wooden floor and the ridged hilt of her dagger and tried to breathe as quietly as possible.

There was a knock at the door. There was a sigh and a creak from the bed, but Doulings didn't get up. There was a harder knock and then the door burst open, smacking into the wall so hard it bounced off and smacked back into the intruder, who cursed loudly. "Doulings!"

"*What*?" said the assassin in a voice that made Sasha, under the desk, flinch, but the intruder didn't back off.

"There was a spy following the duke," said the intruder, who seemed to be a girl. The bed creaked as Doulings sat up. The girl continued, "I scared him off the trail but I lost him." Sasha relaxed a smidgen, her fingers splayed rigidly against the desk's underside.

"What spy?" said Doulings. "How did he find us? This is impossible—improbable. I should've known if there was anyone in the ministry that close to finding out about John."

The girl sniffed. "Apparently not," she said. "It was the spy from Willow Tree; he was poking his nose around up there, too." The bed creaked as she sat down on it. "Your stupid noble probably did something stupid."

"No," said Doulings. A scrape of a heel on the floor told Sasha he was pacing. "Get up, chit. I need to go take a look at the lay of the land."

"*I* don't want to go anywhere with you," said the girl.

"I wasn't asking you to," said Doulings. "But *I* am leaving, and I'm not leaving you in my room to poke through my things. *Up*."

There was a huff and the girl seemed to have done as she was told. Sasha counted whatever footsteps she could hear. Once they were both out and the door shut, she would go for the window.

"What?" said the girl.

Doulings was turning back. "I need a piece of paper," he said, heading on silent feet towards the desk.

When they found her, they dragged her out from under desk by the scruff of her neck like an unruly puppy.

Sasha was cursing like a proper bit of guttersnipe and flailing in the thin man's grasp. Doulings shook her smartly and she glared. Her hat was crammed low on her head and her cheeks dark with street dust and sweat.

"That's one of Rocole's pigeons," said the girl, who was indeed the blonde assassin from the passages. "The spy, Doulings—I saw him with him just earlier."

"Mm," said Doulings. "That's unfortunate. I'll have to do something about this."

Andrea took two steps toward the door and yanked it open, shouting down the hall. "Charlie!"

Doulings nearly yanked Sasha off her feet as he stepped towards Andrea. "What are you doing?"

"It's his—" said Andrea, rounding back on him, and Sasha slammed her elbow back into the part of Doulings' chest she'd been carefully setting up her aim for and dashed out the gap Andrea had left, leaving Doulings gasping in her wake.

Doulings hacked and waved a hand at Andrea, who was staring at him and the empty space where Will Rocole's street rat used to be. "Go—*after*—him," Doulings managed to gasp.

Andrea spared him a glare, and then pounded out of the room and down the stairs, passing a bewildered innkeeper on his way up.

Sasha dodged past off-shift workers drinking themselves red in the face and a short, blonde young man wiping down the counters. She heard Andrea come down the stairs behind her as she pushed out through the main doors and into the sunlight of the cobblestone streets.

Sasha put her feet solidly on the rounded stone and ran. It was a long, straight street, not too crowded, and the stones were wet from the winter rains. Her boots gripped tightly on the ground, but Sasha watched her step when she tore around a corner.

Andrea was not far behind. She had already chased one nosy Nerian today, but Sasha wasn't sure how much of a run Will had put up. Sasha took another corner, catching her hand on a lamppost to help her throw all her speed into the turn, and then dashed down another. The streets were growing dirtier, the cobblestones cracked and missing here and there, the windows boarded up. Sasha took the twistiest route she could, going deeper into the poorest parts of Neria City.

Her lungs were starting to catch, but Sasha knew that pull of strain around her chest. She chanced a quick glance over her shoulder and saw Andrea was gone. Sasha snapped her head back forward, narrowly missing tripping over a missing cobble, and slipped into a side alley, slowing to a breathless walk and listening hard for footsteps.

There was a puff of dirt and slight impact—that was all the warning Sasha got before she was tackled from behind. Sasha managed to land jarringly on her shoulder, instead of on her face. Andrea had one hand on the back of Sasha'a neck, shoving her down, while the other tried to grab her wrist. Andrea had come over a fence, hopping from one alley to the next, cutting Sasha off.

Sasha slammed her elbow up and back, landing glancing blows on Andrea's ribs and not much else. Her cheek was shoved hard into the dirt and she stopped fighting for her head. Sasha squirmed her legs underneath her and then shoved herself upright and flung Andrea off her back. Sasha spat dirt as she ran.

Andrea picked herself up quickly and followed, her right thigh aching from the blow.

Sasha ran faster now, hopping a fence or two herself, Andrea following almost close enough to snatch her heels. There was a demanding burn in Sasha's legs, her lungs, and her forming bruises. She wrapped her fingers around the splintered edge of a fence and hauled herself over.

Sasha collapsed in a crouch in a narrow alley. She sprung across it and tore at a boarded-over window in the wall. Sasha'd made an opening just big enough to squirm through when she heard Andrea come over the fence behind her. Sasha shoved herself headlong through the window, landing in an ungraceful heap. Pushing herself to her feet, she raced through the room, down a hallway, and out a side window.

Around Sasha's thudding feet huddled, sleeping lumps turned into people and raised their heads. This gang nest was largely nocturnal, and Sasha knew their windows were shoddily repaired. By the time Sasha reached the far window, they were almost awake enough to snatch at her feet.

In the open alley on the other side of the building, Sasha picked herself up. The last lump she'd passed had gotten a good grip on her knee and sent her tumbling through the window. This was a minor gang den for a minor gang, but there were enough of them to prove an obstacle, she hoped.

"Ugh!" came the cry from inside. "Get off of me!" Something smashed as the gang began to protest the intruder they were awake enough to intercept and Andrea fought her way out the backside. In the alley on the far side, Sasha grinned and disappeared.

Doulings and John had spoken for a few minutes before Sasha had managed to situate herself in proper eavesdropping position.

Before Sasha was huddling by the next window over and listening in, John had asked, "What about Gabrielle? She saw me," and Doulings had answered, "Not to worry. I'll take care of it."

Gregory was lost. The palace was at least six times the size of Willow Tree and moved in a miserable rat warren sort of quality from wide, paved walks to shade-dappled courtyards to long shining white wings of buildings touched with mosaic and window glass and tiled roofs. The squat old stone tower at the center was a useful landmark, but there were always seas of roofs between him and it, and when he slipped inside the branching hallways of one of the wings, he could not see it at all.

Gregory tugged at the buttons of his borrowed coat—he'd found a little room with rows of uniforms hung on hooks. They were the same outfits the occasional male servant was walking around wearing, though they seemed to Gregory much too posh to wear for doing actual work.

There didn't seem to be enough servants walking between the curving paths, the tall windows, and the little courtyards where nobility and higher-class bureaucrats sipped tea in the afternoon heat. Gregory couldn't see how the few he'd passed by could handle taking care of the whole massive maze. Even Willow Tree had an impressive brigade of maids and craftsmen to repair and maintain, even if some of them were scrawny kids like Gregory.

In a few weeks, it would be spring, time to dust the back rooms and scour the kitchen and scrub down every stone under the chamberlain's tyrannical direction. What was Cook going to say if Gregory missed it? Who would stick his head into the massive soup cauldron and get ash and iron so thick on his arms it wouldn't wash out for days?

Gregory hadn't said good-bye. He had thought they might laugh at him, for leaving, and after all he was going to come back.

Gregory's vaguely ratty pants peeked out from underneath the sleek brushed splendor of the palace servant's coat. He was glad he'd chosen a particularly long one, which came down to his knees. Gregory looked critically around him.

He knew where he *was*—at least well enough he could go retrace his steps all the way back to the courtyard with the tree that came over the wall. But he didn't know where he was going. Where did they keep princesses? Half the rooms he saw had windows, so that didn't help at all. At one place, the windows were a *wall* and inside he could see it was a library with more books than he had known existed.

Gregory paused by the tall glass windows. There was a pointy nosed fellow just on the other side, glaring at a large tome as though it were offending him personally. A waver in the glass made his nose seem particularly long. When Gregory tilted his head just a little in the other way, the nose shrank into a little bulbous spot.

"You're from Willow Tree," said a voice behind him.

Gregory jerked and turned around quickly. The redhead in the black and silver of the Royal Guard was looking at him, puzzled. "What are you doing here?"

"I came with the caravan," Gregory said, somewhat squeakily.

"You didn't come with the caravan," said the guardsman. "And you talked to Sasha, in the halls, that once, and I bet again." He squinted up at the sun and sighed. "You better come with me."

"Are you going to put me in prison?" said Gregory morosely, following.

The guard looked back at him and laughed, startled. "No," he said. "Anyway, prison's the City's Guard province; the Royal Guard gets to put people his Majesty's dungeon. There's a difference." He added quickly, after a look at the boy's face, "I'm not putting you in the dungeon, either. I'm taking you to Sasha."

"Oh," said Gregory. "Good. I was looking for her."

"I thought you might be," said the guard. He offered a large callused hand with slender, long fingers. "I'm Elijah."

Gregory shook the hand with a hesitant rhythm made erratic with the rise and fall of their strides. "I'm Gregory."

When Sasha got back to her rooms, starting to feel her bruises, she came through the back window. There was a very bored guard on the front door of the living suite. The guard had been there since Sasha had entered the room this morning, after a light breakfast with her mother, and as far as he was concerned, she had been there the whole time, too.

Whatever else Sasha had to say about Brown, it was certainly easier to disappear without the sharp eyes of Second on her door at all times.

Sasha dropped down onto the soft carpets of the bedroom with bare feet; she'd taken off her boots while sitting on the windowsill, to keep them from making obvious tracks.

There was a noise in the front room.

Sasha put her boots down carefully and snagged her knife from its sheath. She peeked quietly through the door, easing it open, and then stepped through. "Gregory?"

Gregory's face lit up. He sat on the plainest chair he could find and Elijah hovered in the space between them, his sword loose in his sheath.

"Relax, Eli," Sasha said as she passed him with a pat on the arm. "Stop guarding."

Gregory looked at the redhead, startled, and startled again as Sasha gave him a swift hug. "What are you doing here? No, wait—Will should be here in a moment."

"Sasha," said Elijah. "What's going on? I've got wall duty five minutes ago. This is the kid who gave you the passages, right?"

Sasha nodded.

"You're going after the assassins, still, aren't you? Why didn't you tell me?"

"I told Gideon—"

"And he was going to pass anything on without royal mandate?" said Elijah.

"I'm sorry, I've been busy," she said irritably. "I just ran halfway around the city."

"What are you doing, Sash? This is dangerous. Fill me in, and then let me do my job."

"You're free to go watch the walls anytime you like, Eli," said Sasha.

"That's not what I meant," said Elijah.

Sasha said, "This is my job, too, alright? I don't care if you've got the uniform and I don't. I'm not just going to sit back and watch this happen and you shouldn't expect me to."

Gregory scooted back in his chair, trying to put some distance between himself and the pair of glares.

"I'm supposed to keep you safe," said Elijah.

"That's why you spar with me," Sasha said. "So I know how to do it myself."

Elijah made an angry sigh. "I really do have to go," he said. "Don't do anything stupid without me there to help, alright?"

"Alright," she said.

Elijah looked a little dubiously at Gregory, but Sasha said quickly, "I trust him. Stop worrying, you big nursemaid," which solicited a laugh from Eli before he went, albeit a quiet, rather tense one.

Sasha sagged down onto the couch beside Gregory. There was a thump in the back room.

Gregory had drawn up his legs to sit crosslegged on the chair. "I thought all your guards were silly," Gregory said. He looked uncomfortably over his shoulder, but Sasha didn't seem worried about the thump.

Sasha said, "Eli's a friend too, so that helps. And he *is* silly, some of the time."

"Who's silly?" said Will, who had made the thump by jumping through Sasha's back window. He came out of the back bedroom and stood still. "Gregory?"

Gregory froze. "Hi, Will."

Will crowed happily and said, "What are you doing here?"

"I found a knife, in the passages, a Ceren one," said Gregory. "I thought it might help, somehow, and so I brought it." He drew it out of his bag and put it on the couch arm next to Sasha. "It doesn't seem like much, now that I'm here. I thought maybe it would help somehow."

Sasha touched a clean bit of the hilt, softly. "Well, maybe," she said kindly. "Gabrielle still can't remember anything specific. We found out which noble it was, though—Duke John."

"Oh," said Gregory.

"But you're here," said Will. "And that means more than any knife at all."

Gregory looked at him dubiously.

"It does," said Sasha. "Now what are we going to do?"

"What did you find?" said Will. "And you're not terribly surprised to see me—I *did* run off to distract a dangerous rebel from following you, you know."

Sasha stuck out her tongue, feeling about five years old with the gesture but it made Will laugh, of course. "I never had any doubt in your ability to keep yourself safe—and anyway I heard her say that you'd lost her. Doulings knows your name now, though."

Will sat down. "You've obviously more of a story to tell than me," he said, while Gregory looked at them both wide-eyed.

"John was meeting a man named Doulings, who was the one who had Gabrielle in the passages. Once John's married Lia, they plan

284

to get the rest of us killed. Doulings seems to be in charge of something. The girl Andrea showed up, too, and then she chased me all the way to the slums until I lost her in a gang nest."

"You're not supposed to grin about that kind of thing," said Will. "Not that wide either— your face is going to split, you bloodthirsty heathen."

"We need to keep watching John," said Sasha. "Gideon's keeping an extra guard on Gabrielle, and I don't think they'll try anything until after the wedding, so that's as covered as it can be. We need to find some way to stop them."

Will shook his head. "We know John's game now. I think it's this Doulings character we should be trailing, if we want to find anything of use. He's the one pulling everyone's strings."

"Andrea didn't like him," said Sasha, "but she did what he said. I think you're right."

Gregory looked for clarification. "Doulings is the scary fellow, with the knives in the passages, who Will didn't see *once* in Willow Tree, who's got scary rebel folks terrified of him, and who gave you that scar?"

"No, the blonde girl's the one who nicked my cheek," said Sasha. She touched the thin, crusty scab along one cheek. "And it's not much of *scar*."

"I'm sure it was just a lucky shot," said Will heartily.

Sasha looked at him, reluctant. "Will, in a fight, it doesn't really matter if it was luck or skill. It matters who's bleeding. *Not*," she said, "that this bled much at all."

"So we're to follow this fellow around, then," said Gregory. "The one who's bossing around the girl who didn't make you bleed *much*?"

"He'll lead us to something," said Sasha. "There's got to be some weakness."

"Know thine enemy," said Will.

"What?"

"It was in a book I read once," said Will. "Well, it was something Westel said once, in a lecture, and I think it was from a book."

Chapter Nine
The Execution of a Plan

Early morning light streamed through the window of the office of the Captain of the Royal Guard. Sasha's skin itched, watching Brown sit in Harston's chair.

"I can't arrest a noble," Brown said, squeezing the bridge of his nose. "Not because someone says she saw him in the city—especially not when according to your guard, you were in your room at the time, reading poetry."

Sasha glared at him. This was far from the beginning of this conversation. Even if she hadn't been aching already from the sight of this familiar room with an unfamiliar paperweight on the desk, her temper would still be close to frayed. "But he's a traitor."

"John's a noble. He's one of the oldest names in all three provinces. My grandfather was a cattle merchant. You know what kind of power my word has in this Court? Unless you can give me something tangible, I can't do anything."

"I heard him!" said Sasha. "What else do you need?"

"That's not how the world works. You can't stick old nobility in his majesty's dungeon because a little girl and a petty bureaucrat say something about him."

The conversation continued in time; it didn't get any farther in content, however.

In the morning sun, Gregory swung his legs, drumming them on the side of the wall from his seat in a crenellation.

"You're mighty brave there," said Elijah.

Gregory looked quickly over his shoulder. "Ah," he said, wrinkling his nose. He leaned over his knees and looked down to the grassy slope at the foot of the palace wall. "There're taller trees than this, at home. I'm waiting for Sasha."

Elijah winced. "Don't tell me that. I've spent long years building up the habit of stopping her from doing just this."

When Sasha swept up the wall and over it, a few minutes later, the guardsman pointedly closed his eyes while she and Gregory disappeared into the city.

As they headed for the Drunken Dog, Sasha passed on the news of Brown's stubbornness and she and Gregory set up a watch.

As was easily suspected, room number eight of the Drunken Dog was where Doulings made his home. For the next few weeks, they lurked nearby. Sasha spent more time watching than Will, who actually had a job he was supposed to be doing, and Gregory even more than them, as he didn't have any royal busybodies to placate with afternoon teas and evening banquets.

Sasha could pass as a street rat, while Will could pull off a minor apprentice of some sort or other. Gregory's Willow Tree hand-me-downs were out of fashion, but with their level of wear that didn't make any fuss at all.

With his tattered clothes, Gregory made an even better street rat than Sasha, if you ignored his wide-eyed stares and the twitches at loud noises and fast movements. (Sasha had the proper wiry strength of a hard-knuckled city boy, but if you squinted past her petite bone structure you could see she was well fed). A proper street rat *was* twitchy, but in a way that implied they'd been caught off guard and beaten silly and their crust of bread stolen once and it wasn't going to happen again—not twitchy in a way that simply looked startled.

Sasha winced as a cart clattered over a sunken cobble, sending cages of squawking chickens banging into each other, and Gregory jerked around to stare.

"Eyes forward," said Sasha.

"But what if something's happening on my side?" said Gregory. "What if that was an important cart?"

"It was full of chickens," said Sasha.

"Yes, but what if?" They were standing in an alley, trying to look grungy and as though they would prefer to be nocturnal. They were rather grungy, in truth.

"Then you still have to keep your eye on the door. What if Doulings slipped out and got away because you were looking at chickens? You can keep attention on things out of the side of your eye, if you focus."

Gregory looked at her, dubious.

"Where are you not looking?" said Sasha.

Gregory sighed. "The door. But *you*'re looking at it."

"You should be, too!"

He jumped at *that*, too, and she felt bad.

Sasha grumbled apologetically. "I just don't want you to get caught off guard," she said. "Jumping at things is good, but—you have to keep your aim, Gregory, if you get what I mean."

Gregory didn't, but he nodded. She sighed.

Sasha was busy enough sighing that Gregory had to point it out. "There!" he said. "He's leaving."

Sasha snagged him by the elbow. "We don't go bouncing out after him," she said. "We don't want him to know we're following. And he knows what *I* look like, remember? So you'll have to take point."

Gregory looked at her *very* dubiously.

They managed to work out a system in which Gregory trailed behind Doulings and Sasha trailed behind Gregory, except when she knew a short cut or a good scramble over the roofs or she just couldn't stand staying back any longer. She'd dodge up through the crowd and tap his arm and whisper, "This way," or "Has he spoken to anyone?"

Doulings strolled the markets and bought a bag of the last winter chestnuts, piping hot from the fire. Gregory, who considered the lowland "winter" to be sweltering at the very least, made a face.

Doulings dropped by several seedy pubs, and one nicer one. Sasha whispered in Gregory's ear, "That's a nest," about the second floor above one of the seedier pubs that Doulings passed through. They didn't know if he went up, because street rats weren't quite the clientele, even if it was seedy, and so they had to watch from outside. There was nothing to be seen through the windows.

Doulings went to a burbling fountain and fed pigeons, bought a little block of cheddar from a cheese shop, and stopped at a blacksmith's to look at some knives. Sasha watched this last with faint envy; neither princesses nor street rats spent much time looking at fine knives.

They returned to the Dog and Sasha and Gregory hunkered down in a different alley. "Did we learn something?" Gregory asked brightly.

"A gang connection, maybe," said Sasha. "I can poke about the other places, too, and see if they're affiliated with anyone." She leaned back against the brick, which was warm even in the faint winter sun, and watched the Dog with half an eye. Gregory stood in the shadows, missing snow.

The walls of the palace were stacked solid granite blocks turned a gradient of white with coats of thick whitewash. The wide top could walk five men abreast, with raised crenellations on each side. Torch brackets marked each third crenellation, but it was an hour after noon, so the torches stood dead beside old ash marks up the lime-whitened stone.

Elijah polished a brass button and watched the people entering the small merchant's gate he was on duty over.

Eli had to admit, whatever else he thought of wall duty, he liked the height, four men tall above the ground, looking down. It was a wonderful feeling, even if he liked roofs better, where the people below didn't know they were supposed to look up as well as side to side.

Elijah had always been fond of heights.

There was a constant crush at the smaller gates, but other than nobles, visiting dignitaries, and higher class merchants, the larger gates had little traffic. Elijah knew their flows intimately; Second might not guard the King, but every man among them had guarded each and every step of his royal walls.

The noon rush had faded before the bell tolled one, but the gate was never without movement. Elijah stood proper guardsman straight, hands clasped behind him, and weighed the relative benefits of having gate duty versus patrol. At least if you were walking the walls, the scenery changed a little.

His spine jerked a little straighter. Elijah turned his head, slowly, and watched the figure who had just gone through the gate as he walked on into the palace. Elijah didn't turn his head too fast, because then he might be noticed. Red was a fairly distinctive hair color. Sloppy, Elijah thought with a critical eye on the figure, he should have come in with the rush.

The figure moved on, farther into the palace walks, and Elijah twitched to follow, but held his post, cursing quietly under his breath with a constant rhythm. When the bell tower rang three, Elijah waited until his replacement had mounted the stairs and then Eli moved as fast as he could to the barracks house.

Elijah unlatched Second's door and stepped inside. "Nate?"

His brother had just hauled off his black jacket and flung his sword on his bed. Nathaniel was kicking off a boot and looking at the hard, lumpy cot with undisguised longing. "What?"

Nate said without looking over. He'd just finished a shift as well.

"Probably needs you to tie his bootlaces," said Stearnes. "That's what bothers are for."

"Brothers?" said Gideon, tiredly. He was eyeing his cot, too, but unlike Nate the squad leader wouldn't succumb.

"That's what I meant," said Stearnes innocently.

"Nate," said Elijah. "It's a bit *stuffy* in here."

Nate looked at him, wearily, and sighed. "Yes, I suppose it is." Nathaniel tugged on the boot he'd kicked off and put his foot on Stearnes's bed to tie it, leaving a dirty footprint. The two brothers left Stearnes's promises of vengeance behind and stomped out past the practice field.

"This better be good, Elijah."

Eli ducked under a branch of the scraggly oak and stood in the weak shade. "A city 'sassin came in the east gate, dressed up like a petty merchant. One of Lukas's best."

"Where did he go?" said Nathaniel, very awake.

"I don't know," said Elijah.

"You don't *know*?" said Nate. "Did you let a knife toting thug *lose* you?"

"I was on duty," said Elijah.

"So?"

"I couldn't follow him," said Eli. "And I didn't have any way to stop him, short of dropping a rock on his head when he walked under."

"Why didn't you follow?"

"I was on *duty*," Elijah repeated. "I had a wall to watch."

Nathaniel shrugged. "It's not like anyone's going to launch an armed attack. Who'd miss you?"

"How have you not been fired?" Elijah demanded.

"How could you not follow?" said Nate. "You let a '*sassin* in? What if he was after Sasha?"

"Then he's going to have some luck finding her; she's cityside." Eli glared at his brother. "Don't mark me for an idiot, anyway. He wasn't seriously armed, as far as I could tell, and what kind of hit happens in the afternoon, in the middle of the Royal Guard? There aren't very many suicidal swords for hire out there. Maybe he was here on honest business."

Nathaniel blinked at him, then rubbed his head. "If you're not worried, then why am I not sleeping?"

"I didn't follow, but I watched where he went. He was headed towards the fifth wing."

Nathaniel kneaded his forehead. "John," he said. "He was headed for the noble apartments."

"Do you think it's involved?" asked Eli, wanting very much for Nathaniel to say no.

"Lukas has got business everywhere," said Nate.

"Not near Sasha," said Elijah. "Not if I have anything to say about it."

"Well," said Nate, slinging an arm around his little brother's shoulders. "That *is* our job."

Her mother held tea in the garden again, passing out disapproving sideways looks and valuable smiles while the servants distributed tea cups and tiny pastries. Sasha had to wait until the crowd died down and was sipping tea in small chatty circles.

There was someone she should have talked to, the moment she found out about John, before Brown, maybe even before her ragtag allies.

When her sister was near the edge of a group, Sasha touched Lia's sleeve. "Could we talk?"

They stepped to the edge of the courtyard, out of the queen's hearing.

"What is it?" said Lia.

Sasha took a long breath. "You can't marry John," she said. "He's behind Gabrielle's kidnapping."

"Stop talking nonsense," said Lia, with a quick glance toward their youngest sister. "Stop encouraging Gabrielle—I know she's frightened of John and Dereck *both* now. She has enough nightmares."

"They're not nightmares!"

"They *are*, and you encouraging her isn't helping. It was terrible, when she was taken. Of course she's frightened, someone *took* her. Of course she's afraid of every man who's not her father. She's young, Sasha. Even if nothing had happened—the world is changing and it's hard when you're that age. I remember, even if you don't." Lia flicked her hands over her skirts.

"What do you mean by *that*?"

Lia gave her a sharp look. "Nothing's ever been hard for you—you just stomp over anything you don't like."

"Like you're doing to me now?" Sasha said. "Why don't you believe us? Why don't you trust her?"

"John's my friend, Sasha," said Lia, "and he's my fiancé. I've known him since I was fifteen. Marie used to dunk him in the lily pool for tugging on our hair ribbons. I think I'd know if he was evil."

"You're wrong, Lia. I'm sorry, but this is dangerous. You're going to get us killed. If you marry him, they won't need us around anymore."

Lia pressed her hands against her ears, saying in a taut, quiet voice that felt like a scream, "I'm trying to do the right thing. Stop being difficult. Stop making this difficult for me." Lia drew her hands away from her head, squeezed the brow of her nose, then let her hands fall and clasp nicely in front of her waist. "You always do, Sasha."

Lia said calmly, "I'm marrying John this summer. You'll have to live with it." She swept up her skirts and marched away.

"What about the white?" said the seamstress. Her assistant held up a bolt of fabric next to Sasha and the seamstress pursed her lips. She was an old woman with limbs like elegant fire pokers and fingers run with calluses. "No, makes her look far too ruddy. Less time in the sun would do you some good," the seamstress told Sasha, who blinked at her and continued to hold her arms out while the second assistant fluttered productively around her, taking measurements with a knotted cord.

"And she'd only muss the white, anyway," said the queen from her seat on one of the couches in Sasha's sitting room. Her royal majesty, the royal seamstress, and the royal seamstress's horde of clean-faced, quick-fingered assistants had descended on Sasha unexpectedly with a sharp knock on the door. She had had to send Will and Gregory, with whom she was having a council of war, out the back window. "A more *sturdy* color might be better," continued the queen.

Sasha wished she had grabbed a couple weights to hold while the girl took her measurements with her arms spread wide, so at least she could count the odd position as a kind of strength exercise.

The queen stood up. Sasha, distracted, blinked in her mother's direction as the queen came over and touched her second eldest daughter gently beneath the chin. "You're not ugly," she said.

"Why thank you, mother."

"And despite that mouth of yours, you're quite clever. Yes, I think you'll do fine." The queen smiled softly, patted her cheek and returned to her seat. Her skirts draped around her in perfect practiced symmetry. "I think her highness needs another riding outfit," she told the seamstress. "Green, perhaps. It would look fetching with her eyes."

"Your majesty is astute as always."

"Why do I need another riding outfit, mother?" Sasha asked suspiciously.

"It befits your station to look your best," said the queen dismissively. "Now, darling, I've arranged for your dance tutor to meet with you an extra evening every week. I noticed at last week's ball that you have fallen quite out of practice over the winter. I thought the skills would stick rather longer, or I would have sent your tutors with you. I will sit in on your deportment and elocution lessons to make sure those are satisfactory."

"I didn't trip over my feet," said Sasha.

"No, you never do," said the queen. "And your posture is impeccable. But there is a certain lack of grace I want addressed. No, I think *elegance* is the proper term. You're not clumsy, certainly, but you dance like a..." She pursed her lips, considering.

Sasha grinned. "A fighter?"

"Yes," said the queen. "I am not pleased. The upcoming social season will be important and we all must do our best. The crown prince of Sylia will be arriving in a few weeks and I want him properly entertained by our Court." The queen lifted the slim leather gloves she'd draped over the side of her chair and slipped them on. "Especially by you, my dear."

The measuring cord tightened around Sasha's breastbone, then released as the assistant stepped away to write down the number. Rising from her seat, the queen told the seamstress, "Come speak to me tomorrow afternoon about potential designs—a ball gown, some spring day dresses, and the riding outfit shall be fine for now."

"Yes, ma'am." The seamstress curtsied as did her assistants.

The queen smiled at her daughter as she left the room. "I'm told the Sylian crown prince is quite the enthusiastic horseman."

The seamstress beamed at Sasha, shifting fabrics with thick-jointed fingers. "Perhaps you will be joining your sister in good fortune soon?"

The assistant had finished her measurements. Sasha lowered her arms. "You're going to give me nightmares," she told the seamstress, who puckered her brow in confusion.

Sasha endured their poking and prodding and chatter—the assistants didn't dare gossip and giggle to each other in the queen's presence, but had learned long ago Sasha didn't care—for another half hour before they gathered their bolts of fabric, notebooks, measuring tools and stools and left.

Sasha had heard the bells ring the fifth hour of the afternoon, so she didn't have enough time to do anything useful before she had to be back and start dressing for a Court dinner that evening. She shook out limbs sore from standing awkwardly and too still for too long and headed toward the door.

"I think I'm off for a walk," Sasha told the guardsman at her door, a broad-shouldered fellow from Fifth. What few words she'd managed to get him to speak during his occasional stints by her door were in a broad southern accent. But he was in Fifth, not Second, so he must be a son of a minor country gentry family rather than a farmer. "Do you have a favorite gardens? I just need air, so I don't really care, you see."

"Um," said the guard. "Excuse my presumption, but a friend asked if you might want to pass by the south east merchant's gate."

The redhead on the wall must have been keeping an eye out for her, because when Sasha and the southern guardsman came up the walk to the minor gate, he turned in their direction. "I'll be alright," she told her guard. "You can wait down here." Sasha hiked up her skirts and took the stairs three at a time. Elijah never would have stayed where she told him, but thank all things blessed, not everyone was as stubborn as Elijah.

"Nate?" she huffed when she hit the broad top of the wall. "What's going on?"

"We think John might have had a visitor," said Nathaniel, perching on the edge of a crenellation. "A suspicious looking character came through, about the first bell after noon yesterday, and we think he went to John's rooms."

"I've got a friend who can look into it," said Sasha. "He'll find out what's going on. Thanks, Nate, for keeping an eye open."

"A *friend*?" said Nathaniel, pushing himself off the stone. "A *he*?"

She rolled her eyes at him and headed down the stairs. "Yes, a friend, you dirty-minded thug."

"Are you going to bring him home to meet the family sometime soon?" Nathaniel shouted over the wall. "We wouldn't frighten him *that* much, unless he really deserves it!"

It was easy to ignore Nathaniel, with as much practice as Sasha had. She swept a hand through her hair as the palace wall slipped behind a hedge behind them.

After a moment of silence, the southern guard said shyly, "The wisteria maze, your highness."

She glanced up, startled, and her face broke into a smile. He blushed.

"Yes," she said. "But let me find a friend, first."

A cloth merchant had been to visit the duke. They had talked for a quarter of a bell and then the merchant had left. A cheerful maid had told Will of this, easily. He'd done his best to make friends among the palace staff, for the year that he'd been in the city before Westel had shipped him back to Willow Tree.

Will popped back into her room to let Sasha know. She had a ribbon in her teeth as she cinched up a bodice. She panted at him. "A peaceful private dinner, with half the nobility invited, just so Mother can make a point to other half. Or something; I'm never quite sure." She tied an efficient knot at the top of the bodice, where a bow should go, and dug through a chest of skirts, her pale shift twitching around her feet. "What did you find?"

"Your pigeon guardsman's right," said Will. "John had a private chat with a 'merchant' just after the one bell."

"Do you know what they said?"

"Why would I know what they said?" said Will. "I'm good, but I'm not magic."

Sasha yanked a blue mass of something out of the heap. When she shook it, it revealed itself to be a dress.

"But they didn't talk long," said Will.

She tugged it over her head, disappearing in the swath of fabric. Her head popped through the neck-hole and said, "Hm."

The throne-like chair beside the queen was empty. The king had made his appearance and returned to his study, leaving his Court in the able hands of his wife while he looked after the country.

The queen laid her fingers lightly on the arms of her chair. "Where are my little ones?" Her favorite noblewoman, silvered hair pulled back in an efficient bun, stood at her side. The rest of the Court filled the room with quiet chatter, standing and sitting among the low couches of the softly lit room they'd moved to after the dinner.

The queen's silvered favorite said, "Lia is dancing with John. Your other two are closeted in a bench in the corner, exchanging remarks behind their fans."

"Sarcasm," the queen said with a sigh. "A poor skill in royal women."

Her lady laid her hand sympathetically over the queen's. "They're still young, your majesty."

A painted cat chased the moon on the back of Gabrielle's open fan; a fall of autumn leaves colored Sasha's. "We have to use someone they will believe," said Gabrielle.

"Yes," said Sasha. "But that means convincing *that* person, and we're rather out of people who will believe us."

"They'd believe Lia," said Gabrielle. "And after all she knows him best."

"We've already been down that road," said Sasha, darkly.

Gabrielle made a face at her. "You shouted at her," she said. "It doesn't count."

"She doesn't believe us, and she won't," said Sasha. "There's got to be another way."

"I'm angry with her, too," said Gabrielle. "But Lia's not *stupid*, she's just angry, too."

Sasha made a face. "I'm going to go get a breath of air," said Sasha.

Gabrielle looked over her sister's shoulder at the door to the outside. "I saw some red hair out there."

Sasha grinned. "Elijah's on duty, or so the rosters say." She slipped off the couch and headed for the door.

The cool night was a relief, as was Elijah, who caught sight of her immediately. After Sasha had reported what Will had found, the two of them leaned against the wall. Sasha chewed on her lip.

"It's a check up," said Elijah. "This visitor was the messenger, not the boss."

Sasha leaned back, the fabric of her gown catching on the wall. The blue dress began at a modest silver neckline, gathered at a wide ribbon around her waist and finally fell crinkling down to her boots.

Elijah continued, "They want to make sure John's still scared enough to do what he's supposed to."

"Or maybe the visitor gave John some poison to slip in Mum's supper tonight," said Sasha. "We can't know."

"No, but they wouldn't risk hurting any of you now, not with the marriage still pending." The other guards were on other doors, or hung politely back from the pair. Nathaniel was off duty and elsewhere.

"But are you sure they'd send someone all the way into the palace just to see how John was?" She frowned. "I suppose they've learned not to send *him* out anymore."

"What?" said Elijah. She shook her head. "This is how this man works," Eli explained, "this sort of man. He's careful."

"Who is?" said Sasha.

"Whoever's behind this," said Elijah, shrugging one shoulder.

Sasha frowned at the toes of her boots. "Let's get him more scared," she said. Elijah turned to look at her. "John. If his visitor doesn't come to call, what will he think has happened?"

"That the world has ended," said Elijah. "The sort of folk he's in trouble with always make their dates."

"John's what the whole conspiracy relies on, keeping him scared enough of them to do what they want."

"He's greedy, too," said Elijah stubbornly.

"What?"

"The duke doesn't just get to hide behind *scared*," said Eli. "He doesn't get an excuse."

Sasha shrugged. "So if we break him, we break *them*."

"If his visitor doesn't come, he'll know something's up," said Elijah.

"Yes, but on their side. Something's happened to hurt his scary people. I don't care how frightened he is of them, as long as he's more scared of us."

"Want me to keep the visitor away?"

"I don't want to make trouble for you with the captain."

"Well, Brown's not doing anything to earn his salt," said Elijah. "And it *is* my job. I'll keep him away as long as I can."

"If it happens and there's no noise," said Will the next day, "John'll think Westel's done it."

"Or that the Guard has got to his contact instead," said Sasha. "City or Royal. The important part is that he thinks we've gotten them."

"The Guard makes too much noise," said Will. "If they caught some sort of treasonous fish, they'd have him strung up on the walls by noon. The Royal Guard's worse than the army about noisiness, when it comes to the king."

"And Westel doesn't care as much?" said Sasha.

"Don't get prickly," said Will. Gregory muffled a giggle. "Westel would do *anything* for his majesty, up to and including put up with me. If it's treason, he'll go extra quiet, like, and sneak around in back of them until he can get the hood properly over the traitor's head. Westel doesn't like it when people try to off his king."

"Neither do I," said Sasha.

Elsewhere, Eli and Nate were plotting.

"The problem is the whole underground is scared of Lukas," said Elijah. "It's not feasible to put them all out of commission, just to keep someone from contacting the duke."

"Not feasible?" said Nathaniel.

"We'd need a few more resources," said Elijah. "A good forger, and a boat. What? Yes, I considered it. It was an option. You have to consider all your options."

"And guard all your walls."

The brothers took a break from plotting for a brief wrestling match. (Nathaniel won.)

Elijah said, "So we obstruct whoever of Lukas's men that we can—"

"—the ones we can get in the way of most easily, without attracting attention to it, and the ones he'd be most likely to send, the scary ones," finished Nathaniel. "You talk to

Threefingers, see if the old beggar's heard anything lately. I can query the uncles."

"No," said Elijah. "I'll talk to the uncles. They already think I'm peculiar."

Gregory had added to his collection of stolen palace uniforms. Along with the footman attire Gregory'd snagged for himself his first day, Will had conjured up a messenger's uniform for him, with no legality to the move except for a princess's blessing. It was fancier than home's but lighter and looser than a footman's stiff garb to let the boys and girls of the messenger service sprint through the palace and city.

Gregory tugged down a cap that was much redder than the faded old thing he'd worn at home and felt very far away from his mountains.

But he could live with it. This thick, humid air was breathable enough. He supposed.

"Oy!" said a voice. "Messenger!" A puffing bureaucrat waved him down from an open door—inside Gregory could see desks and chairs, papers and bookshelves, the clockwork parts of a kingdom that governed mountain, valley, and coast.

Gregory slowed, bowed, and approached—this was the palace, surely the secretaries were higher rank than a mountain messenger, except he was masquerading as a palace messenger. And he was friends with a princess—did that count as anything when deciding how deep to bow? He knew nobles had rules about this kind of thing—

In any case, Gregory bowed and the man brandished a folded, sealed paper at him. "This needs to go to the third undersecretary of the minister of trade," he said.

"Yes, sir," said Gregory. He bowed again, backing away, and fell back into the familiar trot of an on-duty messenger.

In an orderly, cork-lined study near the center of the palace, the minister of Intelligence, Westel, was poking holes in Will Rocole's latest report in a biweekly lesson of proper information presentation. Will was poking holes in the minister's patience.

"But this—" Will waggled his finger at a word on the page. "This looks like *suspicious-contact* written in third-and-a-half-level codework, when it implies *safety-hideout* in the second phonetic. Shouldn't someone look into streamlining that? I mean, imagine how confusing that could be."

"They can look at the rest of the report, and see if it's in third-and-a-half or second phonetic," said Westel. "And make a judgment call from there. I have another appointment, Rocole."

Will widened his eyes with eager fervency. "But first-string doesn't have that particular phrasing at all. Someone writing pidgin could bring up all sorts of ruckus that way!"

Westel sighed. "Then write me a report, Rocole. *You* think of a way to streamline it—*and* implement it throughout the ranks. I don't have the time to think about it, or to talk about it with you."

"Uh," said Will.

"I want it on my desk in a week," said Westel, only slightly hiding a cat-smug smile as he sifted through a pile of papers.

"Sir?" said Will. "I have another question?"

"*Yes*," said Westel. He lifted a page, frowned lightly, and laid it on top of a neat stack to his left. He lifted another. "What is it, Rocole?"

"How do you imply a quadruple agent in the circle cipher?"

Westel might have thrown a pen at his young recruit's head, but at that moment a letter had slid under the door. It only took a quirk of the eyebrows for Will to realize he ought to jump over and pick it up. Will handed it to the minister with a flourish and Westel took it impatiently.

I had an informative trip to the city, minister, read the letter in simple, flawed code. Westel squinted, trying to translate the inexperienced hand. *Ask me quietly, at her majesty's evening gathering. You might find it interesting. John.* At the base of the letter was the Silverlake duchy's seal, pressed into matte white wax.

"Nobles," growled Westel. "Must they all be so romantic?"

Outside, Gregory ran with unhurried strides from the office of the minister of intelligence, just an unsuspecting messenger to any watching eyes.

Now, where was the third undersecretary of the minister of trade?

In the one of the city's open markets, Gideon looked at his grinning subordinate doubtfully. "You just want me to walk down the street?"

"Yep. Right past that fellow with the mule and the squint." Nathaniel gestured around the corner, where a travel-stained man was chatting up a fruit stall girl unsuccessfully.

"And this will help Sasha?"

"Yep," said Nate.

Gideon sighed. "Well, I suppose it's not very illegal."

"It's not illegal at *all*," said Nathaniel. "Just try to walk all stern and guard-like. Pretend I just stuck something squishy in Stearnes's boots and you're going to have a talk with me about it."

Gideon considered this. "A frog in his boots, or a jam pie?"

"I would never waste a jam pie on *Stearnes*," said Nathaniel, appalled.

Gideon brushed off his black and silver uniform, squared his shoulders, and walked down the market aisle with his best severe expression. Nathaniel, in street clothes and with a cap over his hair, meandered in his wake, trailing his eyes over stall displays and keeping a child pickpocket from going through his empty back pocket (his coin purse was secured to the inside of his pants, just like his mum had taught him).

When Gideon passed the man with the mule, Gideon slowed a touch, and the man with the mule turned to look tensely in his direction. Gideon narrowed his eyes, then nodded. "I'm sorry," he said. "I mistook you for someone else."

Gideon moved on; and Nathaniel, who had slipped a sealed, travel-worn letter into the tied bundle in the second flap of the mule's pouch, moved on as well, just another man in the crowd.

The man with the mule would not notice the extra letter. He would hand them out to his various seedy friends, one of whom would read that his mother had taken ill and would disappear into the countryside for a three-week round trip.

His mother, who was perfectly hale as far as Nathaniel knew, would surely be happy to see him.

Nathaniel whistled as he continued down the street.

Now, on to the next.

No one had gotten through the gates of the palace to meet the duke, of that Elijah and Nathaniel were sure, and the duke had not left.

Gideon was maintaining a tripled watch on the littlest princess, with the help of men from several squads, and he promised that Brown had not yet officially noticed.

Gabrielle whispered in her sister's ear than the duke had shadows under his eyes and surreptitiously wiped sweaty hands on his doublet, even as he smiled at their sister with elegant grace.

A note from Will and Gregory told Sasha they'd done their part. She found it on her pillow after she had come in late, from a night of noble company under cold, lovely, distant stars. The sky had been framed by the garden's elegant, trimmed and sculpted trees, which were meant for night sky viewing above all.

Sasha tugged out of a corset, feeling trimmed and sculpted herself, rereading the note laid flat on her bedspread. Dropping the corset in the corner next to the silky drape of her overdress, she burnt the note with her bedside candle. She brushed the ashes from her side table and pinched the candle out with wet fingers.

Her heart thrummed in the darkness, noisy and hot. It was spring, not summer, damn it. She tore the blankets off with irritation and jumped up to pace the room, the window's breeze pulling at the billows of her long, pale sleeping pants and loose top. Grumbling a sleepy curse, Sasha tore an overcoat from the closet and leapt out the window.

She knew this part of the Guard roster by heart. Her feet padded quietly up the whitewashed steps than ran along the inside of the palace wall. The torches turned the pale plaster a warm orange and the soot marks an odd deep purple.

"Sasha? It's past midnight."

"I know," she said. "I heard the stupid bell tower." Sasha pulled herself up onto the edge of the wall beside a torch, the fresh breeze off the river and the wall's cold stone seeping into the thin fabric of her pants, sweeping away the lingering, smothering heat of her room. "I couldn't sleep."

"You look like a ghost." Elijah checked each way for an approaching superior, then relaxed his stance a little. "The letter?"

"He got it." She shrugged, shivering a little. "Tomorrow," she said. "We'll see how well we can lie."

Elijah opened his mouth and she slid off her seat with abrupt haste. "Damn stone's worse than the wind," she said. "Sucks the life right out of you." She crossed her arms, cheeks rosy with cold. Elijah linked his hands behind his back. She was so *small*. She would fit right under his

315

chin, if he pulled her close, but that wouldn't be appropriate.

"Tell me about practice," she said. "Has Gideon gotten up his courage to talk to that apple seller girl? Did that skinny fisherlad drop out of the new recruits?" She slid down to sit at the base of the wall's outer edge, her chin lifted to squint up at him.

"They took a walk down by the river last week and nearly got jumped by brigands," said Elijah with a solemn look, betrayed by the laughing crinkles around his eyes. He kept careful attention on the low green slope of the palace hill and the twinkling city lights beyond. "She made him promise to buy her a pasty as penance, on the next market day. The skinny fisherlad did not quit, but that brawly fellow has gone back to his merchant family to settle down for a rewarding life with an abacus."

"Did Gideon use his parade ground voice to chew the brawly one out?" Sasha asked with sleepy glee.

"It was worse—the *quiet* one."

Sasha snickered happily, pulling her overcoat closer about her. Her head started to sag toward her chest.

Eli looked up at bright pinpricks in a blue-black sky and tugged off his uniform jacket. Bending, he settled the heavy folds over the girl. "I'm not asleep yet," she muttered at him. "Leave be."

"Of course you're not," Eli said, tucking the jacket's ends around her feet. Elijah stood and returned to his quiet watch.

The sun rose in the morning to a new shift of guardsmen on the walls and a princess soundly asleep in her bed, her window open to the dawn light.

The day trickled on in quick, anxious minutes and long, anxious heartbeats. The sun set and the stars came out again, shy in the waning rosy light of the sunset.

Sasha sat on a gilded bench in a palace courtyard, moving her feet beneath her skirts in sliding, bent-kneed circles. The courtyard was hung with small tea lights, winking through panes of colored silk, and the tinkling murmur of light noble conversation overpowered the whisper of the leaves in the courtyard's trees. Sasha kept her feet moving in the pattern, meant for circling evasion in a duel.

It was not a large party, but it was an open one. By the time the night was over, every noble in the palace would have stopped by to pay their respects to the queen.

Minister Westel was standing stiffly to one side of the pavilion, eyeing his cup of tea. He had already greeted her majesty. Sasha had said hello to her mother, too.

It was not precisely a ball, but even her majesty's casual evening gatherings could not be ignored. There were rules; Sasha had been told some of them and some she was supposed to figure out for herself, because apparently there were some rules that were just not spoken. She'd mentioned this dilemma once to Nathaniel, when she was a younger child, and the guardsman had looked at her and blinked. "But they're *rules*," Nate'd said. "How are you supposed to break them if you don't what they are?"

The rules said things about which parties one could go to, and which one couldn't, and which one *had* to go to. They also said things about who one should talk to and how deep one should curtsy and what a particular twitch of a fan might mean.

Sasha kept a small knife in her fan sheath.

With a burst of laughter and a burst of color, Lia entered, walking arm in arm with the duchess and the baroness. Sasha lifted her head, feet slowing. The rest of Lia's inner court entered behind them: the count, and the duke with the younger lady politely on one arm.

Westel put down his tea and Sasha stood up, shaking out her skirts.

"Lia, dear," said the queen. "Marie and Gracia, it's lovely to see you."

There was a tap on the duke's shoulder. "Excuse me, but if we might have a word?" said Westel.

The duke smiled at the younger lady and handed her off to the count. "Of course," he said. The duke and Westel stepped to the side. "Did one of your boys find a particularly interesting love letter of mine?" he joked. From across the courtyard, Sasha noticed sourly that he somehow managed to not even look pale.

"You might say that," said Westel.

The duke settled himself on a low wall, casually comfortable. "May I ask what this is about?"

Westel hesitated. "I had meant to ask *you*."

The duke raised an eyebrow.

On the other side of the courtyard, the queen kissed Lia on each cheek and then the princess heir and her ladies drifted away. Sasha moved forward.

"Lia," she said. Her sister turned to look at her. Her tutors had tried to teach Sasha that court mask. Sasha swallowed and raised her chin. "I want to apologize. Could we talk?"

Lia hesitated, surprise showing in the raise of her forehead, and then smiled softly. "Of course." She touched the duchess's arm, nodded to the count, and stepped away from her group.

Sasha drew her farther, toward a corner of the pavilion shaded by a potted tree that made her sneeze. "Can we talk over here?" Her back was to the dull blaze in the sky from the sun, already set.

Sasha hesitated as she walked, looking over her shoulder at her sister. She'd always thought they'd looked very little alike; Lia had been awkward and gangly for a long-limbed adolescent year or two, before she'd gone beautiful. Sasha had never even hit the growth spurt.

Sasha stopped in the small nook at the edge of the pavilion, bundling her hands in long skirts. "I'm sorry I yelled at you," said Sasha. "I shouldn't have." Lia, watching her, obviously agreed. Sasha steeled her chin. "I'm sorry I didn't believe you, Lia. I didn't mean to hurt you, if I did."

Lia folded herself elegantly into the small bench seat beside the potted tree, out of sight of the rest of the pavilion. Even gratefully hidden from the bright attention of the court, Sasha was tense, her fingers knotting anxiously.

"I don't want you to be angry with me," said Sasha, quietly. "But I do want you to listen."

The architects who had designed the palace had obviously loved secrets. Every pavilion had a hidden turn to an out-of-the-way fountain, a bench tucked unnoticed behind a curve in the wall, or a balcony overhead blocked by healthy blankets of ivy. Every servants' path disappeared with quiet efficiency behind hedges and trick walls. There were hidden courtyards, useful for midnight dalliances, of which Lia's friends probably knew every one.

Sasha wondered why the builders had thought it all quite necessary, and thought that while Will probably loved it (if he'd managed yet to lift his head out of his work and notice), Elijah probably liked the twists but not their unimportance.

By the low wall on the east side of the courtyard, Westel was frowning at his tea. "How was your trip to the city?" Westel asked finally. "Perhaps there is something you'd like to discuss?"

The duke slid one foot to the side and looked over his shoulder. "Trip?" he said. He smiled. "I think you're mistaking me for someone else."

Westel frowned. "I'm not looking to play games, boy." Sometimes he missed the army and its directness, the clear and simple hierarchy, the concise reports. "If you have something to say—" The minister halted, scowling over the duke's shoulder. When the duke glanced over his shoulder himself, he saw a slender brown-haired young man enter the pavilion with a slip of paper in his hand.

Westel missed the army *deeply*. Surely they would have been able to whip something of use into even Rocole's head of hot untrustworthy air.

"I'm sorry, sir," said Will when he had gotten close enough, "but I thought this couldn't wait." He hesitated, almost tripping over his feet as he came past a potted tree and saw who the minister was addressing. "But if you want me to…"

Westel twitched an impatient hand at him and Will handed him the paper, not gracefully enough to keep the duke from seeing the ink letters and the holes in the edge of the page.

"It was, uh, coming for *him*, sir," said Will, not quite quietly enough.

"Hmph," said Westel, who hadn't glanced at it. "I'm busy, Rocole." He turned back to the duke, stuffing the paper into pocket.

Will had opened his mouth to protest when Westel frowned and not at him.

Will shut up and took a half step back. When he'd bet on the minister of Intelligence, it wasn't because he'd thought the man was stupid.

"You look pale, John," said Westel.

"I'm a little tired," said the duke. "Could we talk later perhaps, minister?"

"What were we talking about?" said Westel. "Your trip to the city?"

"I haven't been to the city."

Westel looked at Will. "Are you sure?" It was unclear whom he was asking. Will nodded with as much solemn certainty as he could muster and the duke said, "Of course I'm sure."

"Twelve days ago," said Will. "He went to an inn called the Drunken Dog."

The duke spluttered, "I told you, I haven't been to the city since Willow Tree." He took a long breath and frowned thoughtfully. "Twelve days ago—ah, yes, I was with Lia, all that day. You can ask her highness."

Westel glared at Will. "Rocole—"

Will swallowed. "Sir—"

"He wasn't."

Lia stepped out from behind the potted tree, Sasha in the shadows behind her. They had fallen silent half a conversation ago. Lia spoke to

Westel, but looked at John while she did. "He was gone, for two hours in the afternoon, and he had city muck on his shoes when he came back." Her voice was level and soft.

The duke opened his mouth and tried to clean up his messes. "Yes, I went walking with Marie, just ask."

"Did you think I was besotted enough to lie for you?" said Lia. "And I thought you were good at people, John."

The duke paled.

Lia's expression didn't change as she took the sight in. "Marie's not, either, by the way," she told her fiancé calmly. "Besotted, I mean. I wouldn't expect a rescue there."

Lia turned to Sasha, who was trying to contain her crowing glee as the duke's world crashed around him. "That was not an apology," Lia said and walked away with a face like shattering ice.

Sasha stared after her. "Lia—"

The rest of the court was beginning to turn, staring in the wake of the princess heir's exit, at the pale duke and the severe master of the spies.

"Duke John," said Westel. Will noticed it looked like it pained Westel greatly to have to do this in *public*. A new experience was probably good for the old man. "You are under arrest for suspicion of treason, by order of the ministry of Intelligence. Do you have anything to say?"

The duke dropped his head, opened his mouth, then flicked his eyes at the paper tucked in Westel's pocket. The duke raised his head, opened his mouth to speak again, then leapt over the low wall of the pavilion and ran.

There was a collective gasp from the noble audience.

Sasha grabbed her skirts and flung herself off the pavilion after him. "Guards!" said the queen. Sasha heard the creak of the guards' leather armor and the sound of pounding footsteps behind.

Flattened, polished stone flicked under her old, comfortable boots. A few stalks of grass rose up from the crevices, yanked along by the skirts Sasha'd bundled up to let herself run. The duke was stumbling, tearing down the stone path with a speed Sasha didn't know the pampered nobleman had. With long legs and fear John might outrun her, hampered as she was by thick layers of clinging skirts. The guards on the gates didn't know to stop him.

There were only two pairs of footsteps anywhere close behind her, one pounding, one quick and sharp. Sasha pushed her legs faster, bundling up her skirts in her arms.

This was a man who would have seen them all dead. This was a man who could kiss her sister in the gardens, marry her in the vaulted throne room, and close his eyes when armed figures came for her in the night. He had given Gabrielle to a man named Doulings to keep her silent.

324

Sasha was two long steps from him, too far to leap and reach.

The pounding footsteps behind her lengthened their stride, passed her swiftly, and the count tackled the duke to the grassy ground.

The duke landed with a thud, struggling to get up even before he hit ground. Sasha came to a breathless stop as the count levered the duke's arm behind his back, shoving the taller man bodily downward and keeping him there. She was close enough to hear the count hiss in the traitor's ear, as he applied a rather professional arm lock, "My county's on a war front, you arrogant cod."

The duke was still cursing into the ground when the Royal Guard converged around them. Breathing heavily, Elijah fell from a run, to a walk, to a quiet stillness at Sasha's right shoulder. He was hidden just out of the corner of her eye, the only person she'd ever want in her blind spot.

At the pavilion, Westel watched the Guard disappear around the corner, his expression sour. "That was not subtle," he said to Will. "Though it was interesting."

"What wasn't subtle, sir?"

Westel glanced down at the paper in his hand and his eyebrows knit together as he read the coded letter Sasha had stolen from Doulings's desk. The minister glanced up at Will. "This was important—*very*—but not urgent. This did not have to happen *here*."

"It wasn't urgent?" said Will, innocently.

Westel scowled at him. "No, it wasn't, Rocole. He was not going to do anything *tonight*." He shook the paper. "This thing doesn't even prove anything!"

Will peered at the letter. "Well, it's not within my clearance, you see, sir. That code, I mean. I can't read it. I thought I should get it to the proper authorities *as soon as possible*, to see if it *did* say anything urgent." Will said it very earnestly.

His minister looked at him sourly. "I have to go deal with this," said Westel, thrusting the paper at Will and stalking away.

Will whistled cheerily, following. "Can I help, sir?"

"*No*."

Elsewhere, standing behind a princess in the empty pathway where a count had tackled a duke and the Royal Guard had taken the duke away, a redheaded guardsman froze and said, "Idiot." Elijah repeated to himself, "*Idiot*," and took off at a run.

"I'm still catching my breath," growled Sasha and went after him. "What is it, Eli? We didn't catch the wrong one, did we?"

"They're all on duty," said Elijah.

"What?"

"Gideon, Nathaniel, all of Second, that fellow Ferdy from Fourth who Gideon wrapped into it, all the others. I didn't realize the connection before." Elijah was barely looking at

326

the ground in front of him, fingers twitching slightly as he constructed a framework in his mind, reviewed the day's schedule, drew the circles of protection, the gaps in the walls. "They're all on official duties, the ones who have been guarding Gabrielle."

Fear wrapped itself around the threads of Sasha's throat, freezing her breath while the rest of her burned from the run. "So who's guarding Gabrielle? Just one guard?" She shook her head. "But it's just for one shift. What are the odds that someone would attack right *now*?"

Elijah growled, short of breath, "The odds that every single person willing to help with the extra guard on her happens to be either on wall duty or guarding your mother's party for this *one* shift? Those are quite slim." He pushed himself faster. "She should be in her room, has a tutor this evening."

Sasha thought about Gabrielle, the way she hid smirks behind a fan held by small, soft child's hands. She lengthened her strides, heart jumping with dread, lungs and throat burning. What was the *point* of Sasha, if she couldn't keep her sister safe?

She fumbled at the lacings on her overdress, whipping the heavily-embroidered wad of fabric off. Its edges rippled and fluttered as it sank in the quick arc of a fall and tangled into the bushes at the edge of the path that led to the royal apartments.

Sasha had a tiny knife in her fan case and a longer one down one boot. "Why don't you carry a baton?" she asked Elijah, gasping in quick bursts beneath her damned corset. "I need a longer weapon."

They slid to a stop in front of Gabrielle's suite of rooms. Elijah drew his short sword from his belt with two fingers and offered it hilt-first behind him to Sasha, stepping forward to eye the door, listening for any sound of struggle within.

"Your sword," she hissed back. "I'm not taking it."

Elijah gave her an aggrieved look. "Why not?"

Sasha moved forward, heart simultaneously leaping and breaking at the silence and its implications. The door was locked. She went for her lock picks but Elijah slipped past her and shattered the front window with a decorative rock. With his sword drawn and his jacket tossed over the sharp glass left on the sill, Elijah leapt inside. Sasha followed, knife out and ready.

The room was silent. It was unmussed, no carpets askew, no chairs knocked over. The line of quills on Gabrielle's desk had been laid out perfectly parallel by twelve-and-a-half year old hands.

Elijah raised a finger to his lips and then ghosted forward to check the back rooms, inching up beside the door and then moving quickly inside, sword first. He came back a moment later, confused. He resheathed his sword. "No one's here."

Sasha twisted her knife in her hand and then froze. "Which tutor, Eli? Which tutor?"

"History," he said. "Politics, something like that."

"No," said Sasha, took his shirtsleeve in one hand and climbed back out the window with him. "She doesn't need a politics tutor, she's Gabrielle. She lets him spend the time to work on his research paper. They'll be in the library archives."

Elijah took the information in, edited the framework in his mind, and raced after her. He said, "It didn't look like anyone else had been there and found her missing. The door wasn't forced."

Sasha huffed a strained breath. "So maybe we're overreacting? Maybe no one's trying for her tonight."

"Or maybe they knew where to go the first time." Elijah added darkly, "They'll have done their research."

They ran.

"He came in to see John, but he was scouting, too. *Idiot*," said Elijah, who had stopped talking to Sasha awhile back and now was just muttering under his breath. "Idiot, you know how they work. Lay of the land; but they've got to have someone inside, too, to know she wouldn't be where everyone thought she would be, to know which guards to put on duty and away from her…"

"Who was scouting?" Sasha demanded.

"The city 'sassin who came to scare John," said Elijah.

"The *what*? All you said was 'suspicious character'!"

"I'm suspicious when a killer walks under my gate, yes," he said. They bickered quickly and quietly, strained, over which short cut to the library was quicker through the maze of hidden servant's trails and lovers' courtyards.

Sasha had managed to save one sister from a scared, greedy conspirator, but now the other was deep in the archives, with only one guard—her *little* sister, who knew too much about trade agreement subclauses, and ministry politics, and rebel assassins' plots, who was too brave and too clever, who had quill-nub calluses her right hand's second finger and a nose too cute and button-like to thrust snidely in the air, though she did it anyway because she thought she was smarter than everyone else, even if sometimes she was; a little sister whose only importance to the men trying to kill her was the blood in her veins and the fact that she knew too much about *them*.

Sasha left a flouncy underskirt puddled at the base of a sycamore tree. She loosened her corset as she ran, stumbling with haste, her faithful boots stumbling over mosaic tile paths, her fingers stumbling over taut silk ribbon, trying to find the room to breathe.

The library rose, all wide glass windows and whitewashed pillars. Elijah shoved through an unlocked side door, Sasha close behind. The main library room was warm with candlelight and quiet except for the scratch of quills. Over the edges of books, scrolls and stacks of paper wide pairs of eyes watched the half-dressed princess and her guardsman run full speed through the room and towards the door that opened onto the stairwell that led down the archives. One scribe's apprentice goggled and squeaked; the more intense scholars never even looked up, their spectacled eyes pressed close to the inked pages.

"I'll go high," said Elijah, "You go low," and he kicked open the archive's stairwell door. Sasha darted in below his raised sword, knife flashing in her fist.

There was a black and silver guardsman dead on the stairs. He was sprawled across the steps, arm at an impossible angle underneath him, scraggly beard pushed flat against the smooth stone stair. The dark wet hollow on his chest had stopped bleeding. Sasha stared, gasping for air. She could taste the acrid scent of burning paint on her tongue.

"No," said Sasha, and took the stairs three at a time. Her limbs were burning. Her knuckles were white around her knife hilt with the thought of things that couldn't *couldn't* be true. "Gabrielle!" She couldn't hear Elijah's footfalls behind her through the roaring in her ears. Sasha flew into the archives, the smell of wood and paper and oiled leather book covers mixing with the sharp, clean scent of fresh blood.

The guard on the stairs had been dead for far longer than it would take for an assassin to go down into the archives, find a princess, and slit her throat among the high bookshelves.

"Gabrielle!" Sasha tore around bookshelves and long tables, down carefully tended hallways of knowledge, looking for dark curls tossed into the shadows like garbage, still and silent as the books on the shelves. Maybe if she ran fast enough, maybe if she stopped crying, maybe if she listened harder for the sound of a brave little girl fighting back—

Somewhere in the archives, sword crashed on sword.

Sasha didn't know the maze of the archives, but apparently Elijah did because he grabbed her arm and pulled her left, darting around bookshelves towards the sound of weapons.

In the shadows where a bookshelf met the wall, a girl with a head of dark curls had been tossed, like she was something precious to be guarded.

Gabrielle huddled in the corner while the redhead in front of her fended off the two assassins with a sword in one hand and a long dagger in the other.

"What took you two so long?" said Nathaniel and grinned cockily, tired and desperate. He had a cut down one cheek, a slice across his chest and blood dripping down his left arm (his knife arm). Gabrielle made a sound of desperate relief, her hands pressed over her mouth. Her tutor appeared to have fainted at her feet awhile back.

The two assassins eyed the newcomers over weapons that were shining and well-tended, wicked sharp. One grinned thinly. "A *girl*," said the assassin, a short sword in each hand. "I'll take these two."

A short laugh and the remaining city killer pressed Nathaniel forward. "Your cavalry's not quite enough, kid," he told him.

Nate's bleeding left arm was shaking and weak; his knife dropped from his fingers and clattered to the floor, but he raised his sword. "C'mon, bud," Nate said. "Who needs cavalry?"

The assassin with the two short swords swung them both, stalking toward Elijah and Sasha. They glanced at each other once and then they darted in, he high, her low. She went for a belly cut while Eli blocked the right-hand sword; she had to swing her weapon up and dart away to avoid the left.

Sasha circled back as Elijah parried blows with the assassin, looking for a chance to jump in and strike. She scored a deep slash around his back, which made him howl with rage, but then the other killer broke by Nathaniel's guard.

"*Nate!*" roared Elijah as his brother sagged against the bookshelf, red blossoming on one temple, staining half his face, running rivulets down and pooling in the pocket of his collarbone. The killer pushed past Nathaniel and towards the little princess, raising his blade.

Gabrielle squeaked and darted out of her corner and down between the wall and the long table that ran beside it. She ran, but her foot caught on a chair that hadn't quite been pushed back under the table. Gabrielle went flying, falling to her knees and skidding. The killer grinned.

Sasha threw herself away from Elijah's fight and surged towards her sister's attacker, threw a knife that sliced across the man's thigh but didn't slow him down any—but Sasha was on the wrong side of the long table and too slow.

Gabrielle scrambled to push herself up. The assassin lunged forward, knife flashing— and Gabrielle grabbed the chair that had tripped her and threw it at the assassin's head.

It banged off his shoulder; he stumbled backwards and then growled a curse and advanced. Sasha stepped up onto an askew chair, onto the smooth, flat tabletop, and then lunged forward and tackled him.

Sasha hadn't checked her momentum at all in the lunge, so she went head over heels and tumbled into the wall, killer in tow. She heard several of his ribs snap as they slammed down onto the floor together. She didn't bother scrambling to her feet and instead slammed her elbows across the man's face. He wheezed, nose broken and face bloody, eyes fluttering shut.

A ripping sound made Sasha jump and

then Gabrielle tossed her several thick strips of underskirt. Sasha gulped in breath, nodded, and rolled the man over to get his hands behind his back. His struggles were the half-hearted attempts of a mostly unconscious man nauseous with injury.

The rest of the room was quiet, no sounds of a fight. Sasha scrambled quickly to her feet, drawing her little fan knife. Elijah had Nate's jacket bundled up and pressed to his brother's bleeding head; a dark lump had been left in the shadows below a high bookshelf, two shining short swords tossed beside it like garbage.

"Sash?" Eli called. He checked that Nate could hold his jacket himself, and then bent to start tying the ankles and wrists of his unconscious opponent.

"All good," she said, staring at the knife Harston had given her when she turned eleven, slick with another person's blood. Her knuckles were smeared; there was a red speck on Gabrielle's cheek, looking old and dried enough to be from the guard they'd found in the stairwell. Sasha felt a small hand wrap around her elbow and Gabrielle pulled her away.

"We can send someone down for them," said Elijah, grim, an eye on the blood on Nate's face. He helped the waking, quaking tutor stand. "I'm sure Brown will have questions."

Somewhere else in the darkness of the archives, a man named Doulings counted foes and then retreated further into the back bookcases to listen to them gather close and move for the exit. He had recognized the brown haired princess and the younger redheaded guard from Willow Trees passages. "That's the second time you've been trouble," the thin man murmured to himself; he would not forget.

He said *second* and not *third* because Doulings did not yet know his duke was in a small, unmarked room with the minister of Intelligence and the captain of the Royal Guard. He did not know yet that John was whispering, ragged and weary, desperate, "The Dog. They're at the inn called the Drunken Dog."

The two princesses and the two guardsmen moved up out of the archives with jumpy, exhausted caution, past the two bound but breathing killers, past the Royal guard on the stairs. Gabrielle squeezed Sasha's hand so hard as they passed him that she lost feeling in her fingers, but she didn't say anything.

They gave the tutor to a few of his fellow scholars in the main library. They tracked down the nearest messenger and sent him to Brown to let him know he had two criminals to interrogate tied up in the library archives, and then they made their way to Sasha's suite of rooms, eager to be inside four guardable walls.

Nathaniel kept his jacket pressed to his head. The bleeding was garish, but the wound was shallow. "Head wounds bleed," Nate'd told Gabrielle, who'd looked about to faint at the sight of him.

"How were you there, Nate? You were on wall duty," said Elijah, not entirely managing to mask his relief with rule-abiding disapproval.

"And?" said Nathaniel. "This totally trumps that."

"But how did you know where Gabrielle was? We tried her room, first."

"Because you've memorized her schedule or something?" Nate shook his head, then winced and stopped. "See, Eli," he said, settling for a superior, annoying grin instead. "You do charts and take notes, but *I* do people." Nathaniel shrugged as they reached Sasha's suite. "I saw them go under the next gate over and head toward the library. I assumed they weren't there for literature." He trailed off, pale.

"Nate?" Sasha said. They stood at the doorway, Sasha fumbling for the lock with hands she refused to admit were still shaking.

"I can hold," Nathaniel told her. His colors were all pale, silver and black except for the vibrant red streaks of hair and injuries.

"Until Brown sends reinforcements, probably," Elijah agreed, eyeing him clinically.

Nate grinned at him. "I see where your priorities lie." He told Sasha, "We'll hold, and you're a mess. So shoo."

Gabrielle's slender shoulders were shivering, but her hand firmed on Sasha's. Gabrielle pulled her sister through the door when she would've protested. "They're big boys," she told Sasha sternly. "And you don't want Mother seeing you like this, no matter the extenuating circumstance."

"What does extenuating even *mean*?" Sasha demanded, but she sagged into a chair with a sigh.

Sasha's loosened corset was splashed with blood across the front and the neck and hem of her pale shift were stained and spattered with it. Gabrielle eased her out of it and helped scrub her down with clean cloths.

They did Sasha back up again in silk and ribbons. The moment Sasha was clean and clothed, she caught Gabrielle by the shoulders and buried her face in her dark curls. Gabrielle wrapped her arms around her big sister's middle and stopped trying not to shake. They sat there like that until Gabrielle had stilled and Sasha felt like she had finally caught her breath.

Nathaniel stood guard outside, while Elijah stood guard in the center of the sitting room, holding the knife he'd pulled out of the assassin before they'd left the archives. Eli cleaned Sasha's knife with a handkerchief in slow, even movements, scrubbing at the shining metal and smooth-worn leather long after all traces of blood had been wiped away.

When Brown sent men down to the library archives ten minutes later, they found two bound assassins, right where they'd been told they'd be. Their throats had been slit.

Doulings was already on his way back to the city streets, whistling as he went.

Andrea made her way through the crowds a little uncertainly. There was so much noise after Willow Tree, though if she admitted that to her brothers they'd laugh her back to the little castle—except maybe Pieter, who might understand that.

Quant though—Quant would definitely laugh.

The market was thick with dust and sweat, with the sweet smell of spring herbs and baking pastry. A flower seller nodded at her with a smile. "What were you, sick all winter, Andie? The boys have been doing your chores."

"I'm almost better," she said.

Andrea whisked her braid over her shoulder with a fierce nod and pushed through the crowd with accustomed brashness. She was a rebel, a patriot of Ceren. A little noise wouldn't scare her.

Andrea placed the order at the brewery first and paid the last week's bill. The brewer's lads, who would be delivering the heavy barrels, loitered in the front shop while she talked to their father. How did the man ever get anything done? They stopped to loiter and chat in the Dog when they delivered, too. Andrea would flick her braid when they did, scrub the tables down fiercely and ignore them.

Andrea poked her nose in a little spice shop; she'd passed it once or twice since she'd gotten back. The owner, foreign and shy, blinked and beamed as she sniffed the air, uncertain, and fingered the coin purse Charlie had given her.

From there, she went on to the butcher's. The Dog's customary order was already wrapped, a hefty weight of cheap stew meat. Andrea gave the butcher his payment and a smile and, turning down his offer of assistance, started hauling the white paper-wrapped package home.

The first time Charlie had sent a much smaller Andrea all on her own to lug the week's stew meat back home, the butcher had babbled misplaced concern. Maybe she'd sweated and cursed the whole way back, but she *had* made it. And she was seventeen now, not twelve. He should really stop fretting.

Though when Andrea saw the Dog in the distance, she might admit to a single sigh of relief. She pushed her feet a little harder until she swept through the front door. It was late afternoon, the Dog closed and dark before the supper rush. Andrea dropped the meat inside on the kitchen counter and paced back out into the main room.

"Charlie!" The boys were off somewhere—Koen had flour to fetch; Pieter had gotten a second part time job over winter; it was Quant and Nik's afternoon off. "I want to show you something!"

The innkeeper came out of the study he used to squint over finances—the Dog's, and the rebellion's. Andrea rolled her eyes, smiling. Charlie was still wearing his barkeep's apron, rumpled from the day's work.

Upstairs in the inn, Doulings moved to his desk, opening drawers and idly sorting through papers. Yohan looked at him uneasily; the Cerens didn't understand the man's obsession with pen and ink.

Doulings's fingers paused over a stack, and he went through it again, counting carefully. He put his long fingers on the desk and stood up, slowly.

In the tavern on the ground floor, the sound of feet marching in unison brought Andrea to sudden awareness. She dropped her packet of spices on the bar counter and ran to the open door. Silver and black—the Royal Guard, on a city street, coming towards the Dog.

"Charlie!" Andrea shouted over her shoulder, with a serving girl's bored volume, not a rebel's panic, or as best as she could manage. She jerked her head to the door.

An officer stepped onto the doorway. "We have orders to search these premises. No one may leave the building until we are finished." He turned to Charlie who, stepping forward, beamed amiably at him. "Where is room number eight?"

Andrea was already two thirds of the way up the stairs by the time he finished speaking. A moment later, she burst into

Doulings' room. "The Guard's here. Come quick, get out of here. They're searching this room especially!" she screeched when Yohan didn't move. "Get out, all of you."

"But they're downstairs," Doulings said after her, more calculation than panic rising in his voice, as she turned out of the room and ran down the hallway. At the second door from the end she stopped. Instead of unlocking the door, she knelt down and unlocked the hidden trapdoor with a key she'd snatched from behind the bar.

"In, get in," Andrea hissed, gesturing to them. Charlie might be able to delay the guards for a while, but not for very long.

Doulings leapt in. Andrea started down the dim, narrow staircase, but then she heard footsteps behind her, on the main stairs. She turned, not sure what to do—go down or come back up—but Yohan solved her dilemma. Yohan shoved her down the hole and closed the trap door above her. Andrea rolled down the stairs painfully, cracking her head against the wall.

Andrea struggled up to her feet, swaying unsteadily. She tried to jump for the trap door, to hammer on it, to open it, but Doulings grabbed her arms and clamped his hand over her mouth. "Shut up," Doulings hissed. "You're going to get us both killed." She struggled against his hold, but he had her pinned.

Footsteps—heavy, thunking footsteps from thick boots, like those the Guard wore—sounded above her head. Andrea heard Yohan's voice, and the guards'. The open door to room number eight ought to be enough to condemn him—that was how Nerian justice worked.

More footsteps—it sounded like Yohan tried to make a run for it. There was a sound of a struggle and a body hitting the floor and thrashing about in a vain attempt to get free. The officer's voice barked something out and Yohan was dragged away. Andrea had stopped struggling.

When they could no longer hear the guards, Doulings released her. She jerked out of his hold, glared fiercely at him, and did her best to rub at her eyes with her sleeve. Andrea slammed her hand so hard against the wooden stairs the knuckles split, then walked further down the darkness of the passage, blaming any tears on the pain.

Chapter Ten
The Scars that Remain

His Majesty's dungeon was a small polite building near the center of the palace. The whitewashed building, trimmed with neat rows of pansies, had one room on the ground level and one flight of stairs, going downward. A pair of guards stood at the outer door, and a third kept watch at the entrance to the stairs.

Down the stairs was a long hallway. Cold oozed through the walls and dirt, the underground air damp on the skin. Thick wooden doors lined the hallway with slots in their bases to shove food through and small barred windows at eye's height. Each prisoner had a small square of cold ground, a thin pallet, and a chamberpot. Beyond the fifth door on the left, a dark haired duke was sleeping fitfully.

"John," said a voice from the darkness of the hall.

The man in the cell jerked awake. John was not a naturally light sleeper, but sleeping on a thin straw pallet, behind a locked door, had made him so the last few nights.

"John," said the voice in the darkness. "Have they told you they're going to hang you?"

The duke sat up and stared out. "Lia?"

"No. Not Lia."

"Yes," said the duke. "They've told me. I know what the penalty for treason is."

"Are you sorry?" asked the voice.

"I don't want to die," said the duke. "I don't want to *die*. Of course I don't want to die."

"But are you sorry?" asked the voice, as though throwing him a last line in the darkness, intent and desperate behind pretended indifference. "If you hadn't gotten caught, would you have been sorry?"

He was pale, even in the darkness. "I had to. I owed them money once, couldn't pay it—so I paid them in a favor instead. And again, and again. Some of the favors were ugly, so by the time they came to me about this—they could have said a dozen things to the Guard, to my father, that would have ruined me entirely. There wasn't a way out, except to work with them."

"You could have said no."

"They would have killed me, or gotten me exiled."

"You were going to let a lot of people get killed."

"Not Lia," he whispered. "I was going to keep her safe. I—I am sorry, about the little

346

ones, and their majesties, but what could I do?" He put his head in his hands. "What could I do? I didn't want to die. It's not my fault, and I was going to keep her safe, at least. I was going to try. What more could I have done?"

Outside the cell, standing in the hallway with bits of prison straw scattered on the floor, someone stood with one hand against the door as she listened to the man crying quietly inside.

"They were lying to you," she said. "They would've killed Lia, too." The duke didn't raise his head. "But you knew they were lying, didn't you, John? You *knew*."

"What else could I have done?" came the whisper, but by then the hallway was empty.

"Lia!" came the ringing cry, accompanied by dainty thuds of the baroness's fist on the princess heir's door. "Let us in. Let us in at once."

The door creaked open. "Yes?" said Lia. The baroness, the duchess, and the count stood outside.

The baroness smothered her in a hug and then looked at her severely. "You're pale as snow. Have you eaten at *all* today, your highness?"

"I told her to let you be," said Dereck, shyly. "Are you well?"

"Of course she's not *well*," said the baroness. "But it's not to be dealt with by hiding her head in the sand like one of those silly desert birds. We're going for a stroll. Get your girl to do your hair and put a little powder on, my dear."

"If she doesn't want to," began the count.

"It will be good for her," said the baroness with a sniff.

Lia kissed the baroness on the cheek. "Thank you," she said, "but I am very tired," and she shut the door in their faces.

Lia put the back of her head against the door and listened to the sounds of friendly bickering and ruffled feathers. After a few moments, the sound faded away as the baroness went off in a huff and then the count, sighing relief, went the other way. Lia pushed her fingers through her long hair, running them over her scalp.

A quiet tap sounded the doorframe. Lia stood and turned around. The knock came again, the slow somber version of a gleeful rhythm pounded out when a certain noblewoman came to kidnap Lia for a night jumping from young noble apartment to young noble apartment, or crashing a stately dinner of merchant lords and their eager, flatterer sons and making smiles behind their fans. Lia opened the door.

"I knew," said the duchess. She was watching her feet and her hands were bundled up in her skirt, looking very small in the doorway. The duchess raised her head.

Lia took an uncertain step back. The duchess stepped past her, into the room, and closed the door behind her. She said it again. "I *knew*. Lia, I am so sorry."

"You can't have known." Lia shook her head, faintly.

"I know everything, remember?" she said with a half a smile. The duchess shook her head. "I didn't know all of it. But I knew about the debts, and I knew he was desperate. I didn't know he was this desperate. I didn't know he had a heart that would ever let him see *this* as a solution."

"Neither did I."

"Lia—" The duchess's voice almost broke. She clasped her hands behind her back and unclasped them. "I was keeping his secret, but I shouldn't have. I shouldn't have kept it from you. We'd go out to town—he's awful at the tables, and he's worse at cards, and he's worst at knowing when he should just turn around and go home. His father cut him off months ago." She paced the room, small hands fisted in her skirts, raising them up now and again to push through her tight little curls. "He got in deep, with some dark folk, but I didn't want—it was *his* business, Lia. I thought he'd grow up, settle down, once he married you." The duchess looked to her friend for something like forgiveness and looked away. "It was his secret, not mine, but maybe it *was* yours, and I should have— But I shouldn't have kept it from you. I'm sorry. I'm so sorry I didn't warn you."

"Marie," said Lia.

"I *hate* what he did," said the duchess. "I hate seeing you this sad and I hate him and I hate me for helping."

"Marie," said Lia. "It's alright."

"I should've done—*something*. Lia, I'm sorry. I can't—I don't—"

Lia took two steps forward and wrapped her arms around the duchess, who sniffed into her shoulder. Lia smiled into the dark curls, a little wetly. "And you say you don't care."

It wasn't that funny, but they giggled into each other's shoulders until they were gasping for breath.

The office of the Captain of the Royal Guard was a sizable, tidy space in a wing near to the barracks. It did not compare to the minister of War's, but it was at least quite significant in contrast to an army captain's broom closet of a working space.

Sasha had walked in very quietly. Brown didn't look up from the expense report he was writing until she clicked the door shut behind her.

Brown's face furrowed, puckered into a question mark, and then furrowed again. "Your highness."

"Captain Brown," said Sasha. She sat down comfortably on the square chair in front of his desk. "Harston's desk was always very tidy, too," she said as she crossed her legs beneath her petticoats. "Perhaps it's a Guard trait."

"My deepest apologies, princess, but I'm afraid I'm quite busy."

"That's very admirable of you," said Sasha. "The royal family appreciates your dedication to our safety."

"I'm glad," Brown said warily. "If you would excuse me, then, your highness?"

"No," said Sasha. "I have some things I need to say to you." She crossed her hands in her lap and looked at him, chewing her lip. "I can't take on the captain of the Guard," said Sasha. "If he says I can't practice, if he keeps Second off my watches, I can't argue. But I can take on Frederick Brown."

There was a moment of honest surprise before Brown reined it in to a chill, superior stare. "I don't think I agree," Brown said. "Your highness, you haven't the authority to replace me."

"No," said Sasha. "But I can tell my father you knew about the conspiracy for weeks before you arrested anyone."

"I did not."

"You knew one of the noblemen was involved, and you were too afraid of something happening to your own hide to act. I can't destroy you, but I can certainly stop you from being captain."

"Are you threatening me? I don't respond to blackmail."

"*Good*," said Sasha. "I wouldn't want my Guard captain to. I'm not trying to blackmail you—I'm trying to get you to *do your job*."

"That's still blackmail. And I *am* doing my job."

"Not well," said Sasha. "Next time a little girl in your charge asks you to protect her, you do so. You made a mistake here, sir. I don't want you to ever leave her undefended again. Protect my family, captain. Those are my demands."

The captain squared his chin defensively. "I was being sensible," said Brown. "She is *twelve*. No one could have expected…what happened."

"She's twelve and a half and she's my little sister and you're supposed to keep her *safe*."

Brown's hands went to a stack of papers, straightening it with a tap. "I have already sworn my duties to your father—"

"Promise *me* you will take care of them."

Her voice had almost broken on that, but Sasha covered it with a fierce glare. Brown raised his head and looked at her, her stubborn chin, her tired eyes, the thin scar on one cheek. She looked back.

"I promise," Brown said, very quietly. "But not the blackmailer. I won't promise her anything." She blushed and he went on, "Not the princess, either." Sasha looked up. "But to the daughter that you are, to the sister you are—I promise you, I will do my best."

"Thank you," Sasha said, and stood.

"What about you?" said Brown.

She stopped with her hand on the doorknob. "Let me practice with Second," said Sasha. "I'll take care of myself."

Brown nodded slowly, eyes on the scar on her cheek, the calluses on her hands. "I think maybe you're right. But I never said that, your highness, if anyone asks."

She smiled over her shoulder at him and left what had once been Sir Harston's office.

A few scattered grey clouds promised drizzling moments of rain, but the wind was warm for spring. Sasha spotted two familiar figures on the palace walk.

"Lia!" Sasha hiked up her skirts and ran across the lawn. Lia leaned on the duchess's arm and looked at her. Her hair was a long fall of dark brown; her face was a mask of careful courtesy.

"Lia," said Sasha. "I'm sorry. I didn't mean to hurt you. I think I did the right thing, but I didn't mean to hurt you."

Lia's hand tightened on Marie's arm, and then her face relaxed into a long sigh. Lia stepped forward to kiss Sasha on the forehead. "You're not the one who did."

The mornings were beginning to lighten again. Of course, half the morning practices this winter had been held in the Willow Tree mess hall with torches that looked the same before sunrise and after. But it was good to be in open air again, and to notice the turn of seasons.

When Elijah had finished jostling his big brother awake and stepped out of the two-storey wooden barracks house and onto the careful dirt square of the practice yard, there was a grey lightness to the sky. The scraggly oak was in one corner, twig branches catching the light and shadow. Gideon was checking over practice swords. The rest of the squad was gathering sleepily. A smallish, female figure in practice gear was standing on the field, grinning at him.

Elijah stopped where he stood, and then he grinned back.

The lumpy mattress that was the focal point of Will's room in the city was thin and uncomfortable, but the floor, where Will had been sleeping since Gregory had come, was much worse. Gregory lay on his stomach on the mattress and looked at the blank paper in front of him.

There was a crumpled paper beside him, with lines drawn out and scribbled over, crooked. Gregory heard Will enter the room, but kept squinting. "Ungh," Gregory said.

Will crouched down to look at the crumpled paper. "Maps?" he said. He tilted his head at the markings. "That's Willow Tree. I think."

"It doesn't look right," said Gregory. "I know what they're like in my head, but I can't put them on paper."

"Want some help?"

Gregory shrugged. "It's alright. I just wanted to make sure I hadn't forgotten."

Will squatted down next to him, reaching for the quill. "Let's see if I have."

Gregory shook his head. "I'm trying to write a letter to Cook," he said. "I just got fed up and tried mapmaking instead, until I got fed up with that."

"Writing to Cook?" said Will.

Gregory shrugged again, switching the quill form one hand to the other. "To let everyone know not to worry, if I don't come home right away."

"Gregory..."

Gregory sniffed haughtily and scrawled out *Cook* in big letters at the top of the page. "You'll just get in trouble if I'm not here to watch your back."

Will rocked back on his heels while Gregory stared at the paper and tried to pretend he was thinking about sentences.

"I'm still going to get in trouble," Will said finally. "That Sasha kid, she's bad news." He was grinning. Gregory wrote out *I am well and in the capital* before he had to drop the act and grin widely back.

"I knew it," Will said. "I knew you'd get worn down eventually." Gregory rolled his eyes at him. Will rubbed his hands together with distracted glee. He said to himself thoughtfully, "If I talk to Westel about letting you join the ministry, will that make it more or less likely for him to say yes?"

Gregory cleared his throat. "Actually, Will, I'm not joining the spies."

Will looked confused for a moment, and then cleared his face. "Don't worry, I'll find some way to—"

"Don't, Will," Gregory said. "I don't want to join the ministry."

"But, you—"

"I, what? I find secret passages, but there aren't any here for me to find. I pull pranks with my best friend, but I don't have to be a spy to do that."

"I don't understand," said Will.

"We're friends, Will, right?"

"Always." Will sounded shocked at the question's existence.

"But we're different people. I spent a lot of time trying to be just like you, but I'm not and I never will be. I'm *me*, and I want to do something that's *mine*. I'm not a spy, Will." Gregory grinned. "I'm just a spy's mouse."

There was a knock on the door. Will got up to open it while Gregory pulled himself into a seated position. In the open doorway, Sasha glared. "Check who it is before you open the door," she said, shaking her finger at him as she stepped inside. "Don't you know what part of town you live in? Hello, Gregory."

Gregory put his letter to the side to dry. "Hello Sasha." She grinned at him from under her battered cap. It was good to see her in normal clothes again.

Sasha leaned on the door frame. "Want to see the best view in the city?"

It was at the height of the market day and the noise from sellers shouting their wares, customers haggling over profits, and children scampering underfoot inundated the square. Farmers and merchants had come from many miles around to set up shop here, in the heart of the capital city.

A trio walked together between two rows of stalls. Few paid them any attention; their clothes warned they would not be buying much of anything that did not come from the two-day-old pastry box at the bakery.

The tallest was a gangly brunet. The next, a few years younger, hid under brown curls and behind dark eyes. His brown skin stood out far less here than it ever had at home and Gregory curled into that thought, grateful for some little blessing. The third appeared to be a scrawny boy, who wore a bulky cap.

Sasha pulled the other two through the crowd. Will was starting to get the feel for maneuvering in crowds, but Gregory—well, she kept to the side roads as much as she could.

The bell tower rose out of the center of the main market square, looming brick, stone, and greening metal. Gregory eyed the ornate door to its stairwell suspiciously. "Sasha, I don't think they're going to let us in there."

"You're right," she said brightly.

"I'm frightened," Gregory said. "You're smiling."

Sasha tugged them behind a bakery. Smoke from the great stone ovens slanted in the wind, trailing upward and away. She made her way up a sturdy trellis, an eye on the bakery's back door. She disappeared over the lip of the roof and then stuck her head back over, waving at them. Will clambered up the trellis after her. Gregory gave a long, weary sigh and followed.

The wind was a little stronger on the roof, whistling through mostly open air, rising warm from the plaza floor. Gregory gripped the tile and scuttled crouched-over after them. Sasha lowered herself down to a high fence, tiptoed across it, and climbed onto another, steeper roof.

"You're kidding," said Gregory. He crawled across the high fence, wobbly-kneed. Will fared about the same, but laughed while he did it.

The next roof rose close and high enough that Sasha could leap for the stone and brick buttresses of the clock tower. She got herself settled on a protruding, carved slab of stone, then reached back and down to pull the boys up.

"The view's even better the next ledge up," she said. Will stood eagerly, looking out over the city rooftops.

"I like *this* ledge," said Gregory.

Sasha laughed. She gripped the side of the building with one hand and leaned out, her toes pressed into the edge of the carved whorls of

358

rock. The wind tugged at her, sweeping dust over the toes of her boots.

"Doulings has disappeared from the inn," said Sasha. "I want to find him, and to find whoever else he was working with in the city."

"You're worried he might try again?" said Will.

"That's one reason." Gregory pulled his knees in under his chin. "But she's after him because he tried at all."

Sasha stood with her back to them, looking out over the city. "He's dangerous. He might try again." The knuckles of the hand holding her to the tower were white. "But— you're right. He's responsible for Harston's death. He got my captain killed."

The wind must be blowing west; the smoke from the bakery was getting in her eyes. Sasha could smell it too, on the air, but it smelled more like burning paper than burning bread. Her fingers were pressed tight into the brick grooves of the wall as she leaned out farther over the drop at her feet.

She said, "I'm not asking you to help. I couldn't ask you to cross Westel again, Will, and, Gregory, I know you want to go home. But if you hear anything, or see something suspicious, or—would you let me know?"

"You think I'm afraid of Westel?" Will demanded.

There was a careful rustle behind her as Gregory rose shakily to his feet and took a wobbly step forward. "I'm not going anywhere," he said.

She whirled around. "You're staying?"

Gregory nodded and flailed backwards under her gleeful tackle. "Ack! We'll fall off!"

Will clung to the ledge's edge and laughed until his side cramped. When they'd settled, Sasha adjusting her cap, Gregory hunching his shoulders and putting his back to the nice, secure, steady tower wall, Will said, "And we're both staying with *you*. You think we'd let you fight this alone?"

"It's not your fight," said Sasha, but the wind was rising. It pulled at the smaller hairs curling out from beneath her cap and swept acrid, unseen smoke away into clear air.

Gregory put a shy hand over hers. "Yes, it is."

Epilogue
A week later

Candlelight reflected on the face of Yohan's widow. Two children—a girl, maybe twelve, and a younger boy, about three years old—stood behind her. The girl clenched the boy's hand in hers. The youngster only looked sleepy and confused.

The widow began the slow march to the singer. The slim white candle she held trembled. Her two children followed, the girl's chin stiff but quivering. Andrea remembered walking along that same path, alone, carrying her father's candle. She had been nine years old.

Around them, a hundred other candles burned, of all colors and shapes and sizes—but none like the elegant, tapered, white candle that the widow held. The candlelight lit up the thick wooden beams of the Dog's basement, the dirt floor, and the barrels and boxes of food and beer.

361

This was the only place they had deemed safe to celebrate their old Ceren rituals. If found, all of them would be strictly penalized, if not even locked away as disturbers of the peace. There had been a time when such things were done in the open air—in holy places and with great honor and ceremony. If the floorboards of the Dog weren't quite so thick, they would be hearing the sounds of intoxicated butchers and blacksmiths shouting drinking songs.

There had been a time when Andrea didn't have to sneak in the back entrance of her own home for the farewell of a friend, out of fear the Crown's watchers knew her face (Rocole did) and that they might realize the inn hadn't *just* been Doulings's lodgings. Because Rocole knew her face, Andrea was sleeping on the floor of a washerwoman, a fellow rebel, until the king's men stopped watching the Dog so closely. Her brothers were covering her chores.

The widow handed her candle to the singer, who took it carefully. He closed his eyes and began to sing. It was quiet enough that no one above them could make it out, but with the mourners in perfect silence, it was easy for them to hear. The words were in the lilting speech their ancestors had used; few here knew it. Andrea could only recognize a few words herself.

The widow lifted up her boy and pressed him to her, hiding her tears in his hair. The singer's voice rose and fell. Beside her,

Andrea heard a woman sniffle, a man blow his nose. The singer's voice fell silent. The whole crowd joined in, murmuring together the last final words of farewell to a good and loyal man.

The singer blew out Yohan's spirit candle and the smoke rose to the rafters. Around Andrea, people were crying. A few went to comfort the widow, to stroke the girl's hair, and hold the little boy. Andrea remained where she was.

She knew she would not cry tonight, or any other night, over Yohan. He had been a friend, and Andrea would miss him. But tears, she had decided long ago, solved nothing. What scars could be healed by salt water? It was quite possible her scars could not be healed at all, and she had learned to live with it.

Wax pooled in her palms.

Andrea had sworn an oath to the seasons, to the earth, sea, and sky, and in her world oaths were holy. But more important than those sacred pledges to higher powers was the unspoken promise she had made to her father and all her beloved dead, to continue the struggle they had believed in, the cause they had died fighting for.

This war was not over, not yet.

The story is continued in the second book of the Alliance Trilogy—

Liar.